EVIDENCE TO DESTROY

A VIKING NOVEL OF MYSTERY AND SUSPENSE

EVIDENCE TO DESTROY

Margaret Yorke

VIKING

VIKING
Viking Penguin Inc.
40 West 23rd Street
New York, New York 10010, U.S.A.

First American Edition
Published in 1987

All the characters and events, and most of the places in this
story, are fictional. Resemblance to real people is
coincidental.

LIBRARY OF CONGRESS CATALOGING IN PUBLICATION DATA
Yorke, Margaret.
Evidence to destroy.
(A Viking novel of mystery and suspense)
I. Title.
PR6075.07E94   1987   823'.914   87-40028
ISBN 0-670-81776-7

Printed in the United States of America by
Arcata Graphics, Fairfield, Pennsylvania
Set in Palatino

EVIDENCE TO DESTROY

1

She carried the moss in an old, stained strawberry chip, walking along the narrow path that curved between rose beds and past the vegetable patch to the boundary. The day had been overcast, though mild, and now the young moon was obscured by cloud, but Lydia Cunningham could have found her way down the garden blindfold.

She stood by the fence and took aim. A handful of moss – it was thick, dank stuff which had formed on the roof of the garage – soared silently through the night air towards the huge expanse of bright orange tiles that roofed the new chalet bungalow which blocked her view beyond the Manor to the distant hills.

The bungalow had been named *Mauden* in a blend of its owners' names, Maureen and Roger Dennis. Lydia hurled more moss in the direction of the offending tiles. If it took root, it would spread and mask some of that hideous terra cotta. Much of what she threw simply rolled down to the gutter, but she hoped that some would lodge between the tiles. Would lichen attach itself, too? She could try it; there used to be plenty growing round the church porch. She never went there now except, for form's sake, to lay a holly wreath on Henry's grave at Christmas.

Her ammunition spent, Lydia walked back to the small house which had once been the gatekeeper's lodge at the Manor. Boris, an elderly basset hound, snuffled along beside her, his bandy legs splayed out beneath his low-slung, heavy body.

Gerald, Lydia's son, had been forced to sell the Manor after he and Iris had separated in order to meet her claim for a large settlement. Lydia thought he should have resisted her excessive demands, for it was she who had walked out of the marriage, but, as always, he was generous. The

Manor House and its land had been bought by a property development company. The house itself was a listed building and so protected from demolition; its new owners had sold it, with enough acres to ensure seclusion, to a small hotel group which ran several similar establishments in what had once been large country houses. Because, in the perception of the local authority, it constituted in-filling, planning consent was given for an estate of bungalows and houses on the remainder of the land, and work had only recently been finished on the last of them.

The weather this year had been dismal; cafés and tourist shops by the coast, five miles away, had had a disappointing season, though maritime activities had gone on as usual; the estuary was full of boats. Now, in mid-September, the roads were coming back to normal; life was quietening down as holiday-makers departed from the district.

Lydia's fate had been determined by Henry's extraordinary will, in which he had left everything to their son Gerald 'in the confident knowledge that he will provide adequately for his mother'. A trust had been set up for Thelma, funded by an insurance policy in her favour, but there was no provision for the widow beyond the expressed wish that she should live in the lodge. When the estate was sold, one of the clauses in the agreement was that she should be permitted to rent the house at a peppercorn rate for her lifetime.

Lydia had endured more than two years of din from cement mixers and earth-shifters; now she had lost her view and had acquired noisy neighbours.

She could have contested the will; dourly, the solicitor who had drawn it up had so advised her, knowing, as Henry had done, that she would never stoop to such an action.

She had always known that if Henry were to die before her, she must leave the Manor. It was only right that Gerald and Iris should live there, but she had hoped to turn part of the stable block into a small house for herself; thus, she would keep in touch with him and his family and retain her position in the village. However, the development of the new estate had transformed not only her life but had altered the whole character of Milton St Gabriel, and the lodge was not hers to sell in order to move away. Besides, where would she go? She had lived in the village nearly all her life.

Gerald had explained that it had all been done to save capital transfer tax. The house, with the land that still remained in the estate, was extremely valuable, though Henry had left little else except some heavy debts. Gerald now paid Lydia's small rent and provided the allowance that supplemented her state pension.

When Henry Cunningham died, Gerald and Iris were living in Surrey, from where he commuted to London and his city office. Elegant in black, her hair a froth of russet curls around her pale, pointed face, Iris had attended the funeral and assessed her future. After less than a year of living at the Manor, she had left Gerald, and within weeks of their divorce being made final she had married a former neighbour from the Surrey area where they had spent so many years. Iris and her new husband, who had himself left a wife and three young children, had opened a business dealing in art materials and stationery and, according to Gerald's son and daughter, they were prospering. People seemed to think nothing of chopping and changing partners these days; things had been very different in Lydia's youth.

She entered the lodge through the back door and set her chip down in the lobby. Some things in life must be endured but others could be altered; she was tied to the lodge, but she could attempt to improve the outlook.

Her bungalow neighbours were not the first newcomers to Milton St Gabriel. It had once been an agricultural village with farm workers living in the cottages that clustered near the church and by the pond. For several generations the Cunninghams had owned them and most of the surrounding land, but during the thirties all the farms except one were sold. Later, the old cottages were bought by retired colonial servants and ex-service officers who restored and renovated them, darkening their sturdy beams and displaying ivories and Benares wear. Then, weekenders who stripped and bleached the ancient oak and excavated ingle-nooks arrived, and a few new houses were built in former paddocks or over-large gardens. The recent arrivals were not pleased when the Manor was sold and a new estate was proposed within its former grounds, but when it became clear that the expansion would be separated from the original village area and that it would include two shops and, eventually, a modern health centre serving several neighbouring villages, objections dwindled. One couple had even moved from a beetle-browed thatched cottage to an airy modern bungalow. The old village hall had been refurbished and was used more frequently; there were folk evenings and bingo, and even an occasional disco.

Formerly, Lydia and Henry had entertained the retired tea planters and colonels, the old admiral and his wife, even some former civil servants at the Manor, and were invited back, but since Henry's death she had seen little of the survivors – some of them had also died – of this village nucleus. Few had money to spare and after suitable condolences had been expressed, both sides were relieved to let the socializing lapse. In Henry's lifetime, Lydia had conscientiously tried to undertake the role expected of her; she had led committees, run the Guides, arranged the flowers in church. Now, a new élite managed such affairs.

Several of the newcomers were retired people lured south by the prospect of a mild climate. The fitter ones played golf; some played bridge. Lydia knew a few of them by sight. The Dennises at the bottom of the garden were younger and they both went out to work; she did not know what their occupations were. To the west of the lodge, away from the Manor entrance, a row of six small terraced houses had been built. One day the lodge itself would be pulled down and more bungalows or some other new construction would fill up the space. Lydia drew some satisfaction from denying the developers this expansion for the present.

Her immediate neighbours in the terraced block were a long-distance lorry driver and his wife, the Whites. Their daughter Karen liked pop music and she played it loudly. Tonight, as Lydia closed the back door, a pulsating burst of sound came from next door. If it continued after midnight, she would telephone to complain. It wouldn't be the first time, and she was wearily aware that neither would it be the last.

She glanced round the kitchen. Everything was orderly, the tea towel hanging on its rail, the draining-board wiped down and gleaming, nothing out of place.

'Goodnight, Boris,' she said, and was answered by the thumping of his tail against the side of his basket.

Before she went to bed, Lydia returned to the sitting-room where, on a card table, was a nearly completed jigsaw puzzle depicting tigers in the jungle. She stared at it for a moment, then inserted three pieces into position; if you returned after an interval, you could often see where something fitted. Finally, she slowly climbed the stairs, a thin, tall woman in a much-washed Marks and Spencer's sweater and an old grey flannel skirt.

Her preparations for retiring were a ritual: swift undressing, followed by the washing of underwear and tights which she hung on a rail above the bath to dry. She put her skirt away in her wardrobe on a hanger. Her sweater was neatly folded on a chair and covered with a lace-edged piece of silk which her mother had always used for this purpose. Latterly, the thought of sudden death had become a spectre in Lydia's mind. If she were to die in her sleep, whoever found her must discover no confusion, even in the last extremity.

Gerald Cunningham was an ugly man. He was short and solid, looking almost stout although he was, in fact, merely well-muscled. All his life he had striven to overcome his physical disadvantages where there was any chance of success, and even where there was not, and with his failed marriage behind him, he had quickly looked for sexual comfort.

His present partner was preparing for the night as Gerald lay in bed and watched her. He saw the bright face, the blusher and the vivid eye-shadow, disappear, replaced by pallor and a tiny pimple on a cheek, and sighed. Without her paint, her thick mascara, she was just a very average woman and no longer young, but he had felt good at being seen with her in the restaurant where they had dined. In an expensive dress, her hair-do sleek, bracelets on her arm and earrings dangling, she had seemed to be a symbol of success, evidence of conquest.

But he knew that it was his money that had attracted her. Iris had made it plain not long after they were married that no woman could be drawn to him for any other reason.

Gerald had learned that he was ugly when he was four years old. Another little boy had come to play. The visitor was blond and fresh-faced, with large blue eyes. When he fell over in the garden and grazed his knee, Gerald's mother had comforted him and had even kissed him. She had bathed the knee and taken the casualty on her lap to read him a story till the pain had eased.

Gerald had later deliberately cast himself upon the same paved path and wounded himself more severely than the guest.

'Duffer, aren't you?' Lydia had said. 'Be brave, Gerald.'

His ruse had failed. She ignored his quivering lip and, as usual, Gerald blinked his tears away. He did not flinch when his wound was cleansed with TCP, which stung.

'You're ugly,' said the visitor when they were again playing in the garden. Seated in Gerald's pedal car, the other child was intent on running down his host in every way. Quoting the ultimate authority, he added, 'My mummy said so.'

'What's ugly?' Gerald asked Betty, the girl who at that time, during the war, helped his mother in the house.

Betty was busy washing behind his ears.

'Not nice to look at,' she replied, concentrating on the task in hand. She'd missed some honest grime before and Mrs Cunningham had been cross.

'Is Thelma ugly?' Gerald inquired.

'Course not, silly,' said Betty, who had no idea what lay behind this interrogation. 'Your sister is a lovely little girl.'

'She's fat,' said Gerald.

'It's only puppy fat. She'll lose it,' said Betty, who was still waiting for her own to disappear.

After that, Gerald would now and then inspect himself in a mirror, facing up to what was so repellent. He had thick, straight brows above brown eyes and his hair fell naturally in a heavy fringe, refusing to lie back in the manner decreed by his stern father who occasionally appeared on leave during those years.

If you were good, and rather small, you could hide in

corners. If you kept quiet, people often didn't notice you. Gerald had learned this before he was six. He had also learned to read, taught first by Betty, who thought the sturdy child a manly little fellow, and then by a retired schoolmistress who gave lessons to several children in the village. At that time his mother was working as a nurse at the Manor, which had become a convalescent home; wounded men, in rough blue suits, with bandages and crutches, walked about the grounds and sat beneath the trees. Gerald's grandparents had moved into one of the cottages, and his mother, with the children, was living in the lodge.

After the war, when the house was returned to the family, Gerald's grandparents decided to remain in the small, convenient cottage, and, on a dwindling income, his parents moved into the Manor when Henry was de-mobilized from the army. Soon, the old man died and Gerald's grandmother moved to a flat in London. Henry, with a manager, ran the farm and became a JP. Gerald, at the age of eight, had been sent away to school. There, he found there were other boys whose appearance caused comment. One, with red hair and freckles, was called 'Carrots' but he did not seem to mind; he won popularity by telling ghost stories in the dormitory after lights-out.

Gerald never shone at anything at school, but he held his own at work and on the playing-field. At fourteen, he ran a book on any event which caught the fancy of his peers – the Derby, the Boat Race, inter-house matches – and so earned their respect as well as making quite a little profit.

After university, determined to escape the genteel poverty in which his parents strove to maintain appear-ances – by this time the last farm had been sold – Gerald became a merchant banker. He met Iris at a dance, one among many she attended in pursuit of a husband with money and, with any luck, position. Even when Gerald understood her reasons for accepting him, the marriage had superficially worked. Iris's material wishes were granted; they had a son and daughter and, eventually, a small house in a Surrey suburb from which they later moved to a large one in a green-belt area, complete with swimming-pool. Though Iris had liked the grandeur of the Manor, it was in such a state of disrepair, so cold and draughty, and so inconvenient, that when she went to live there she soon grew to hate it, and she missed her friends. It was too far for Gerald to travel every day; he had a one-roomed flat in London and, with the children both away at boarding schools, perhaps her defection was inevitable.

Gerald stared at the woman as she brushed her copper-coloured hair, one white arm moving slowly to and fro, her brush strokes languid. He had met her at a conference; she was personal assistant to a business manager. Now he sensed reluctance in her unhurried actions and realized that she too was bored.

'Were you ever ugly?' he inquired as at last she came towards him.

'Hideous,' she answered cheerfully. 'I was fat and spotty and had braces on my teeth.'

But she'd got over that and now she could paint on a mask to face the day, Gerald thought, preparing to embrace her.

What if she should plan to marry him? The idea was appalling. It wouldn't do, and he must end it.

Money always helped at such a moment. A cheque to take her to Bermuda or Marrakesh would soften any disappointment. Meanwhile, there was a ritual to be performed, and he had learned to do it skilfully.

2

Thelma Hallows, Gerald's sister, had noticed the young man when he boarded the late train. He wore jeans and a bomber jacket, and he carried a small canvas bag. He was narrow-hipped, with long, thin legs, and his short brown hair was curly.

He took a seat at the rear of the same coach and she was able to watch him over the magazine she pretended to read. He was perhaps twenty-two, or less – a student, maybe. He sat very still, staring out of the window at the dark night through which they passed, his own reflection gazing back at him. Soon he grew aware of Thelma's interest and began to play the game of gradual response. By the time the train reached Swindon they were the only two left in the coach, and he moved up to sit facing her.

She was quite a looker – older, he now saw, than he had thought her from a distance, but with clear, fresh skin and deep blue eyes, her blonde hair styled in near-Afro fashion. Her suede jacket was the real thing; the high-heeled sandals on her bare feet with their scarlet-painted nails not cheap. It was a long time since he'd had social contact with a woman, and talking to her would pass the time.

He had told the probation officer that he was going to stay with his sister after his release, but Julie didn't know that he was on his way. He hadn't warned her, afraid that she would tell him not to come, though she must know he was due out soon. If he turned up in the small hours of the morning, she would have to take him in, he reasoned. There'd be a corner for him somewhere.

She hadn't been to see him since she took this job, though she'd gone on writing regularly. Throughout his life, she had always stuck by him, and she had visited him at first, after his arrest and then his sentence.

He was frightened that he'd gone too far this time, that she had run away and left him. Without her, he had nothing.

Lydia was dreaming the dream when the telephone woke her.

In her dream, workmen were decorating the house into which she was to move. Cans of paint in colours she did not like – reds and browns and violent purples – stood about, and she moved around the unfamiliar rooms with dread, unable to halt their actions. All the while heavy beat music assaulted her ears, and a nurse with a hypodermic syringe in her hand steadily followed her, needle upraised.

She had telephoned the Whites' house next door at ten minutes past midnight and asked them to tone down their so-called music.

A male voice had answered the telephone and called out, 'Hey, Karen, some old bag's complaining. Tell her to get ear-plugs if she doesn't like it.'

Then Karen White had come to the telephone. She had once seemed a nice girl, yet now she wore her hair spiked out like the spines of a hedgehog, often dyed in strange colours or with blue or red tufts at the front like a cock's comb. She would come up the road after school with several schoolboys, giggling and indulging in horseplay. What were her parents thinking of to allow such behaviour? But they were seldom at home: the mother worked as a barmaid in Heronsmouth, and the father was often away. Karen was obviously having a party tonight. Surely the mother was back by this time?

Girls asked for trouble, these days, but if they fell into it, they could climb out. Years ago, there had been no such chance.

Well, once again she had survived the first hours of sleep without dying, she thought, reaching out for the telephone extension beside her bed. Who could be calling her at this hour? A wrong number, probably, or perhaps Karen's friends wanting to taunt her.

She hadn't expected it to be Thelma.

'But you're in Los Angeles,' she said.

'No, mother. I'm at Cheverton station,' said Thelma. 'It

didn't work out with Lucian, so I've left him. Will you collect me, please?'

Lydia fetched clean undergarments and tights. She put on a warm sweater and her grey skirt. Then she did her hair, taking trouble to arrange the long grey strands with care, securing them under a snood of velvet ribbon so that they concealed the bald expanse of skull above her forehead. She had lost her hair soon after Thelma's birth and it had never grown again.

'You're not going to get your mum to come out and fetch you at this time of night – or morning – are you?' Edward Fletcher had protested when together they left the train. 'Won't you take a taxi?' In which he'd cadge a lift, since they had discovered that they were both going to Milton St Gabriel.

'I've no money,' said Thelma. She'd got a few dollars left, but no sterling, and anyway, why pay good money for something her mother could provide at no cost? That was what mothers were for.

'Oh!' That was a surprise to Edward, who had been intrigued by what seemed to him her worldly air and her poise.

They got better acquainted while they waited for Lydia's arrival. She would be forty minutes or more by the time she had dressed and got the car out, Thelma informed him, leading him into the deserted waiting-room. When the small dark blue Metro arrived, it seemed to be agreed that Edward would go with Thelma to her mother's house, for, she told him, it was far too late to disturb his sister.

Lydia's rapid heart-beat and her raised blood pressure had settled somewhat as she drove to fetch her daughter. Mist hung between the high banks that bordered the narrow lanes before she reached the main road, and she went slowly. No useful purpose would be served by having an accident now. As she neared the roundabout where one road led to Heronsmouth and the other to Cheverton, her headlights picked up a hedgehog waddling across the tarmac. Lydia steered to avoid it, her wheels passing either side of its rotund body; it would probably be run over before the night was done, but she need not be its executioner.

It was typical of Thelma to arrive at an anti-social hour, and with no warning. In the past, Lydia had met her at airports and stations after various phases of her life had ended either in failure or disaster. This last was only the latest of several romantic escapades.

On the strength of two walk-on parts when she was nineteen and a brief stage-managing spell when she was also an understudy and appeared as Nina in *The Seagull* for four performances, Thelma described herself as an actress, but she had had no paid dramatic role since those early years. Lucian, whom she had gone to America to visit with a view to remaining there, was an actor she had once known. They had exchanged some letters after his marriage ended and Thelma had been certain that when they met again, all would be roses.

'He's begged me to come,' Thelma had told her mother.

Lydia had remained unconvinced by this assurance. Thelma tended to arrange versions of events to suit the scripts she structured in her imagination. She had been away only three weeks, having sub-let her flat in Clapham for two years.

As Lydia drove into the station yard, two figures stepped out of the shadows.

'This is Edward,' introduced Thelma, without greeting her mother at all.

'Hi,' said Edward, who had not been told the old woman's name. As Lydia struggled to open the car door, preparatory to getting out, he added, 'Please don't move. I'll see to the bags.'

Thelma had a lot of luggage. He managed to stack it all in the small car, putting what would not fit in the rear compartment on the back seat; then he got in beside it, fitting his skinny legs around a duty-free carrier bag and a soft holdall. However had she managed to get on to the train with all this load? Maybe someone helped her; most blokes would want to help a bird like her.

Thelma sat in front beside her mother and they set off in silence which, to Edward, soon grew oppressive. Had they nothing to say to each other after their separation?

'How far is it to Milton St Gabriel?' he asked at last, and was answered at once by seeing a signpost which announced a distance of eight miles.

The old lady drove well and smoothly, at a steady forty miles an hour or so until they reached the lanes, where she dropped her speed. Steep banks on each side of the car reminded Edward of high walls. He felt hemmed in and nervous.

'What happens if you meet a car?' he asked.

'There are passing places,' said the old lady.

He couldn't see them in the misty darkness, but they met no other traffic.

'Did you have a good journey?' Lydia eventually inquired.

Edward had not had much of a look at her so far; she was wearing one of those khaki-coloured padded anoraks you saw on real battle axes of the female sex, and perhaps she was one, but at least she hadn't got a superior-sounding penetrating voice.

Thelma was describing her long flight and her landing earlier in the day.

'Why didn't you come straight down?' her mother asked.

'I had people to see,' Thelma answered curtly.

She had spent the day ringing round old friends. The last of her sterling had gone on drinks at a pub frequented by resting actors and actresses. No one had offered her a bed, with or without strings attached. She hadn't rung Gerald, who might have been expected to take his sister in for the night. He would only have preached to her about using prudence in her life and not sponging on their mother.

They ran out of the mist as they entered the village, passing quiet, darkened cottages and the two original shops, one housing a sub-post office, and came to wide entrance gates with a discreet sign which advertised *The Manor Hotel*. Beyond them, Lydia drew up at the lodge.

As Boris lumbered out to greet them, wagging his tail, the young man carried in Thelma's bags. Meanwhile, Lydia went into the kitchen and put the kettle on. She would not sleep without a hot drink to settle her.

'The beds are made up,' she said. She kept them ready and aired, used to Thelma's sudden arrivals and ever hopeful that Gerald or a grandchild might turn up unexpectedly, but they never came without warning and then not often enough for her.

'Show your friend the way to the yellow room,' Lydia told her daughter. This was more tactful than describing it as the small bedroom.

They'd take no notice; she knew that: but at least she was not openly condoning their liaison. This man looked young enough to be Thelma's son. Where had she found him? She'd lost no time in replacing the rejected Lucian. How long would this one last?

'Would you like something to eat?' she offered. 'Some sandwiches?'

'Oh, thanks,' said Thelma. 'Got any Scotch?'

Silently, Lydia went to a cupboard and took out a half-empty bottle of Dewar's. Then she built a pile of sandwiches with what was left of the bread, some cheddar cheese and the last of the butter. She had not been expecting guests and supplies were low.

'I'm going back to bed now,' she told the pair when this was done. She would have liked to ask Thelma what had gone wrong in America, and what her plans, if any, were, but such things could not be discussed in front of a stranger. Besides, she was too tired. Explanations must wait.

Thelma and Edward finished the whisky before they went to bed, and both were rather disappointed with what followed.

Edward woke early the next morning. He stretched out in the bed; it was soft, and his head rested on a down pillow. This was better than the nick. He lay savouring the sybaritic bliss of physical ease until a faint sound came from the other bed. Then he remembered. During the night he had found himself perched on its edge, with Thelma, curled into a ball like a hibernating dormouse, occupying the middle. He had moved out to the second bed.

She hadn't woken. He had heard faint, snorting little snores.

They had not talked much. She had no settled job and did not know how long she would be staying with her mother.

'Till something else turns up,' she had said.

If she was thinking of making him the something else, he'd have to make sure what he was in for, Edward reflected.

He swung himself out of bed and dressed quickly, then let himself quietly out of the bedroom. His trainers made no sound as he padded down the stairs. When he opened the kitchen door, the fat old dog waddled over to him, wagging his heavy tail and making small sounds of welcome in his throat.

'I suppose you want to go out, boy,' said Edward, and opened the back door.

Boris sauntered into the garden, and Edward followed him down the path. The air smelled fresh and damp; he inhaled greedily. Beyond the fence he saw a bright orange roof rearing up almost like a wall; there were similar high-vaulted roofs on either side. Last night, when he arrived, Milton St Gabriel had seemed to be a picture postcard village with its stone cottages, thatched roofs and the pond that he had noticed, driving through. Here was total contrast.

Boris blundered up to him and sniffed at the ends of his jeans. Edward bent and patted him, then walked back towards the house, followed by the dog. He shut the animal in, then set off down the road. He meant to look for Julie now.

Lydia had slept very little when at last she had returned to bed. She heard Edward's quiet movements in the house, and she watched him from the window as he studied the outlook. He seemed pleasant enough, and he was well-mannered, but he would need a lot of food, if he was staying.

She sighed. Your children were supposed to be off your hands when they were adult, but Thelma had never stayed away for long. Lydia hoped she was always pleased to see her daughter, but it was a pleasure seldom untinged with dismay as she waited to learn the nature of the latest crisis that had brought her home. She had always been a creature of sudden enthusiasms, swayed by whims, and when she chose the stage as a career she had selected a life of insecurity. The wonder was that Henry hadn't put his foot down and forbidden it, but then she had always been able to twist him round her little finger.

She must be still asleep.

Lydia went downstairs and made herself a cup of tea which she took back to bed with her. She needed time to prepare herself to meet the day and all its new demands, and until Mrs Dodds's shop, up the road, was open, there was no bread for breakfast.

Edward walked past the row of terraced houses next to the lodge and turned down the road beyond them. This led through the estate which backed on to the garden of the lodge. The new bungalows all seemed steeped in sleep, the curtains drawn across their picture windows. The mist had gone and thin sunlight filtered between the young shrubs and sapling trees in their freshly landscaped gardens.

He came to a sturdy fence, strong chain-linked wire which stretched between solid posts where the new road turned to the right past another row of bungalows. On the farther side were tall trees and well-established shrubs. Edward, no gardener, could not identify any of them. He walked along until he saw a strong bough within his reach, grasped it and swung himself over the fence, landing on the leafy ground. He must have worked his way round towards the hotel by now; this fence had to be its boundary. Staying within the cover provided by the undergrowth, Edward went on, his trainer shoes by this time sopping wet.

He came to the house quite soon. It was a large, square-fronted building made of the local granite, dark grey and with a darker roof of slates. It had been built in the days when merchants and ship-owners prospered by shipping goods in and out of the estuaries along the coast. A glossy virginia creeper covered one wall of the house. Some cars were parked outside.

Edward retreated into the shelter of the bushes so that he could circle the place and approach it from the rear. The guests would still be sleeping, but the staff must be about, preparing breakfast and cleaning the public rooms. Moving quietly, Edward eventually reached a rear drive just as two scooters puttered by bringing staff in for the day's work.

He followed them, walking confidently now. He had every right to come and see his sister.

There was a row of outbuildings, once stabling, behind the house. Edward passed an open door and saw two enormous washing machines and a tumble drier. There was a mechanized ironer like one he had used in the prison laundry where he had worked during part of his sentence. Maybe they could use a temporary laundryman here, though really he didn't fancy being cooped up in that damp, steamy atmosphere again; he'd rather be out of doors. A few weeks in the country, while he got used to his freedom and before winter set in, was what he wanted, if he could find some work. Edward never stayed long in any job, though he worked well enough until the feeling grew that someone was gunning for him, picking on him, finding needless fault. Then he'd leave, but he hadn't always managed to do this before the compulsion to light a fire overwhelmed him. He'd told the doctors at the prison about it; he wanted to punish someone, they'd explained, and it all went back to the fact that his mother had abandoned him when he was only six. This had made him want to get back at the world. He had done a great deal of damage by yielding to the urge.

Through the kitchen window he could see the breakfast cook and her assistant hard at work. Julie wouldn't be among the white-coated people here; she worked on the domestic side.

Edward slipped in through the unlocked back door and walked silently along the corridor into which it opened. A flight of stairs led off to the left, and he ran swiftly up them, finding himself in a long passage with doors punctuating either side. It would be easy to do this place; there'd be plently of casual pickings. He padded on and at the end of the passage saw another door, half open. From within came chinking sounds, and as he approached, out came Julie with a laden early-morning tea tray.

She gave a single shriek and dropped it when she saw him, sending scalding tea over her legs and smashing most of the china. Edward grabbed her before she could yell again and pulled her back into the housemaid's pantry where she prepared the trays.

'Eddie, what are you doing here?' she gasped, when her first shock had abated. Her words came mingled with little wails as she dabbed at her legs with a damp tea-towel.

'Well, I'm out, aren't I, so I came to see you,' he said

reasonably. He bent down and began to pick up the broken crockery. Most of the damage was on the landing. 'Oh, the carpet,' he tutted, like an anxious housewife. A soggy section of patterned Axminster confronted them, with two teabags marooned in the midst of the swamp.

'It'll wipe off,' said Julie. 'There's a floorcloth in the cupboard under the sink. You just get on with it, Eddie. Use plenty of hot water.'

This was how she had always talked to him, his elder sister behaving like a mother. After their own mother had gone, Julie had done her best to look after him and their father, although she was only twelve. Then Dad had re-married and had another family, and he and Julie became outsiders.

'I wish you wouldn't call me Eddie,' he grumbled.

'I always have, and I shan't stop now,' said Julie. 'You haven't escaped, have you?'

'Of course not. I've served my time,' he said. 'I'll take that tray for you. Where's it got to go?'

'What? And terrify the guests out of their lives?' she said. 'Look at you! Not shaved and with your jeans sopping wet. Do you want to get me the sack?' Then she began to laugh. He had always had the trick of making her feel happy, even though he never seemed able to stay out of trouble.

'How're the legs?' he asked.

'Better,' she said, though they still stung. She poured boiling water into a fresh teapot. 'I won't have enough crocks now,' she added. 'Mrs Thomson will have something to say about that.'

'What do you need? I'll go down and nick them from the pantry,' Edward said. 'Let those folk down there do the explaining.' He studied the tray. 'What's missing?'

'You'll do no such thing,' she said. 'Stay here till I get back.'

She went off with another loaded tray and Edward made himself a cup of tea while she was gone. There were Osborne biscuits in a tin and he ate six of them.

'You can't stay here,' she said when she returned, having tried to think constructively while she drew the curtains in the room where a retired doctor and his wife were staying for a restful week.

'There's no need,' said Edward, taking another biscuit from the tin. 'I've got friends in Milton St Gabriel.'

'You can't have, Eddie. That's impossible,' said Julie.

'I have, too. And what's more they used to live in this house,' said Edward. Thelma had told him some of her family history. 'I'm staying with Mrs Cunningham.'

'I don't believe it!' Julie stared at him, amazed.

'Well, it's her daughter I know really,' Edward said. 'She's just back from Los Angeles.'

'How could you have got to know her? Wheɪ ɪid you get out?' asked Julie suspiciously.

'I got out yesterday, and I met Thelma on the train. She invited me to stay,' he said. He was on the point of boasting about his conquest, then thought better of it; Julie would be sure to disapprove.

'How long are you going to be there?' she asked, while the familiar cloud of anxiety about her brother descended on her once again.

'Oh, I've no definite plans,' said Edward.

'You've got to stay out of trouble,' said Julie.

'I mean to, don't you worry,' Edward told her. 'I understand my motivation now.'

Julie was not reassured, but she felt guilty herself because she had travelled all this way to escape responsibility for him. She had let him down. Until his prison sentence, she had always managed to protect him from the consequences of his actions, pleading for him with the headmaster when he put lighted matches in the waste-paper basket at school, and keeping it a secret when she later learned that he had set fire to some rubbish in a disused warehouse. He had confessed to that offence when he was arrested for firing a car. It had gone off like a bomb and he had been sent to prison for two years.

'Well, for God's sake keep on like that,' she told him. 'Now, I must finish my trays or they'll be screaming. Number seven will have finished hers; I'll fetch that to make up for what you smashed. Stay here while I'm gone.'

Julie knew he meant what he had said, but was he strong enough to stick to it? He'd always said he was sorry when caught out in any minor misdemeanour as a child and he didn't like upsetting people. But he loved the sparkle and the glitter of the fires he made. He stood and watched them burn and that was how he had been caught. A man who could do a thing like that, the judge had said, had shown a total disregard for human life.

3

Thelma woke with a headache and a sour taste in her mouth. She'd overdone the whisky, but she had hoped that it would help her through the inevitable ending to the evening. Nothing ever did, however; she should know that by now.

He wasn't still in her bed: that was something to be thankful for, and perhaps he had even left the house. She peered around her, blinking in the pale light which filtered through the printed chintz curtains. Then she saw the hold-all that had been his sole piece of luggage standing in a corner of the room.

She had done none of her own unpacking yet; her cases stood where Edward had left them in what she regarded as, in perpetuity, her bedroom. Some of her possessions remained here wherever she herself might be and now she found an old blue quilted dressing-gown in the cupboard. She put it on and, barefoot, went downstairs in search of coffee.

Her mother was standing by the table in the sitting-room where her current jigsaw was set out, a jagged fragment in her hand. She turned as her daughter entered the room. Thelma's hair stood out in an aureole around her pale face; her eyes looked haggard. Once, she had been a predictable if sometimes sulky little girl, and was always pretty, but her mother had found it hard to love her and for that reason was perpetually consumed with guilt and self-reproach, aggravated by Thelma's failure to build herself a happy life.

Lydia had put the percolator on, using the last coffee beans; normally, she drank instant coffee, which Thelma scorned.

'Good morning, Thelma,' she said, and did not ask her daughter if she had slept well; least said about the night's activities the better. 'There isn't any bread,' she added. 'But Mrs Dodds will have opened up by now, though she won't have had a fresh delivery yet. Still, there may be a loaf left over from yesterday.'

'I don't know why you don't keep some in the freezer, Mother,' Thelma said.

'I do, often,' said Lydia. 'I've run out. That's all.' With Thelma in America, it hadn't seemed necessary to be equipped against a sudden siege.

Lydia put the jigsaw segment into her skirt pocket and accompanied her daughter to the kitchen, where she poured her out a cup of coffee. Boris, half asleep, opened one eye and regarded both of them benevolently from his basket.

'That dog's getting old,' said Thelma.

Lydia ignored the comment.

'Your friend's gone out,' she said. 'Will he be staying long?'

'I've no idea,' said Thelma carelessly. 'I only met him yesterday. In the train, as a matter of fact. We'll have to wait and see.'

Lydia would not give Thelma the satisfaction of registering shock, but her hand shook as she put down the percolator. She always sought excuses for her daughter's waywardness: poor Thelma had been married less than six years when her first husband, Charles Hallows, was killed in a motor accident. No other car was involved; he had run off the road and hit a tree one Tuesday afternoon. He had left the office early, suffering from flu, but the spot where the crash had occurred was not on his route home. No explanation was forthcoming; the post-mortem showed no evidence of alcohol, or of heart attack or other seizure; it had all been very difficult to understand and accept. Within a few months Thelma had married again, but her husband had left her after only three weeks. She had reverted to her earlier married name and, as soon as it was possible, had obtained a divorce. Her father had bought her a flat in London where she had lived on and off ever since, reappearing in Milton St Gabriel at frequent intervals when pressed for cash or emotionally suffering. She had taken various temporary, often insubstantial jobs, sometimes as a demonstrator at trade exhibitions or in stores, always hoping to get into the theatre again. There was much talk of Equity; Lydia was uncertain whether Thelma had qualified for the essential card or for want of it failed to secure any parts, or whether there was some other cause for her lack of professional success.

Thelma finished her coffee. She was longing for a cigarette but had smoked her last; her mother did not smoke and did not care for others to do so in her presence or in her house.

'There's some Ry-Vita,' said Lydia.

'I don't want anything to eat,' said Thelma. 'I've got a stinking headache.'

Lydia had seen the empty whisky bottle.

'Have you, dear? I'm sorry. There are aspirins in the bathroom,' she said.

She left the room to avoid losing patience with Thelma. That must never be allowed to happen. Boris levered himself out of his basket and trundled after her into the garden. She was standing under an apple tree turning the jigsaw piece round in her pocket when she heard a cheery whistling, and the young man, Thelma's latest acquisition, came towards her. Boris waddled towards him, tail wagging; he, at least, approved.

Edward, coming up behind her, had whistled to announce his presence for she had been standing so still, her back towards him, lost in thought, that he did not want to startle her by suddenly appearing. He wondered how old she was; nearer seventy than sixty, that was certain. Her soft, fine hair was nearly white. She wore it in an odd, old-fashioned style with that band around her brow.

'I've been to see my sister,' he volunteered. 'Did Thelma tell you she lives here? She was ever so glad I didn't turn up in the middle of the night. She hasn't got a bed for me just now.' Julie would find a corner for him later, he was blithely certain; in a place that size there must be some odd spot where he could sleep unnoticed. Meanwhile, he'd hope to stay here. 'It's really nice of you to put me up,' he added. 'What can I do to help? Shall I cut the grass?'

He'd had a smashing breakfast at the hotel: fried egg and bacon, sausage and tomato. The going rate for that, if you were a guest and came in casually, was four pounds ninety-five, but for residents it was included in the bedroom price: thirty-five pounds at least, depending on the room. The staff seemed a friendly crowd: he'd met Victor and Mavis, both friends of Julie's who worked in the dining-room, and a nice old man, Ferdy, the barman, who had some sort of foreign accent. Edward foresaw no problem about getting the odd meal up there. Now, with his first fears lulled, he was full of goodwill towards the world and in particular his hostess.

'That would be very kind,' said Lydia. 'It's still growing fast; all the rain has meant it's needed cutting more often than usual this summer.'

'What sort of mower have you got?' asked Edward.

'It's one that doesn't mind damp grass, if that's what you were thinking of,' said Lydia, and her face softened slightly; she did not smile, however. Did she ever, Edward wondered, and wondered more at having such a strange thought himself.

He ran his hand over his chin and realized that he had not shaved yet; an old girl like this one wouldn't like that.

'I'll have a wash and shave first, if that's all right,' he said. 'Sorry if I look untidy but I got up rather early and didn't want to wake anyone up.'

'There's petrol in a can in the garage, if the mower needs refilling,' Lydia said.

A fragile amity between them, Lydia and Edward returned to the house.

Thelma had gone back to bed. She would be the problem, Edward decided, not her mother. Still, not to worry; he'd sort something out to keep them both happy.

Thelma wanted something from him now, he discovered when he went into the bedroom to collect his razor.

'Not while your mum's about,' he told her sternly, but he gave her one of his most winning smiles as he left the room.

Thelma pouted sulkily, rolling over in the bed, but she was really quite relieved; it was just a way to pass the time and meant you didn't have to talk.

That evening, Gerald telephoned to invite himself down the following weekend.

'Thelma's here,' said Lydia.

'What? Oh, no! What's happened now?' Gerald was taken too much by surprise at the news to hide his dismay.

'It didn't work out.' Lydia repeated her daughter's explanation.

Gerald could imagine his mother sitting by the telephone, lips pursed as she finished speaking, perhaps fiddling with a pencil, or fragment of jigsaw, or other small object which she would suddenly set aside as she disciplined herself not to fidget.

'Oh dear!'

'She's got a friend with her,' said Lydia.

'Male?' As if he needed to ask: Thelma had no female friends.

'Yes.'

'Hm. You're not being very forthcoming, Mother. Can't you talk freely?'

'No.' The telephone was in the hall and while they were talking, Thelma was watching television in the sitting-room while Edward was doing Lydia's jigsaw. He had an eye for it.

'What's the matter with this one? Is he another lame duck?' asked Gerald.

'I don't know,' said Lydia.

Sometimes they were; there had been two alcoholics, an unemployed steel-worker, a monk who had returned to the world and whom she'd met when she'd spent some weeks in a commune in a remote Cotswold village.

'You aren't happy about it,' Gerald stated. 'It's as well that I'm coming down.' He swiftly reshaped his thinking; he had intended the weekend as a chance to get away from things, or rather, from himself, for he was not proud of the manner in which he had ended his recent liaison. Now he must accept the new problems posed by his sister. The first one that came to mind was purely domestic; no doubt she and this man, whoever he was, were occupying the double spare room in the lodge and this would leave the small room free for him, but it might not be safe to assume overt arrangements which his mother would certainly not approve, even though it would not be the first time she had had to accept such a situation. Whatever the circumstances,

there was only one bathroom and Thelma would be unlikely to consider the wishes of himself or even their mother
in the demands she made upon it. He would be much more
comfortable at the hotel, and his absence would remove
some strain from his mother as she juggled with her sense
of duty towards them both. 'I'll stay at the Manor,' he told
her. 'If they're full, I'll go to the Swan in Heronsmouth.
We'll all have dinner at the Manor on Saturday. How does
that appeal to you?'

'Very much,' she answered. 'Thank you.'

Gerald sat staring at the telephone after he had replaced
the handset. Her voice was never warm or enthusiastic.
When she was young, had she been eager and ardent? He
found it impossible to imagine intimacy between her and
his father, a stern man forced by the death of his elder
brother in the war to settle for farming the land and running
the estate he would inherit. He'd wanted to make the army
his career but had told Gerald that there wasn't money
enough for him to join the sort of regiment he would have
chosen, where a private income was essential. He had read
law before the war, and was a territorial soldier.

Henry Cunningham had failed to run the farm with profit
and had let the estate decline, but he had seen Gerald prove
his own business acumen and died hoping that he would
rescue the family fortunes.

He had not foreseen Iris's defection.

As it was, Gerald had invested in the hotel group so that
at least he kept in touch with what went on there. Once his
decision to sell was made, Gerald had quite enjoyed
imagining his father's disapproval. The old man had been
so strict: Gerald had never won praise for any achievement
and had soon learned to conceal his small sins which were
usually of omission. All Henry's warmth was reserved for
Thelma; he had adored the pretty little fair-haired girl with
her big blue eyes and had indulged her every whim. He had
found excuses for her scholastic failures and had revelled in
her sporting prowess, for Thelma was good at all games and
she loved riding. Gerald still remembered the birthday
when their father had given her Rondo, a liver chestnut
pony which had subsequently helped her secure many a
rosette at local gymkhanas and hunter trials. Thelma was a

good horsewoman, and fearless; Gerald acknowledged that, while admitting that he was, himself, a poor performer, except at golf where the ball was attacked while stationary.

After Charles was killed, Thelma had come home. She had ridden about the place on an old cob which was the only mount her father was then able to provide for her, and had got herself involved with the stockman. Even Henry had had to pay some attention when the stockman's wife had come to the Manor in tears to protest; he had interviewed Thelma who had then been sent to London to do an advanced cookery course. While there, she had met and married her second husband, and Gerald had been made to feel that he was at fault for not keeping more of an eye on her during that time.

It was no good dwelling on past old jealousies and resentments. Gerald determined to rise above prejudice when he went down to Milton St Gabriel, and to deal with the present while he was in it. He telephoned his daughter Fiona, who lived in a mixed flat in Shepherd's Bush and was, at the moment, unemployed. She was pleased to accept his invitation to lunch.

They met at a French restaurant in the City. Fiona arrived wearing what seemed to Gerald to be a romper suit in pale pink cotton, rather crumpled, and an enormous baggy sweater which she unpeeled when they sat down. Her long dark hair was secured in a thick plait, and she wore a lot of eye make-up. She looked striking, attracting notice from others in the restaurant as she entered, and causing the waiters to hover round her in a covey.

'Hullo, Daddy!' She kissed him warmly. 'This is fun.'

'I want to be sure you get an occasional square meal,' he told her, trying not to show too much delight at being in her company.

'Oh, I don't do too badly,' said Fiona airily. 'I get given my dinner most nights.'

Looking at her more attentively, he saw that beyond the first impression of general health and energy, there were faint shadows under the large brown eyes, and that the colour on her cheeks came from blusher sparingly applied.

'Who gave it to you last night?' he asked.

'Oh, just a man I know,' said Fiona carelessly. 'Can I have steak, please? Any kind, but large and rare.'

She looked as if she could do with a month in the country. If he still owned the Manor, she would automatically go to Milton St Gabriel when no more attractive prospect offered and, as her Aunt Thelma still contrived, be nourished and refreshed. Well, he couldn't put the clock back. Nor could he turn her once again into the little girl who loved her pony to distraction and was going to be a show jumper when she grew up. About the age of fourteen that artless child had disappeared, to be replaced by a young female stranger keen on pop music and who wore wild, freaky clothing when she could get away with it.

Had he spoiled her, over-indulged her, as his own father had Thelma? Was she destined to follow her aunt's feckless example, and if so, would it be his fault?

Such thoughts made Gerald uncomfortable.

'She'll marry well,' Iris had declared. 'She must have her chance in London. She'll meet young men with prospects there.'

But Gerald wanted her to marry a man who loved her and would want to make her happy.

'As you met me,' he had attacked, and Iris had smiled.

'Of course,' she said. 'And I did my bit – you can't deny that.'

It was true. She had run the house efficiently, and she was decorative. She had played her part in the circle of similar couples among whom they had lived for most of their married life, giving tasteful dinner parties and getting the children's teeth dealt with by a leading orthodontist. She had known that one day the Manor at Milton St Gabriel would come to him and had pictured herself as a potential leader of county society; what she had not expected was that the house would be so badly run down, so much in need of restoration; and she had not known about sea mists which clung damply round the hills, the pervading chill, and the winter gales. Very soon, she gave in to boredom. She enjoyed exciting admiration; men were attracted to her, and she had had several discreet affairs with wandering neighbours before she made her bid for freedom.

Fiona, eating pheasant pâté before her steak arrived,

revealed, under her father's gentle questioning, that she rose late most mornings and idled away the day, sometimes shopping, sometimes pottering into a museum or a gallery, going occasionally to see a film, all the while waiting for the evening. It seemed to him a pointless way of life. He gave her an allowance which was enough to cover her share of the flat's rent; there could be little over. Was she drawing the dole? He dreaded to hear that, in her parasite existence, she was entitled to it, so he did not ask. What if he docked her monthly cheque? Would she then be forced to find a proper job or would it drive her into something worse?

'These men – ' he hesitated. There had been mention of Gavin, Robert, Peter. 'Any of them special?' he essayed.

'Not really, Daddy,' she declared, smiling sunnily.

'I wish you knew what you really wanted to do,' he told her.

'I'm having a good time,' she said. 'Isn't that enough, at my age? It's OK by Mummy. She says it's only what girls of Granny's generation did, waiting to get married.'

'Some of them,' said Gerald grimly. 'Your grandmother helped in the parish – looked after her parents. Then, in the war, she was a nurse.'

'I didn't mean Granny C. I meant Granny,' said Fiona patiently, referring to her maternal grandmother who had done the season properly and been presented, wearing ostrich feathers. She had married an impoverished younger son of a baronet after her third circuit.

'Girls can do anything, these days,' said Gerald. Various able young women were steadily rising at the bank; only if they succumbed to family demands would they fail to maintain a continuing ascent. 'You could be Prime Minister,' he added.

'Don't be silly, Daddy dear,' said Fiona. 'Of course I'll get married in the end and be a mother all my days.' She sighed. 'But twenty years is a long time.'

'Is twenty years all you give your marriage?' Gerald asked her.

'It's a long time to live with one person,' said Fiona. 'Must get boring, doesn't it?'

'Your mother thought so,' Gerald said. 'But Granny – Granny C. and Grandfather were together for over forty years.'

'Yes, and it was hell, I bet,' said Fiona. 'At least nowadays, if things go wrong, you can get out of it without a lot of hassle.'

'I'm sure Granny C. and Grandfather never contemplated such a thing,' said Gerald, truly shocked.

'I don't suppose they did,' said Fiona. 'Granny C. is much too proper. Do you suppose Grandfather had affairs?'

'Of course not. What gave you that idea?' asked Gerald.

'I don't know. He was a lusty sort of man, wasn't he? Vigorous? And Granny C. is rather decidulated.'

'There's no such word,' said Gerald. 'What do you mean?' But he knew, and she was right.

'Her leaves have kind of dropped off, right?' said Fiona.

'She wasn't always old,' said Gerald sadly.

'Oh, I know, and she was always nice to me, showed me lots of things, like birds' nests and how to knit,' said Fiona. 'But even now I'm afraid of blotting my copybook with her, and you are, too, Daddy. Don't deny it.'

'Thelma's come back.' Gerald flung the information into their conversation, where he was rapidly getting out of his depth. 'I'm going down to Milton St Gabriel on Friday – staying at the hotel to leave room at the lodge.' He wouldn't mention Thelma's boyfriend in case that provoked more uncomfortable remarks from Fiona.

'Oh dear. I thought she'd gone to America for keeps,' said Fiona.

'Your aunt never goes anywhere for keeps,' said Gerald.

'She got tired of Lucian, I suppose. Didn't fancy twenty years of his tickly beard and yellow teeth,' said Fiona.

'I didn't know you'd met him,' Gerald said.

'Oh yes. She had a party once, and in a fit of auntly duty, asked me along. She had a thing going with someone else then. A painter, I think it was.' And Lucian had fancied Fiona and she had let him kiss her in order to try out the beard. She hadn't liked it much.

'Why don't you come with me?' Gerald said, on impulse. He looked across the table at her pretty, bright face. How lovely it would be to drive down with her, hear more talk, have a chance to deal better with her opinions, mend bridges between her and her grandmother. 'I'm sure the hotel will have another room,' he urged her.

'Sorry, Daddy. I've got people to see and things to do this weekend,' said Fiona. 'Thanks, though.'

What was she going to do? Whom would she see? Gavin? Robert? Peter?

'Another time, then,' Gerald said.

'Mm. Rather.' Fiona looked at her watch, a tiny gold one he had given her for her eighteenth birthday. 'Wow, it's late. I must dash. Thanks for lunch, Daddy.'

Where was she rushing to? She had no typewriter waiting for her, no tutor, no essay to write, no angry supervisor or executive with dictation to impart.

'I'll ring you in the week,' was all he said as she kissed him on the top of his head and left, with three waiters supervising her departure from the premises.

4

Edward had put more petrol into Lydia's old mower. He had found the mixture wrongly adjusted and had corrected it, then oiled the machine thoroughly. He cleaned it well when the job was done before putting it away in the garden shed. There was a big tin of paraffin there, under the shelf; she used it for bonfires, he supposed.

Edward liked putting things right and had a feeling for engines; as a schoolboy he had sometimes done odd hours on the pumps at a garage where he had learned what went on under a bonnet. He had thought of becoming apprenticed there, but the owner had found out about his escapades with fire and had turned him down. Edward had got off, then, with being put on probation, but in the end, as the magistrate had said, he had had to be properly punished. Now he was an ex-con and would receive no mercy if he offended again. He was running scared: the sensible thing would have been to go into the approved lodgings suggested by his probation officer, let her help him towards a job. But who would take him on when there were plenty of other young men without records also looking for work? He had fled to Julie, as usual relying on her help, but when he saw her dismay that morning he had suddenly understood what a burden he had become.

Mrs Cunningham was nice, in her odd, stiff way. She wouldn't turn him out at once, not if he gave no trouble and helped about the place; there were plenty of little jobs that needed doing. He'd sign on at the nearest DHSS and perhaps he could get some work in the village to supplement his social security. It wasn't Edward's way to look too far ahead: the next week was enough. He'd postpone the problem of Thelma, too; he'd been stupid to play her game but it had seemed the only thing to do at the time.

The old lady had gone off shopping now, in her Metro, which needed a wash. He'd do that when she came back, and check its oil and water and tyre pressures. She might be careless about things of that sort. Edward had finished the jigsaw she was doing, all but one piece which was missing, too late for her to take it with her to Cheverton. She'd taken a pile of others, some with battered boxes, to return to a charity shop. It seemed that when people donated them, they had to be sorted out and assembled as pieces got mixed. If any were incomplete, that had to be stated on the outside, and Edward wrote carefully, in ballpoint on the lid, that one piece of the jungle scene was missing. Then, reluctant to face Thelma when she decided to get up, he went off to the new estate through which he had walked that morning and began knocking on doors in search of odd jobs. He told potential employers that he was staying with Mrs Cunningham for a while and needed work while he looked for a permanent post. Thus he established credentials; everyone knew who Mrs Cunningham was, even if they had never met her, and that first day he got several offers. It was not easy to find casual help in the village because the hotel employed so many local people; only a nucleus of staff lived in.

Edward was well pleased with his morning's canvass, although he found no one at home at some of the bungalows. He was shocked to see half-lights open at windows and other invitations to prowlers. Just because the place seemed so quiet and peaceful didn't mean it was immune to visits from villains. After all, he was an ex-con himself.

There were fire hazards, too; piles of rubbish in garages and weedkiller in bags in garden sheds. A puff of flame was all it would take.

After she had delivered six jigsaw puzzles to the charity shop and collected several more, Lydia did some shopping in Sainsbury's. There was no comparable supermarket in Heronsmouth, where she went for what could not be obtained in Milton St Gabriel. When she was alone she needed so little, but now that Thelma and Edward were staying, she must stock up. And there would be Gerald at the weekend. Lydia wrote a cheque in Sainsbury's shuddering inwardly at the amount. Then she went to the bank and cashed another cheque for money she was certain to need for day-to-day expenses. Even the milk bill would be double; she used only two pints a week but Edward would probably pour half a pint on his cereal, if he was anything like her grandson, Christopher. A young person needed good food, and plenty of it.

Her tasks done, Lydia was reluctant to return home, where she would have to face the problem of Thelma. She decided to have lunch in Cheverton's big department store; it needn't cost much if she chose her meal with care, and it would be a small treat. Now and then she allowed herself this, or a bar snack at the Manor. It was nice to eat something she hadn't prepared herself and need not wash up.

She took Boris for a run, then left him in the car in a parking lot near the store. While she was sitting at a small table in the no-smoking area of the self-service restaurant, eating an egg salad attractively garnished with pineapple slices and cress, she saw a small girl wandering between the aisles on her own. The child could not be more than two years old. Lydia looked about for the mother. It wasn't easy to collect a tray and keep an eye on a child at the same time, but surely one so young could be attached to a harness?

As the child's lower jaw dropped and her mouth opened to cry, Lydia got up and approached her.

'Now, dear,' she said, bending down. 'Where's your mummy? We'll soon find her, don't worry.' She took the child's hand and peered round.

The child was comforted by the firm grasp but she did not know this person who had stooped down to her level and was now asking her name. She let out a loud yell and at that moment there was a flurry of movement beside Lydia as the little girl's hand was snatched from hers.

'What do you mean by getting away from me?' demanded the mother, yanking at the child. She glared at Lydia. 'And what do you think you're doing?' she demanded. 'Poking your nose in where it's not wanted?'

Before Lydia could reply, the mother had swept the child, now bawling, away to a table in a far corner.

Lydia returned to her own place, her heart thumping fast in anger. The incident had sent her appetite away and spoiled her fragmentary pleasure in what she was doing, but she forced herself to eat the food she had paid for and to drink her coffee, which was now cool. It was so tiresome having to collect everything all at once; coffee never stayed hot while you ate your main course. She was unaware of any reaction to the small episode, and indeed few people had paid any attention.

Later, Lydia went to the store's hosiery department where she bought herself a pair of warm navy wool tights for the winter. As she paid for her purchase, she saw the same mother walking through the department, dragging the child by the arm. The small girl was still crying; sobs of grief, not of temper, rent the air.

Lydia glared at the mother, and the mother glared back.

Thelma knew that she was alone in the house. She had heard the mower outside and had seen Edward's busy activity; then there was silence. Her mother had gone off in the Metro and after that, apart from an occasional car passing in the lane, there was no noise.

Then the radio next door came on. Beat music throbbed through Karen White's window, opened because she had been doing her hair and had filled the room with spray. Thelma liked pop music; it drove away thought. She welcomed the noise.

She had a bath, put on trousers and sweater, then filled the washing machine with the clothes she had travelled in from America and switched it on. Her hangover had abated and she felt hungry, but when she looked in the fridge there seemed to be nothing to eat. Surely her mother could have gone along to Mrs Dodds's shop by now and stocked up, before going out?

Thelma decided to go to the Manor for a drink and some food.

She still found it strange to walk down the drive of what had been her home, with the colony of bright new dwellings away to the right behind the rhododendrons. The place was so familiar, yet so changed. Here, she had ridden her pony around the grounds. Here, on the somewhat uneven grass court, she had learned to play tennis, hitting the ball across the frayed, mended net to her father. They had never been able to afford a hard court, but now there was one, and a swimming pool. In his study, now the bar, her father had pretended to be cross when her school reports were poor, but his disapproval had never lasted long.

'You'll soon get married,' he'd say. 'You won't have to worry about a career.'

He hadn't taken her wish to go on the stage very seriously but when she was turned down by various recognized drama schools, he paid for her to go to one more obscure. Marrying Charles Hallows, the son of the local doctor, rescued her from the failure of her early career but supplied her with fresh problems. Charles, who had failed to get into medical school and was anyway not keen to follow his father's profession, was working as an estate agent, learning the business from the bottom up, with exams to be passed as he progressed. He was serious about his work, studying at home in the evenings, and was reluctant to take Thelma out dancing or even to the cinema. She was lonely and bored, but she enjoyed her married status and being able to refer to 'my husband'. Occasionally they gave dinner parties, returning the hospitality of other young couples encountered mainly through Charles's work, and Thelma enjoyed these. She took cooking lessons at a local college but gave up after less than a term; the course was not geared towards entertaining and she found it dull. Her mother had taught her the essentials and it was more amusing to try out recipes from books and magazines. She enjoyed dabbling about in the kitchen in an unstructured way.

She and Charles were both disappointed in their marriage. He had always admired Thelma. When they were children she had been a tomboy – first up the highest tree, able to swim faster and further than either he or Gerald could manage. When Charles saw her performance as Nina, he had felt a sudden love for her, but she only agreed to their marriage when no more parts came her way. Charles had expected things to work out easily after the wedding; after all, they had known each other so long and all girls wanted to settle down, or so he had thought. But it didn't happen like that; Thelma was bored at home and didn't want children, and she didn't enjoy Charles as a lover.

He flung himself more and more into his work; she haunted the local pubs and went frequently up to London in quest of theatrical work.

He did not know what would follow if she were to win a part in a London production, but it didn't happen. Then he was killed. He never knew what sometimes went on when she was supposed to be at an audition; nor did he know that within two years of their marriage she had had an abortion. She took care not to need another.

Thelma was truly shocked by Charles's tragic death, but now she attracted pity and she enjoyed her role as a young widow. After the episode with her father's stockman, several men attempted to console her and as she missed being one of a conventional pair, she tried marriage again.

Since then she had lost count of how many lovers she had had, but she had never found whatever it was that she sought. Her pleasure came from knowing that she could enchant; she swiftly grew bored and moved on. But it was to have been different with Lucian. After he left for America, he had written her several amusing letters. She'd read, *You should come over*, and had taken this as a serious proposition when he had meant it as merely an idle suggestion. After she arrived, at first he had made the best of things; but because they had been incompatible both in and out of bed, he had brought the affair to an end.

The arrival into her life of Edward had restored Thelma's confidence, and now she stepped optimistically across the Manor threshold. She'd nearly ceased to expect her father to appear and greet her with a cool kiss on her cheek. She had liked the feel of his scratchy tweed jacket, the scent of the special stuff he used on his hair.

'Well, poppet, and what have you been up to?' he would say. He was gentler with her than with anyone, but now he had gone.

She went into the bar, where Ferdy was behind the counter polishing glasses. He was an elderly Pole who had served in the Army during the war and had lived in England ever since. He seldom went off duty, serving tea in the afternoon and morning coffee as well. He lived in a council flat in Heronsmouth, where he had worked at the Swan until they retired him because of his age. Gerald had been instrumental in getting him the job at the Manor where his experience was useful. Most of the staff were young, and guests found Ferdy's presence reassuring.

'Well, Ferdy,' she greeted him. 'How're you?'

'Splendid, splendid, Miss Thelma,' said Ferdy, who had known her since the days when her father used to treat her to lunch at the Swan. He smiled at her. The sight of a pretty woman still cheered him up.

Thelma ordered a double gin and tonic.

'I haven't brought any money,' she said. 'Chalk it up, will you, Ferdy? And have one yourself.'

'Thank you,' said Ferdy, but he frowned. Miss Thelma never had any money when she came in alone and he didn't like asking her mother to pay, which was what had to happen. Miss Thelma seemed to forget that her father wasn't around any more to pick up the tab. He did not take up her invitation to himself.

'Busy?' asked Thelma, gazing round.

'We're half full,' answered Ferdy. 'It's been a bad season. There have been a lot of cancellations because of the weather. It's not been a summer to sit by the pool and sunbathe.'

'No.'

Thelma picked up her drink and looked round. Two middle-aged couples were sitting at a table in a corner; otherwise, the bar was empty. She sighed. Well, something – or someone – might yet turn up: it was still early. She'd order some lunch and see how things went.

The bar filled up while Thelma was eating a prawn salad. She was suffering from jet-lag and the scene around her had a touch of unreality about it; she could almost imagine that this was some party her parents were throwing. Everyone seemed to be paired; she saw no one alone.

When she had finished her meal, she went upstairs for a prowl. She often did this on her visits home. No one challenged her. She tried the door of what had been her father's bedroom but it was locked. In the renovation process, bathrooms had been added to all the main bedrooms and an efficient heating system installed. No guest would get chilblains now, as she had done as a child. Along here had been her room. It was one of the nicest, with a view towards the distant sea. Her mother had let her choose material for new curtains when the room was done up just before her six-teenth birthday. No one else's had been refurbished at all; Gerald's had stayed just the same as it was in her grand-parents' time. Some of the furniture had been valuable, and what hadn't been bought in by the hotel had been auctioned by a branch of the firm in which Charles, if he had lived, would by now have been a partner.

Why had he gone and got killed like that, hurtling her into widowhood while she was still a girl? It wasn't her fault that he'd come home early that day and found that she wasn't alone. He'd rushed off and given her no chance to explain that the man had been no one important; it was only because she was bored.

She still sometimes wondered if he had driven into that tree on purpose or if it was really an accident. But it didn't matter now. Only the other man knew that Charles had come home first, and he wouldn't tell for he had been married. Thelma couldn't even remember his name.

She wandered about the upper floors of the Manor for quite some time. Luckily Mrs Thomson did not emerge from her flat; Thelma always felt that the manageress did not approve of her visits, though why shouldn't she return to her former home? She tried several doors and found one or two, in the staff quarters, unlocked. There were posters on walls, make-up on dressing-tables, made beds, unmade beds; signs of alien life. Why had it all had to go?

When her thoughts turned this way, Thelma felt des-perate; movement helped, and she hurried downstairs again, coming into the bar once more.

'Coffee, Miss Thelma?' asked Ferdy.

'Yes, please.'

Thelma sat at a table drumming her fingers until it arrived. What was she going to do? If she stayed with her mother, the sparks would fly. Thelma had always wanted to shock her, beginning when she was quite young and had climbed all over the roof of the Manor, with Gerald so frightened that he had fetched their parents. She had come down fairly easily, the way she had ascended, over the parapet above the gallery and in through a window, and her father had secretly been delighted although he had made her vow never to do it again. As for Gerald, he was beaten for tale-bearing.

Thelma scarcely noticed an elderly man sitting in a wing chair near the hearth, but he saw her.

When she had finished her coffee, she went out into the garden and down to the pool. Some wet towels hung over lounger chairs at its side, but no one was swimming. Only the hardy would bathe today.

Thelma peeled off her clothes. She loved swimming naked and there was no one about. Even if there had been, she didn't much care. She dived in and swam up and down until she was out of breath.

The elderly man from the bar came up to the pool while she was in the water. Her back was turned to him as she climbed out of the pool, shook back her wet hair and grabbed a towel from a nearby chair. He thought he was dreaming.

5

Edward went out after dinner that evening.

It had been an excellent meal. Walking home from the Manor, Thelma had decided to give her mother a treat by cooking her something delicious. She had persuaded the new butcher in the village to bone her some lamb, and had stuffed the fillet thus obtained with herbs and small mushrooms. They had zabaglione for pudding.

Lydia knew that the various items would all have been charged up to her. In fact, she no longer ran an account anywhere in the village; her wants were few when she was alone, so it wasn't worth while, and she liked to pay as she went along. She was, however, such a respected resident that Thelma would have encountered no problems about shopping, like royalty, without money. After her visits, Lydia always went round paying whatever was owed.

But Edward knew nothing of this. He revised some of his harsher thoughts about Thelma in the light of what seemed to him to be generous conduct.

He'd discovered, however, that there was a disco in the village hall that night, and he had decided to go. After his time inside it would be a real thrill, and he might meet some girl who'd be more his style than Thelma.

He helped clear the table and wash up – he had always helped at home, Julie had seen to that – and slipped out while Thelma was making the coffee.

She put the television on when she brought in the tray. Any sound was better than silence.

'Where's Edward?' she asked, when she had poured out three cups and he had not appeared in the sitting room.

'I've no idea,' said Lydia.

Thelma went to the foot of the stairs and called him. She tried the cloakroom door, then went into the garden and called again, in vain.

'He's not here,' she said.

'How odd to go out without saying where he was going,' said Lydia, but she spoke placidly. She had enjoyed her dinner; Thelma was certainly a very good cook. There was quite a lot of the lamb left; it would do for two more meals at least.

'He's probably gone down to the Bell,' said Thelma. 'I'll go along later and see.'

But he wasn't at the pub. Thelma knew some of the people who were there, however, including the Dennises from the bungalow beyond her mother's garden. She ended up playing darts and didn't come home until closing time.

Her mother was still up, putting pieces in a jigsaw; she seemed never to weary of this occupation. She had let Boris out for a final run in the garden and had washed up the coffee things.

'Edward is not back,' she told her daughter, who was flushed and animated, but at least had returned alone. 'Will you be sure to lock up when he does return?'

'I will. Don't worry,' said Thelma. 'I'm not going to bed yet myself – my metabolism is still running on American time.'

Lydia left her watching the late film.

She was very tired, herself, and fell asleep over her book, a biography of Florence Nightingale.

Edward left the disco when it finished soon after midnight. The swirling lights and loud music had excited him, and he had revelled in the movement and contact provided by the entertainment. Young people from neighbouring villages had come in cars and on motorbikes. Julie and her friends from the hotel came in when the restaurant closed; Edward left with them and a girl he had met who lived near the lodge.

'I'll walk you home,' he told her. 'I'm going your way. You shouldn't go home on your own.'

'Why ever not?' asked Karen White. 'Nothing ever happens in Milton St Gabriel.'

'You can't be sure it won't, one day,' said Edward. 'A stranger may come to the village and turn the place over.'

'One like you, you mean,' said Karen.

'Exactly,' said Edward, grinning in the harsh light from the street lamp outside the hall. There were now eight strategically placed street lights in the village; one faction on the parish council said more were needed but another declared that the old-world charm of the original area would be spoiled by this modern intrusion.

'You must be joking,' said Karen. 'You're Julie's brother.'

'That's my passport, is it?' asked Edward, laughing. He took Karen's arm. 'Well, you're safe enough with me, but it doesn't do to be too trusting of blokes you've just met, you know.' He'd come across some very unpleasant customers when he was inside.

'I've got some wine in my room,' said Victor. 'Let's keep the party going.'

'Why not?' agreed Edward.

They went back with him to his room in the stable block, where Victor produced cans of beer and a bottle of rough red wine. He put on a tape of Duran Duran and they all sat round enjoying their drinks. The music removed any need to talk, but it was too loud for Julie who worriedly told Victor to turn it down. Sound travelled across the yard to the hotel, she explained, and the guests might complain. It had happened before and she did not want Mrs Thomson to come storming across. Julie was reluctant to account for Eddie's presence among them.

Karen thought this was really living. Here she was, in the early hours of the morning, drinking wine from a plastic mug and smoking, though it was nothing more daring than ordinary tobacco.

Not much happened, however. There was no kissing or cuddling. Perhaps that would come later, on the way home. Boys always wanted it. She swallowed her wine, which was rather nasty, and held out her mug for some more.

It was Julie who broke up the evening, sending Edward and Karen off into the darkness and reminding Victor that she and Mavis had to get up early, in her case to attend to the tea trays, and in Mavis's, to serve breakfast.

Edward and Karen walked hand in hand down the dark drive. There was no moon, and the air was mild, as if it was still summer. They kept wandering from the tarred track on to the grass, giggling as they stumbled along. Soon Edward's arm was around Karen's waist and they stopped now and then to kiss.

They had both had a good deal to drink, and one thing led to another, so that they took some time to reach Karen's house, next to the lodge.

'How convenient,' said Edward.

She giggled, then put a finger to her lips and said 'Ssh.'

'How are you going to get in?' he asked. 'Have you got a key?'

She had, and opened the door quietly. Her mother was probably back from Heronsmouth by now, but she never cut up rough if Karen was late; it was her father who wanted to know chapter and verse.

'Can I come in too?' Edward whispered. 'Just for a minute?'

She had sobered up enough not to let him. Edward didn't insist; they arranged to meet the following evening instead, at the Bell. The landlord knew she was under age and he wouldn't let her in if he recognized her, but Karen decided to think about that tomorrow.

The door at the lodge was unlatched. He let himself in and crept quietly up to the small single room at the top of the stairs, where he fell happily asleep and did not wake until he heard Mrs Cunningham go to the bathroom at seven o'clock the next morning.

Betty, who during the war had helped Lydia to look after the children and thus freed her to work at the hospital which the Manor had become, came from Heronsmouth once a week to clean. She did not need the work but she liked to keep an eye on Lydia, for whom she felt a sort of affection.

During the intervening years, Betty had married, raised a family and been widowed herself. She had never lived far from Milton St Gabriel, and now occupied a bungalow in the outskirts of Heronsmouth. Lydia drove her each way because the buses were few and inconvenient; she did shopping errands after she took Betty back. Betty's husband, a chief petty officer in the Royal Navy, had opened a newsagent's shop when he retired. Their son, an accountant, was now with a multi-national firm, and their daughter, a teacher, had married a lecturer at the University of Durham. Betty had never lost touch with the Cunninghams, and often during her husband's tours at sea had helped out at the Manor.

She was waiting at the corner of Malplaquet Drive when Lydia drove up, as she was every Thursday morning at a quarter past nine, a small, dumpy woman with neatly waved grey hair and today wearing a smart pale green raincoat. She carried a holdall in which were her apron and the slippers she wore at the lodge.

'Good morning, Mrs Cunningham,' she said brightly, getting into the Metro. Long ago, when she had just left school and used to bath Thelma and Gerald and read them stories, she had addressed Lydia as 'Madam'. This had ceased when her husband was no longer a mere naval rating.

'Good morning, Betty.' Lydia engaged the gears as Betty buckled her seat belt.

'Wretched thing, I'll never get used to it,' she grumbled, as she did every week, and Lydia felt comforted. One thing which never altered in the changing world was Betty and her reactions.

'How are Brian and Pat?' Lydia inquired, in her own ritual.

A report on the lives of Betty's children followed. Over the years, Lydia had followed their progress through measles, mumps, examinations and courtship through to parenthood and their present satisfactory positions in life. Today's chapter contained no startling news: Brian and his wife were off to a villa in Corfu for a late holiday; Pat and her family had earlier rented a *gîte* in the Dordogne.

As she talked, subconsciously Betty noticed how thin and veined were Lydia's hands on the steering wheel, how bony the wrists that protruded from her carefully washed blue cardigan. Did she eat enough? Betty hated taking money from her, aware that her own income probably equalled or even surpassed that of her employer. It had not been possible to conceal the terms of Henry Cunningham's will: the *Cheverton Gazette* had given its details and Betty had been shocked, but she was sure Gerald took good care of his mother. He'd done well, but then that Iris had cost him a packet. Betty had never taken to her and she'd been proved right in the end. She, Betty, had been lucky. She'd had a good life with her Bill, a cheerful, kindly man, whereas what she had seen of Mrs Cunningham's marriage depressed her. There didn't seem to be any laughter. Mrs Cunningham, always quiet during the war years when he was away, had later grown quieter still; she had had no glow about her. Betty and Bill had laughed a lot and there wasn't a tiff or a disagreement that hadn't been resolved with a smile from one or the other. Some years before the old man died, Mrs Cunningham had moved out of the main bedroom at the Manor to quite a small one in another wing. She had given no explanation and Betty had not commented on the change, but she felt sad. She had spent many a lonely night when Bill was at sea, and all the more precious had been those last years together, curled up in their cosy bed like spoons; she missed him still in every way.

Now, Betty could tell that something was wrong. Mrs Cunningham was tensing herself up to raise some distasteful subject. Was she to be given the sack in an economy drive? Betty resolved not to take it, if so. She settled her holdall more firmly on her lap and waited for the disclosure.

At last, as they entered the village, Lydia found the words.

'Thelma's home,' she said.

'She's never! I thought she was gone for good, this time,' said Betty, who had been to the States herself, three times, to visit her sister, a GI bride who had stayed the course. 'What happened?' she asked.

'It didn't work.' Lydia repeated Thelma's explanation.

'Why ever not?'

'I don't know. She hasn't told me,' said Lydia.

No, and I bet you didn't ask, thought Betty.

'And there's someone else here,' Lydia managed to add. 'A young man whom Thelma has invited to stay for a while – he has relatives in the village and they haven't a spare bed at the moment. I think they let rooms.'

This was a long speech for Lydia, and a lot of information for her to give at one time. Clam wasn't the name for her;

safe deposit, more likely.

'I see,' said Betty.

'He's pleasant enough,' said Lydia. 'He cut the grass and adjusted the mower so that it works better.'

'Good,' said Betty.

When they arrived at the lodge, Edward was to be seen up a ladder cleaning the windows.

'There he is,' said Lydia.

'Well, now!' Betty was pleased. A window cleaner occasionally came to Milton St Gabriel, but he sometimes forgot to call at the lodge. The bungalow windows were easier to clean if he was pressed for time. 'I'll soon find him a little list of jobs that want doing,' she promised, getting out of the car.

Edward had decided to carry out one useful task for Mrs Cunningham every day. In that way, she would feel awkward about asking him to move on, and besides, it was only right that he should do something for her in return for his bed and board. He'd noticed how smeary the windows were after the rain. The job wouldn't take long and he polished away with a will, whistling.

Thelma was in the kitchen finishing a late breakfast when the two older women entered.

'Well, Betty, you see the bad penny's turned up again,' she said.

'You're lucky to have your mother to take you in,' said Betty, taking off her Dannimac and hanging it on the back of the kitchen door. 'Now, what's the trouble this time?' After knowing Thelma all her life, she had no inhibitions about questioning her.

'Oh – men,' said Thelma largely.

'You liked him enough to go all that way, didn't you?' Betty said, putting on her house slippers. She tied her apron round her generous waist.

'You can't tell till you live with someone,' said Thelma.

'Well, I know that's the modern way, more's the pity,' said Betty. 'But at your age you should act more respectable.'

'Come off it, Betty,' said Thelma. 'Life begins at forty. Didn't you know?' She got up as Betty began to clear the table.

'Time you settled down,' said Betty, but she spoke in a
tolerant tone. Thelma hadn't been lucky; she'd married that
second husband on the rebound, for sure, after Charles's
death. Her father had been anxious about it right from the
start, but even he hadn't been able to prevent her from
going ahead. It was all very sad and just showed you could
never tell how things would work out. Thelma had been
such a pretty child, with appealing ways; she'd twisted her
father round her little finger and even her mother let her get
away with blue murder, though they were both always
picking on Gerald, who was such a good little boy. Betty
hadn't seen much of him after his marriage; she'd thought
that Iris a stuck-up sort of girl but the two children, Fiona
and Christopher, were nice enough. Really poor Mrs Cunningham didn't get much joy from her family, Betty
thought, getting the vacuum cleaner out of the cupboard.

She plugged the machine into a socket in the sitting
room, then, before switching it on, began moving the furniture away from the walls. Perhaps that young man would
look at the cleaner; it hadn't been working very well lately.
If it needed a part, Mrs C. could collect it that afternoon
when she took Betty home.

But Thelma decided that she would do that.

'It'll save you the trouble, Mother,' she said.

She'd scream if she spent another whole day in the
village. Besides, she wanted to get her hair done and buy a
few things. She'd got her bank card which she could use to
save paying now; the next instalment of her income would
reach her account on the first of the month.

'Where'd you find that young man, then?' Betty asked as
Thelma drove her, much too fast, down the lane. Various
signs, as she tidied up Thelma's room and made her bed,
had revealed to her the nature of their relationship which
they seemed to be having the tact to conceal from Mrs C.,
poor blind soul.

'In London,' said Thelma airily. It wasn't a lie; the train
had begun its journey at Paddington.

'Hm.'

'Oh, Betty, you and your "hms",' said Thelma, and
laughed. 'Where's your sense of adventure? You only live
once.'

'Yes, and you only die once, too,' said Betty. 'And then you've got to account for it all.'

'Do you still believe that?' Thelma asked, changing gear roughly. Her mother was a far better driver, Betty reflected, glad now of the support of the seat belt as Thelma hurled the car round corners. She had to jam on the brakes hard when they met a delivery van head on with no room to pass. The van driver reversed to a passing place and Thelma gave him a cheery wave as they drove by, so that he smiled.

'Of course, and so should you,' said Betty, a staunch Baptist. 'I'm sure your mother always brought you up to do so.'

'Well, she's given it up now,' said Thelma. 'She never goes to church.'

'How can you say that? Of course she does!' exclaimed Betty. Regular as clockwork, off they'd gone every Sunday, and Mr C. had been a churchwarden right up to his death, reading the lesson each week.

'You're wrong, Betty. She gave it up after Daddy died. I don't think she's been since the funeral.'

The church had been full then; local dignitaries, the Lord Lieutenant, the Chief Constable and representatives from the council had turned out that day, as well as most of the village, and Thelma had wept throughout the service while her mother had remained dry-eyed and stony-faced, exhibiting the stiff upper lip for which women of her and earlier generations were renowned. Thelma had not seen her shed a single tear.

'I didn't know,' said Betty. 'Are you sure?'

'The vicar spoke to Gerald about it,' said Thelma. 'Typical of the church – always wanting someone else to do its dirty work. Why couldn't he ask Mother direct?'

'Did Gerald?'

'No, and quite right too. She still supports the good causes – goes to the fête – all that sort of thing,' said Thelma.

Perhaps she thought the Lord had deserted her, Betty reflected. Poor soul, denying herself such a source of comfort. Betty didn't know where she would be without the support her religion gave her. Still, that was the way of it, these days. All the same, she was surprised that Mrs C. was to be numbered among the heathen.

6

Thelma swirled the Metro into Malplaquet Drive and dropped Betty outside her bungalow.

'See you next week,' she called, thus answering Betty's unspoken query as to whether she planned to stay on in Milton St Gabriel.

She drove towards the town and left the car in a side road before sauntering into the main street. The day was grey: clouds lowered over the estuary where the boats lapped at their moorings. Thelma felt chilly in her cotton boiler suit. She saw an end-of-season sale on at Liza's, a fashion shop, and went inside, where she bought a voluminous sweater knitted in heathery shades of mohair, and not reduced. She paid for it with her bank card and put it on, feeling warmer straight away. The climate here compared unfavourably with that of California. Her departure from the States had left no time for general maintenance and her hair needed a fresh brightening rinse; she went along to see if The Copper Nob could fit her in this afternoon. Her mother never went to the hairdresser; she trimmed her own hair, pulling it over her shoulder and clipping the ends. Thelma had once caught her doing it, had seen the bald dome of her mother's head and been shocked by its ugliness. Lydia had put her hands to her skull to hide it and shouted to her to go away, quite frightening Thelma.

Her luck was in. The hairdresser had a cancellation and soon Thelma was leaning back over a basin being shampooed.

The atmosphere soothed her; while she waited for Luigi to attend to her, she listened to the talk around her and heard another customer, who was being dyed, talking to the girl daubing her hair about a new drama group which was going to put on *The Seagull* in November. They were casting now, and she hoped to secure the role of Arkadina.

Immediately, Thelma knew what she must do. That part shall be mine, she decided; and everything else went out of her head as she listened hard, hoping to learn who the producer was, or any other relevant details. She was unsuccessful; the salon was busy and most of the clients were chatty, their voices drowning the one she wanted to hear. The other woman was still being worked over when Thelma left, her own hair now standing out in a gleaming mass of golden spirals.

She walked down the road wondering how to find out more. In the Public Library, perhaps?

Her attention was caught by a billboard outside the newsagent's, once owned by Betty's husband. RATE RISE FORECAST, she read, and wandered in. She wanted to order *The Stage*, and it occurred to her that the shopkeeper might know about the dramatic society.

He did. There was a feature about it in the latest *Cheverton Gazette*. The new group replaced one that had withered away some years ago, prone as it was to putting on Brecht and other difficult works of limited appeal. The newsagent thought *The Seagull* sounded good; he supposed it to have a maritime theme of local interest.

Thelma did not disabuse him. She bought the paper and took it away to study. There were details of a meeting that evening at the producer's house in Willow Close; some parts would be cast then, and if necessary there would be readings. Thelma went to the bookshop, and rather to her surprise, found that they had a paperback volume of Chekov's plays, which she bought, again paying by cheque. By now the bank was shut and it was too late to get any money. She walked on up the hill to the Swan Hotel, where years ago she had so often been with her father. A treat had been lunch in the restaurant, or tea in the panelled lounge – toasted tea cakes sopping with butter in winter, by the fire; clotted cream and jam with scones in summer.

The lounge was unaltered. It contained comfortable chairs, and Thelma sat there reading the play, thinking herself into the part of the vain and beautiful actress as she refreshed her memory.

She had just enough cash to pay for her tea. When she

went back to collect her mother's car, there was a parking ticket under the wiper blade. Thelma tore it up and drove off to Willow Close. A number of other cars were drawn up outside, and she saw the woman from the hairdresser's walking ahead of her up the path.

Thelma displayed confidence; she mentioned that she had been a professional actress before her marriage, and when several scenes were read, she performed with attack. The dark woman, who had failed to prepare the part, was cast as Masha, and Thelma secured the role of Arkadina.

Edward had spent the afternoon with Julie. She usually had the afternoon off because she came on duty so early, but she sometimes had to turn beds down at night and be ready to help out elsewhere.

They'd got a lift down to Worton Bay with Victor, who had a girlfriend there. Her parents ran a café lying back a short way from the beach in the huddle of tourist shops and fishermen's cottages which clustered in a fold of the hills. Because of the poor weather, they had had a bad season, and the place was empty when the trio from the hotel arrived. After they had all had tea, Julie and Edward went for a walk on the beach.

The tide was coming in. Edward picked up a stone and flung it as far as he could towards the horizon. A ship in the distance moved slowly along, a dark smudge against heavy clouds.

'Bit miserable, isn't it, when it's not sunny,' he said. 'Still, it's nice to get out.'

'Mind you stay out,' said Julie.

'Oh, I will,' said Edward. 'I'm going to light a bonfire for Mrs Cunningham tonight, or maybe tomorrow. She's got a pile of stuff waiting to be burnt. That'll do me.' He was looking forward to it, had planned how he would lay paper and the drier stems and stalks at the base, touch it off with maybe a little paraffin to obtain a blaze, then stoke it and allow it to smoulder.

'See that it does,' said Julie. She had never been able to understand his compulsion which came on when things weren't going too well for him. He had fired the car after a girlfriend he'd been going out with for several months threw him over. At school, when exams loomed or when he found work difficult, he had started blazes in waste-paper baskets and once in the boiler room. He'd gone to a psychologist then, and had been suitably penitent, but it hadn't lasted. It would be dreadful if something went wrong at the lodge. Suppose he annoyed the old lady in some way, and she got cross? He might want to kick back at her. There was something fishy about his being a guest of the daughter: Julie had never seen Thelma, but she had heard about her; she didn't sound like a do-gooder or prisoner's friend.

'How long are you planning to stay here?' she asked.

'I don't know. I'll see how it goes,' said Edward. 'I've got myself a few little jobs, mowing lawns and painting, things like that. Some of the folk in the new bungalows are wanting help in the garden. They'll pay me well.'

'Has Mrs Cunningham said you can stay on?'

It seemed that putting him up at the hotel had not crossed Julie's mind.

'We've not discussed it,' he replied. 'I'm doing jobs for her, too. She needs someone to help her along.'

'Be careful,' Julie warned.

'Why wouldn't I be? She's a nice old bat and Thelma doesn't treat her any too well,' said Edward. 'She went off in the car taking the cleaning lady home, and she wasn't home when I left just now. Mrs Cunningham's meant to be going to supper with some friend in Wilcombe. I hope Thelma comes back in time.'

'Oh, she will, surely?' said Julie. She hesitated, then had to ask. 'What about you and Thelma?'

'Oh, that's nothing,' said Edward. 'Bit of a turn-off, as a matter of fact.'

'Oh, Eddie, you don't mean to say you and she – ?' Julie's heart sank. What had he got himself into? 'Why, she must be years older than you.'

'I can't help it if she fancies me,' said Edward smugly. 'But if you ask me, she doesn't like it all that much. I had to go along with it, didn't I? It'd have been rude not to.'

'Just fancying isn't enough,' said Julie curtly. 'You've got to like the bloke.'

'Oh, is that right?' Edward was put out at the thought that Thelma had found him wanting. 'I'd say it won't happen again,' he added, promising nothing.

Julie was only partly mollified.

'Watch it,' she repeated.

'What's her brother like?' Edward thought it was time to change the subject.

'I don't know. I haven't seen him,' said Julie.

'Well, he's coming for the weekend. Staying up at your place, it seems,' said Edward.

'You just watch your step, then,' Julie warned. 'You may have got round the old lady and her daughter but he'll know what's what. He'll have you out in minutes if he takes against what's going on.'

'Nothing's going on,' said Edward. 'And you don't have to worry. I don't want another stretch, believe me.'

'But you said you couldn't help yourself, before. You could get like that again.'

'No way. I just flipped,' said Edward.

But that hadn't been the first time and he might flip again. Julie watched worriedly as he suddenly ran away from her down the beach, arms waving like a small boy pretending to be an aeroplane. He let out chortles of pure joy at his physical freedom, swooping and swerving and leaping into the air, thin legs in faded jeans twinkling as he pounded over the band of seaweed at the tideline and across the foreshore towards the café where they had left Victor.

Julie followed more slowly. He had inveigled his way into Mrs Cunningham's house, whatever he might say about having been invited. What if she found out about him? Challenged him? Turned him out? For she wouldn't knowingly house an ex-con.

Julie shook herself. If she wouldn't believe in him, who would? She had a duty to him, like it or not, and she'd run away from it during his sentence. What if he were to get a regular job here, in the district? Would he settle to it or would he become bored in the winter, when there was so little to do? Thelma Hallows was only slumming, taking up with him; wouldn't she throw him away as a dog might an old bone?

Filled with foreboding, Julie followed her brother across the road, passing the souvenir shop with its racks of fading postcards but no customers, to the deserted café.

7

Gerald Cunningham's emotions as he turned into the Manor drive on Friday evening differed from Thelma's, but he too regretted that this was no longer his home.

If things had been different, he could have contrived to stay on, striking a deal over selling off some of the land to provide funds for putting the house to rights, as in fact had eventually happened. But on paper the place was worth a great deal and the smart divorce lawyer Iris had hired had pressed her entitlement to a very big settlement, so that now she and her new husband occupied quite a large house and had been able to open their business. Gerald hoped that, since he had subsidized this, the other family – Iris's step-children and their mother – were suitably supported too. It was all a sad pity.

It pleased him to find the Manor restored and fully used, and with his investment he still had a stake in its future. He took his bag into the hall, registered at the desk and was allotted his room, following the porter up the wide front staircase and along the passage to number eleven. This had been a spare bedroom, seldom used. Part of it had been sectioned off and turned into a bathroom. A television set was supplied for the guest, and brochures advertised places of local interest; there were potteries and gardens, museums and a few stately homes all within a moderate radius. Gerald glanced idly through the leaflets; he hadn't known about half these places.

He wasted no more time in nostalgic reflection. All his life he had got on with the next task as soon as the last one was finished, and now he washed, shaved quickly – his beard was so dark that he looked unkempt by evening – put on a clean shirt and then walked down the drive to the lodge. It was good to stretch his legs after spending so long in the car, and he gratefully inhaled the warm night air. In spite of the appalling summer, autumn was delaying its arrival. All the extra rain must have persuaded the leaves to cling longer to the trees, he thought.

As he approached his mother's house, he reminded himself of some facts. I am a successful banker earning a high salary and attempts have been made to head-hunt me to other concerns where I would earn still more. My advice is asked for and listened to with respect by eminent persons. Therefore it is foolish to feel now as though I were ten years old, returning from school and longing for an affectionate, approving welcome from my mother. I didn't receive it then, and I won't now. I'll never please her, he decided, but at least I can do a little to help her, unlike Thelma, who turns up whenever the fancy takes her and expects a welcome like that given to the prodigal son – and gets it. That story had always seemed to him an example of grave injustice.

Squaring his shoulders, Gerald approached the house, where lights showed behind the curtains. The garage doors were open, the light above them on, and the car was out. It was irrational to expect his mother to be at home waiting as eagerly to greet him as he was to see her. He had said he would stop for a meal on the way down and might be late arriving. Why shouldn't she be out? Though she rarely was, unless she went to see Dorothy Butler, her one real friend, a retired schoolmistress who lived some thirty miles away.

His spirits had already slumped as he moved to the front door. It was Thelma whom he must now prepare to meet. He nearly turned back, putting it off till the morning, but Gerald was one who always saw things through.

The door was on the latch. Gerald opened it and went into the small hall. Boris at once came to welcome him. Friend and foe alike, Boris would greet any visitor with joy.

'Well, boy.' Gerald stooped to pat the dog. The sitting-room door was ajar, and he went into the room, followed by Boris still wagging his tail.

His mother was seated in front of the table before an incomplete jigsaw puzzle. The outline was filled in, and she held a piece in her hand as she turned to him. Sitting close to her was a young man in jeans and a red sweater. Gerald immediately sensed the accord between the two. It did not cross his mind as he advanced, his features arranged in a warm smile, that this was Thelma's friend, and his head was full of questions.

'Ah, Gerald. There you are,' Lydia said. She stood up, moving easily, with no sign of arthritis or rheumatism. They did not kiss; she was taller than he was, and it would have looked ridiculous. 'I never heard the car,' she added, and he detected reproof in her tone.

'I went straight up to the house – I needed a wash,' he said.

'There is a bathroom here,' Lydia observed.

Two put-downs in less than a minute: that must be a record.

'Well, I'm here now,' said Gerald firmly, and looked towards the stranger, who had risen to his feet. He was thin and rather pale, with short brown curly hair.

'This is Edward Fletcher,' Lydia introduced. 'My son Gerald.'

'Pleased to meet you,' said Edward. He beamed at Gerald, anxious to create a favourable impression.

'Thelma's friend,' Lydia supplied in level tones.

'Where is Thelma?' Gerald asked.

'She went out,' said Lydia.

'She's acting in a play, in Heronsmouth,' said Edward eagerly. 'She's the star.'

'What, already?' Gerald's thick, dark eyebrows rose.

'It's a rehearsal tonight,' Edward explained. 'It's all about a seagull. By some Russian.'

Gerald looked at his mother, who nodded.

'She's Arkadina,' she told him.

'So she'll be staying here a while,' said Gerald, with misgiving.

'Where else is she to go? She's let her flat,' said Lydia.

'And how long are you staying?' Gerald turned to Edward, smiling pleasantly to take any hint of challenge from the question.

'I'm not sure,' Edward answered. He hesitated, then took a gamble. 'Do you want me to go?' he asked Lydia.

'Only when you're ready,' said Lydia equivocally.

'You're on holiday, I suppose?' said Gerald, who supposed nothing of the sort. The young man's much-washed sweater and his faded jeans were no real guide to status, but his wrists were gaunt; he looked – what? Unloved was the word that came into Gerald's mind as he surveyed the visitor.

'No. I'm unemployed,' said Edward. 'I've a sister in the village and Mrs Cunningham is very kindly letting me stay so I can see her. I'm hoping something in the work line will turn up.'

'Edward has done a lot of useful jobs since he arrived,' said Lydia. 'Cut the grass, mended the mower, cleaned the windows, repaired the vacuum cleaner, unblocked the sink – ' she paused to think of another achievement to add to the catalogue.

'Splendid.' Gerald admired the interloper's frankness. The length of his sojourn depended, no doubt, upon Thelma's whim. What was their relationship? 'Are you performing in the play too?' he asked.

'Oh no,' said Edward hastily, and to avoid further questions he offered to take Boris out for a final run, leaving mother and son alone.

The whisky, brandy and sherry that Gerald had brought for his mother were in the boot of his car. He did not suggest they had a drink as Thelma might well have used up all his mother's supplies. Here was his chance, though, to have a proper talk with her, find out what was in Thelma's mind, but he could not take it; instead, he asked about the jigsaw and, tentatively, tried to put a piece in position.

Now that she was a member of the drama group, Thelma was more cheerful. After she had secured the part, she had gone with her new associates to the King's Arms, where some of them, Thelma included, made it a prolonged session. She was unaware of the fact that her mother had wanted the car to go to Wilcombe for supper with Dorothy Butler.

Thelma had held court in the pub. She had told amusing tales of life in Los Angeles, repeating stories she had heard from others, mimicking them and using their success to achieve her own. Her blue eyes sparkled, her cheeks grew flushed, and the man cast as Trigorin, a dentist with a practice in Cheverton, thought himself lucky to be playing opposite someone so full of life and charm.

Left at home, Lydia had eventually telephoned Dorothy, who was Thelma's godmother.

'I didn't make it clear to her that I needed the car,' she excused, when Dorothy made tutting sounds on the line.

She had rustled up omelettes for herself and Edward. He went out after they had eaten, not telling her that he was meeting Karen White from next door lest she might think him faithless.

In the morning, Lydia did point out to Thelma that she – and what was worse, Dorothy – had been inconvenienced.

'You should have said you wanted the car,' Thelma answered sulkily.

'It never occurred to me that you wouldn't come home fairly soon,' said Lydia. 'Never mind. Let's just make sure we don't misunderstand one another again.'

'I'd like the car tonight, then,' Thelma said. 'And I don't know what time I'll be back.' On the excuse of reading through the play in preparation for the first rehearsal, some of the company had planned to meet again.

'Gerald's coming down,' her mother pointed out.

'Well, I'll see him in the morning,' Thelma said.

For different reasons, Lydia and Edward were both relieved to be spared her presence and were content to spend the evening together. Karen's father had come home and she was staying in; there was nowhere else to go, except to the pub or the hotel. Edward washed up, whistling; then he made coffee for Lydia, sending her into the sitting-room while he did so.

Interrupting their concentration on the jigsaw only to watch the television news at nine, they had spent a harmonious evening until, at last, Gerald arrived.

'That's Thelma's latest, is it?' Gerald said, after he had failed to fit any pieces in the jigsaw.

'I think she's lost interest already,' Lydia said. 'It was just a passing fancy.'

'Well, he is a bit young for her, isn't he?' said Gerald lightly. It was better not to make too much of it. 'I expect she was upset at that American thing not working out.'

'She's so unlucky,' Lydia sighed.

Oh, of course, thought Gerald. There's always an excuse

for her.

'Don't let her take advantage of you, Mother,' he said aloud. 'She'll wear you out, if you give her half a chance.'

'This is Thelma's home,' Lydia said. 'She is welcome here.'

It had happened again. The atmosphere between them had become strained within minutes of their meeting. Gerald stood up, turning away from her as Edward returned.

'I'll go now,' he said. 'It's late and I'm sure you're tired.' It would not occur to him to plead fatigue himself after his day in the City and the long drive, although he suddenly felt totally exhausted.

'Nice guy, your son,' Edward observed when Gerald had gone. 'Successful, too, isn't he?'

'Yes,' said Lydia. 'I suppose he is, in a way.'

But he had not been able to keep his wife, and he had lost the family home which had meant everything to his father.

As Gerald was walking away from the lodge, Thelma returned. She braked, with a scurry of gravel, her headlights picking up the short, stocky form of her brother, his hands in his pockets, trudging towards the entrance to the Manor. Thelma pipped the horn, making a lot of noise.

'Hullo, Gerald,' she called.

He walked back to meet her, his resentment giving way to rueful affection as he focused on her, blonde hair in alluring disorder, a light coat worn over her pale tracksuit. She was a pretty woman.

'So it didn't work,' he said bluntly.

'No. Lucian isn't good husband material,' said Thelma.

'Good thing you found out in time, then.'

'Yes, well, I'd rather live in England, anyway,' said Thelma, who had just thought of this idea.

'I hear you've landed a fat part,' Gerald said.

'Mm – only amateurs, but still, it'll be fun, and I'll add strength to the company, with my experience,' she said.

It was years since Thelma had performed, even with amateurs; still, Gerald answered kindly.

'It'll help you get back into the swing, I expect,' he said.

'Like a lift up the drive?' she offered, in her turn making

an attempt to bridge the divide between them.

'No, thanks. The walk will do me good,' he replied.

'Suit yourself,' said Thelma.

Gerald walked away from her full of anger at himself. This was not how he had intended things to be, with discord between his mother and himself and now a surge of hostile feelings towards his sister. Trying to capture a more positive mood, he walked past the house across the garden to the swimming pool. A pale blue bubbled plastic sheet covered it now, retaining warmth until the morning. They wouldn't keep it going for much longer, with this dark, dank weather. Behind the wall that sheltered it, well-tended beds produced vegetables for the hotel guests. He turned to look back at the building, where lights showed at several bedroom windows and were still on in the public rooms. Inside was comfort, if not company, and he slowly walked towards it.

The receptionist was listening to someone on the telephone, and before she saw Gerald, he heard a burst of laughter from her. The sound was such an unusual one to Gerald, in his present life, that it startled him.

She put the telephone down and came towards him, smiling still.

'Yes sir?' she asked, an ordinary girl of twenty-five or so, with unremarkable features and brown hair, but a person who was happy.

'I've got my key,' said Gerald. 'Room eleven. I didn't hand it in.'

'Oh, that's all right, Mr Cunningham,' she answered. 'Would you like tea in the morning, or a paper?'

'I'd like *The Times*, please,' said Gerald. 'No tea, though, thank you.' Then he hesitated. He always woke so early. Why not have a cup of tea and a lie-in, for a change? His mother wouldn't want to see him very early.

He asked for it at seven-thirty, and the cheerful receptionist wrote it down.

8

Next morning, Gerald's tea was brought by a pale girl in a grey dress. Her dark hair was tied in a ponytail and she had sandals on her bare feet.

Julie knew who he was, of course. She glanced curiously at the dark man who, when she entered, was already sitting up in bed with his glasses on, reading a very thick book. He wore pale cream pyjamas piped with crimson, and a forest of dark hair was exposed at the neck.

Would he find out about Eddie's past and send him packing?

She worried about it all the morning, and in her agitation she broke a saucer, which meant that she had yet another breakage that week to confess to the housekeeper.

Gerald went for a swim before breakfast. He had to uncover the pool first, rolling the plastic back, a task better done by two people. He must mention it to Mrs Thomson, discover tactfully if energetic guests were catered for when the weather was better; they should not have to do this themselves. It was quite useful to stay in the hotel, find out its merits and flaws for himself.

The water was pleasantly chill, refreshing him. He swam a great many lengths, not enjoying it much but aware that it must be doing him good. By the time he had showered, shaved, and had breakfast, he was feeling more relaxed than for several weeks. The same cheerful receptionist was on duty. He wondered what shifts they did; it was something like hospital doctors, he thought: long spells on and then a good break.

'I shall have some guests for dinner tonight,' he told her. 'I should have mentioned it in the dining-room but the head waiter wasn't on duty.'

'No. He doesn't do breakfast,' said the girl. 'I'll see to it for you, Mr Cunningham. How many will you be?'

'Oh – four, I think,' said Gerald. 'Yes.' That was right, with Thelma's young man. 'About eight?' His mother did not like eating late.

'I'll pass it on to the dining-room right away,' she said.

Gerald walked briskly down the drive in a much lighter mood than that of the previous evening, but when he reached the lodge, no one seemed to have time for him. Edward was out in the garden trimming the tufted grass beneath the trees which the mower could not reach, his mother was arranging some late roses in a bowl in the sitting-room, and Thelma was in the kitchen, ironing. His mother went on with her flower arranging after her usual cool greeting, and even Boris barely looked up.

Gerald went into the kitchen to talk to his sister.

'Want to tell me what happened in America?' he asked.

'It's none of your business. I told you as much as you need to know last night,' said Thelma.

Gerald counted to five in his head before he replied.

'I'm not just being curious,' he said, successfully keeping impatience out of his tone. 'I thought you might need some brotherly sympathy, that's all.'

'I'm not asking for any,' said Thelma, thumping the iron down hard on the sleeve of a shirt.

'I don't like to see you unhappy,' said Gerald.

'I'm not unhappy,' said Thelma. 'Not at all. Unlucky, yes, but then we're an unlucky family.'

'Why do you say that?'

'Well, Daddy dying and losing our money,' she said.

'Father was getting on for seventy. He'd had a full life,' said Gerald. 'And he didn't lose money. He never had a lot of it.'

'He should have married a woman who had some, then,' said Thelma, now tackling a green cotton skirt. She poked the iron into a fold by the zip. 'Not a penniless vicar's daughter.'

'What a dreadful thing to say!' Gerald was outraged.

'I don't know why you're so shocked,' said Thelma. 'People have always done that.'

'You know perfectly well that theirs was a wartime romance,' said Gerald.

'It wasn't like that at all,' said Thelma. 'Daddy was never in love with mother. He married to carry on the line. He was afraid he'd be killed, like his brother, before he had an heir.'

'Good God!' Gerald exploded. 'You talk as if he was a duke or something. His family had a manor house and some land. That was all.'

'It was very important,' said Thelma. 'But it didn't mean a thing to you or you'd have never let it go.' Then she smiled, a sly, smug grin. 'Anyway, he made sure she could have children before he married her,' she said. 'Got her pregnant first. He told me he was very disappointed because I was a girl but as soon as he saw me he forgot about that, and you arrived ten months later, so it was all right in the end.'

Gerald stared at her. She was saying that it had been a shotgun marriage. Surely that couldn't be true! Not his parents! He realized that he had never known the actual date of their wedding, only the year. They had never celebrated their anniversaries, and even their birthdays had passed without the exchange of gifts and greetings, though the children's were suitably marked. As he grew old enough to realize how swiftly his own birth had followed that of his sister, Gerald had decided that he had been premature and that this was why he was so short, a notion he had held for many years until Iris laughed it to scorn. She had been shocked when she discovered that Gerald was vague about his parents' birthdays and she had found out the dates and seen that they were greeted thereafter. Their silver wedding had already passed by the time she and Gerald were married.

Thelma was pleased with the effect of her words.

'Daddy told me. It's the truth,' she said, ironing on.

His mother seduced, misled: Gerald couldn't take it in.

'Well, he didn't get killed,' he said, and abruptly turned the conversation. 'How long are you staying?'

'I haven't decided,' said Thelma. 'I'm doing this play in November.'

November! There was the rest of September and all October to get through first! Gerald looked round the kitchen. Thelma's clothes lay about on every surface, some ironed, some awaiting attention.

'Doesn't Mother want to get into the kitchen?' he asked.

'Couldn't you do your ironing in your room?'

'I shan't be long,' said Thelma.

'I think you should let Mother know your plans,' he said.

'It makes no difference to her,' said Thelma. 'I'm sure she's glad of my company. Besides, this is my home.'

This was just what their mother had said. Gerald's patience snapped.

'We've left the nest, Thelma,' he said. 'We've both been married, for heaven's sake. If you are going to stay, you should make some contribution towards your keep. Maybe Betty could come more often. It's a lot for Mother, having two extra. She's getting on, you know, and she's used to a quiet life.'

'She's as fit as a flea,' said Thelma. 'She walks miles with Boris. It'll do her good to be dug out of her rut. Besides, I'll do most of the cooking. I'm a much better cook than she is.'

'Well, as long as you do,' said Gerald. 'Don't just let things drift. Couldn't you get a job?'

'Doing what?'

'Well – cooking,' said Gerald. 'You could be a country cousin, or whatever they're called. Go as a temporary live-in cook and be paid very well, and all found.' What an inspiration, he thought, pleased with it.

'I wouldn't be able to go to rehearsals then,' said Thelma. 'Besides, I'd be just a skivvy.'

'You wouldn't. You'd run the house,' said Gerald.

'What – for someone like Mother? Some senile old woman who can't manage her own affairs?' Thelma set the iron down hard and glared at him.

Gerald felt his blood pressure rising.

'Mother is anything but senile, as you very well know,' he said. 'And she could perfectly well manage her own affairs if Father had left her any to handle. If you can't stand working for a woman, find yourself some old man to look after, a rich widower. That might be just what you need.'

So saying, he angrily left the room. Thelma was distracted from replying only by the smell of singeing as she scorched her skirt.

'You bloody man!' she yelled after him as Edward came into the kitchen through the back door.

'Not quarrelling with your brother, are you?' he asked.

'Dear, dear, that won't do.'

'He's a pompous, interfering ass,' seethed Thelma. 'Thinks he's so bloody marvellous because he sits in a damned bank all day deciding who can and who can't buy companies. Well, he can't tell me how to run my life, that's for sure.'

'He seems all right to me,' said Edward, and then, 'Oh look, you've scorched your skirt.'

Thelma picked up the dish cloth and flung it at him.

'Don't you start,' she shrieked, but Edward had already retreated.

Lydia had heard the sounds of her children's raised voices as she finished arranging the roses. She gathered up the paper containing the stripped-off thorns and snipped leaves and stems and went through the french window into the garden. Would they never learn to agree? Their hostility had been limited in their adolescence because they had spent most of their time apart at separate schools, and in the holidays pursued different activities. Gerald had preferred riding his bike to ponies; he had liked watching birds, and helping the men on the farm.

Edward had intercepted Lydia as she set off down the garden to put her rubbish on the bonfire pile.

'I'll take that for you,' he offered. 'I'll burn up what's there, too, before it rains and gets soaked.'

'Make sure it won't blow across any of the neighbours,' said Lydia.

'There's no wind,' Edward pointed out. Then he laughed. 'My word, you wouldn't think Thelma had such a temper, would you? What are they fighting about?'

Lydia thought it might very well be him and his un-suitability as a partner for Thelma.

'I don't know,' she said. 'Gerald isn't always very clever with Thelma.'

'Nor are you, are you?' asked Edward, holding the bundle of clippings to his chest and regarding her quizzi-cally.

'What do you mean?' Lydia's invisible hackles rose, and the tone of her voice ascended in response to this im-pertinence.

'Let her walk all over you, don't you?' said Edward. 'She takes your car without so much as a word – turns your place over – even moves me in without a by-your-leave. It's not right.' He backed off towards the bonfire spot as he spoke. He might have gone too far.

But Lydia followed.

'She's my daughter,' she said. 'She has a right to be here and to borrow my car. This is her home.'

'Well, you've got rights too, haven't you?' Edward said.

Sometimes this very thought had occurred to Lydia, when Thelma returned in tatters at the end of one of her sorry adventures, but she had always banished it; a mother's obligation to a child was the greater.

'She's been unlucky,' she said. 'Have you matches?' She nodded towards the rubbish dump.

'Oh yes,' said Edward. He wasn't comfortable unless he had a small pack or a lighter, though he didn't smoke at all.

Lydia returned to the house, disturbed. It had been wrong to discuss Thelma behind her back, and she never permitted adverse criticism of her daughter.

Gerald had been cooling down in the garage, where he checked the Metro which shone after Edward's ministrations. Oil and water were in order. When he could prolong this activity no more, he walked the length of the garden to where Edward had started the bonfire. Gerald watched him for a while without speaking. He was rapt, absorbed.

'You're quite the boy scout, aren't you?' Gerald said at last.

'What? Oh!' Edward rubbed a grimy hand across his forehead and laughed. 'Sorry – I didn't realize you were there,' he said.

'It's all so damp, I'm surprised it burns,' said Gerald. 'I'd never have got that to go without paraffin, I'm sure.'

Edward did not reveal that he had used some, pouring it liberally over the kindling base, watching it flare up high before piling on refuse.

'It's got a good bottom,' he said. 'That's the secret.' Oddly, a memory came to him of helping his old grandfather with a fire at the end of the long, narrow garden in the part of Birmingham where his grandparents had lived.

He'd forgotten about that until now.

He heaved a forkful of rubbish over part of the blaze; it was a pity to douse it like that, but still, the fire had a purpose. Smoke rose in a plume as he stacked on more rubbish.

'You're a useful guest,' said Gerald.

'It's ever so good of Mrs Cunningham to put me up,' said Edward, and went on quickly, 'I've fixed myself up with some gardening and decorating jobs in the village. It'd be just temporary, for the next week or two. I was going to suggest that I might be a proper lodger – pay for my room and that – if you don't think she'd be offended?'

'Hm.' Under such an arrangement, would Lydia be able to turn him out if she tired of his presence? Present-day laws favoured tenants over landlords and criminals over their victims. But a couple of weeks shouldn't be enough to establish squatter's rights.

Edward had sensed his hesitation.

'If she wants me to go, she's only to say,' he assured Gerald. 'My sister will be able to put me up later. She can't at the moment.'

'Where does she live?' asked Gerald.

'Over there.' Edward pointed vaguely in the general direction of the Manor.

He was saved from having to give more details by Lydia, who came out to say that the Dennises had rung up to ask if the bonfire would be alight long. They were having a barbecue that evening, and would prefer it to be extinguished by then.

'Funny, that. They'd be within rights to complain because we'd lit it before six o'clock,' said Edward. 'Or it may be six-thirty. I'm not quite sure.'

'What do you mean?' asked Lydia.

'He's right,' said Gerald, chuckling. 'In built-up areas, you're not meant to light bonfires until the evening. On the principle, I suppose, that people will have gone indoors by then.'

'We don't worry about things like that in Milton St Gabriel,' said Lydia regally. 'But now I suppose we're to put up with the smell of fried onions wafting across the fence.'

'Well, that won't bother you. You'll be tucking into a

good dinner down at the Manor,' said Gerald. 'You and Thelma are coming too, of course,' he told Edward. 'Would you like to invite your sister and her husband?'

What a thought! Julie, a chambermaid at the hotel, to be included in the evening! As it was, it would be quite a turn-up for him to be there, himself.

'That's kind, but she's busy this evening,' said Edward. He couldn't begin to explain.

'Some other time, then,' said Gerald.

'Right,' agreed Edward.

'You're not going to be able to get into the kitchen, Mother,' Gerald told Lydia. 'Thelma's got half her wardrobe draped all over it. Why don't we take Boris for a walk on the shore and leave these two to it? We could have something to eat at the Crab and Winkle.'

'Oh, that would be nice, Gerald. Thank you,' said Lydia. 'Boris will enjoy that.'

'And so will you, Mrs Cunningham, won't you?' Edward prompted her. 'Get you away from her for a bit.' He nodded his head towards the house. 'She'll soon cool down. Leave her to me.'

He always felt powerful when in control of a fire.

Perhaps some attention from her latest conquest would soothe Thelma's ruffled feelings, Gerald thought; he was amused at the young man's masterful advice and happy to take it as he drove off with his mother.

'Do you know Edward's sister?' he asked as he edged his BMW carefully down the main street past the mail van, parked while the postman made deliveries. A couple from the hotel, in strong shoes and raincoats, tweed hats on their heads, trudged along for the good of their health, and old Admiral Hughes tottered towards them on his way to Mrs Dodds's shop, a basket over his arm. As a young man the admiral, then a lieutenant, had been responsible for the destruction of at least two German submarines in the Mediterranean.

'I know very few of these new younger people,' said Lydia.

'He wants to stay on with you until she's got space for him – as a paying lodger, I mean,' Gerald told her.

'Oh! He's said nothing about it to me,' said Lydia.

'No. He thought you might be offended,' Gerald explained.

'I don't think anyone's offended at being offered money these days,' said Lydia, who for some years had acted as custodian at a stately home not because she enjoyed mounting guard over the treasures, but because she was paid a small sum for attending. This year, for no given reason, she had been told that there were enough guardians and it would be unnecessary for her to put herself out to take on the duty.

Lydia had bitten back protest: what was the use? Their minds were made up to exclude her from the clique that had developed among the group of women and the few men who annually acted as guides and supervisors.

'I can hardly take money from one of Thelma's friends,' she said.

Gerald thought that she could, and from Thelma, too, if she planned to stay long.

'I think he means this independently of her,' he said. 'It wouldn't be for more than a week or two, I gather.'

'Well, we'll see,' said Lydia.

Gerald parked the car on the cliff above Worton Bay and hurried round to open the door for her. Boris tumbled out of the back, and they set off down a narrow track to the beach. Gerald was reminded sharply of past expeditions to this spot laden with beach towels and picnic baskets, himself always overburdened in his perpetual endeavour to exhibit masculine strength while Thelma skipped ahead empty-handed, her fair hair bouncing about on her shoulders. She swam better than he. He sighed at the recollection.

'Are you lonely, Gerald?' Lydia asked suddenly, as they walked along on the shore.

Gerald was startled. He could not remember her asking him anything so personal before.

'I've plenty of company during the day, at the bank,' he replied.

'You know that's not what I meant,' said his mother. 'You must miss – er – being married?' Her voice rose at the end of the sentence, demonstrating that she expected an answer.

She meant sex, of course.

'Well, now and then, perhaps,' he said carefully. 'But I have friends, mother.'

Women friends were implied: Lydia did not wish to pry.

'You might marry again,' she said, and added quickly, 'Your private affairs are your own business. I'm sure you're discreet.'

He didn't think that he was, particularly.

'There's no one special,' he said.

'It's all so different, these days,' Lydia said, with unusual feeling in her voice. 'People – er – taking up with one another and then moving on.'

'Like Thelma, you mean?' he dared to say.

'And most of the population, from schoolgirls upwards,' said Lydia tartly. 'If one can believe what one hears. It makes for a very unstable society.'

'People have always had affairs,' he said gently, not wanting to snub her but anxious to turn her observations into a discussion, and prompted, too, by Thelma's earlier remarks into feeling tentatively curious.

'But with much more serious consequences than today,' she replied. 'Girls took risks. They didn't have the opportunities that they've got now. Not that it makes for happiness, all this freedom. There's no sense of duty.' As she spoke, she walked faster, head poking forward studying the ground ahead. 'Ttch – look at that rubbish.' A plastic detergent bottle, some carrier bags, an old tin and other detritus adorned the band of seaweed rimming the beach.

Gerald was more interested in watching the sand dry out around his feet under the pressure of his weight, a phenomenon that had always fascinated him. He thought of his daughter, whose way of life worried him.

'I don't think people today work at their marriages much,' he said. 'That's a generalization, of course. But I'm sure Iris and I didn't. I just took it for granted that she was content, but she wasn't.'

'People demand such a lot,' said Lydia. 'In my day, girls adopted the position in life their husband provided. Some bettered themselves, others didn't, but each knew her duty.' And if you didn't marry, you were reckoned to be on the shelf at twenty-two, a doomed old maid. 'You were provided for,' she continued aloud, 'and you vowed to be faithful and obedient.' She paused. 'It meant total submission. For better or worse, and if worse you just knuckled under and didn't complain.'

'No young girl makes that sort of promise today,' he said. Then, cautiously, he asked, 'Was father a hard taskmaster to you, like he was to me? When you were young, I mean?'

'Oh yes!' Lydia addressed her reply to her sensibly shod feet in their K Skips.

The admission could cover so much. Gerald waited before adding a gentle prompt.

'I suppose as a child I wouldn't have noticed,' he ventured at last. 'I mean, if Father and you quarrelled.'

'We didn't,' said Lydia. 'I had promised to obey, you see. Soon, as a person, I ceased to exist. I'm what he made me – a robot, you could say.'

'Oh Mother, no!' Gerald was appalled, yet even as he protested, he realized that what she said was true. When had he ever heard her, until this moment, express her own views?

Now that she had at last started to speak, Lydia's words began to flow, somewhat jerkily, like a stream breaking past a dam.

'I'm probably shocking you, Gerald, but your generation needs reminding what life was like for mine. How things were between your father and me wasn't untypical. And one carried on, you see. Divorce was a scandalous thing and took place for one reason, adultery.' The word spilled harshly into the damp, salty air between them. Two seagulls spiralled nearby, raucously calling.

Gerald remembered the easy dissolution he and Iris had obtained two years after they parted; there had been no contumacious argument, very little rancour. Of course, he had surrendered without a struggle.

'Girls have it too easy today,' Lydia pronounced. 'Things were too hard in my time – if you left a marriage, you got no support and what could a young mother do? It's quite the thing to be a single parent these days, it seems – even without ever having been married. A whole generation of lost, unanchored children will be roaming the world.'

Gerald sometimes shared this view, when he woke in the night depressed about Fiona.

'Any infidelity is serious,' Lydia went on. 'It's a symptom. It happened in the war because people couldn't stand the loneliness. That's a reason, not an excuse. People took risks and marriages broke up later over things that were only a matter of consolation.' She walked on, head down, marshalling her thoughts. 'Girls married – or sometimes they – er – anticipated marriage because the man might be killed the next week. Often they'd only met a few times and then they had to try to build a whole life together. Like Betty's GI bride sister.'

'But you and father had known each other for years,' Gerald said, unable to relate any of this to his parents, even after what Thelma had told him.

'We were acquainted,' Lydia said. 'The age gap between us would have kept us apart anyway as children, but later I was thought suitable to be asked to tennis. Then we co-incided once on leave. I was doing my nursing training then. I never finished it.'

'You were good at tennis,' said Gerald. 'I never managed to beat you.'

'No. You weren't much good at games,' his mother said dismissively.

To his horror, Gerald felt his male middle-aged eyes prickle with sudden unbidden tears at the familiar disparagement.

'Thelma was,' he said with an effort. 'Is, I mean. Perhaps she'll take it up again. Tennis.'

His mother sensed the strain in his voice and knew that she had made a mistake. She too withdrew, changing the subject to ask about Fiona.

'Isn't it time she found something worthwhile to do?' she said. 'She should train for a career.'

'I agree,' said Gerald. 'But Iris has other ideas. She wants her to make a good marriage. In a material sense, that is. So you see, it still goes on.'

'Well, she won't get pregnant, will she?' said Lydia. 'However she occupies her time. She won't have to marry in order to save herself and her family from shame and disgrace.'

Was that why she had married his father? Soon afterwards, her father had moved to another living some distance away. Gerald did not remember his maternal grand-parents at all. Had they failed to treat their daughter with Christian charity?

There were so many questions he wanted to ask, but he did not dare; his mother's mood had broken.

Surely, whatever the truth of the later years, there must once have been passion between his parents? Why else had he been conceived so soon after Thelma's birth?

The passion, of course, had died, as passion tended to do.

9

Perhaps the insurance company would pay for her scorched skirt, Thelma thought, banging the iron down hard on a pair of slacks. She was annoyed because her mother and Gerald had gone off in his car without saying where they were going, but Edward seemed to know when he returned to the house.

'He's taken your mum off for some peace,' he told her. 'And she needs it, poor soul, with you two at each other like that. Can't you get along?' It seemed sad to him; his own sister had been his best friend until he went to prison, and her failure to visit him latterly had been part of his punishment.

'I don't know why he had to come down here, poking his nose into what isn't his business,' Thelma grumbled.

'He probably wanted to make sure I wasn't going to rob you both, or murder you in your beds, or something,' said Edward cheerfully.

'Why ever should he think you might?' Thelma briefly emerged from her self-absorption to marvel at such an idea.

'Well, you haven't known me long, have you?' said Edward. 'For all you know, I'm an escaped murderer.' He pulled a face at her, gibbering.

'If you were, it would be on TV,' said Thelma flatly. 'Don't be silly.' She hung her slacks over the back of a chair and asked, 'Have you any washing?'

'Gee, thanks, I thought you'd never ask,' drawled Edward in what he thought was a Hollywood accent.

'I'm not offering to do it. I'm suggesting you should put it in the machine while Mother's out,' Thelma snapped.

'You're too kind.' Edward swept her an exaggerated bow. 'But I've already taken it to my sister. She's only too pleased to do it for me, knowing how helpless I am.'

Julie had grudgingly accepted a bundle he'd put in one of the hotel polythene bags supplied to guests for their laundry, and agreed to pass it into the system.

'Oh,' said Thelma. 'That's good.'

Edward bowed again, and this time, in spite of herself, Thelma's scowl was replaced by a wintry smile.

'You look pretty good when you smile,' he told her. 'Let's see you do it again.' He went towards her, set a hand on either arm, and kissed her nose.

Thelma laughed and melted against him. She felt no desire herself, but was always consoled if she aroused it in others, and they were alone in the house.

Edward had not meant things to go so far, but he had nothing better to do at the moment, and lighting that bonfire had made him feel rather good. Besides, he owed her something.

Thelma was rather ashamed of her conduct and wanted to drive the memory of it out of her mind. Her mother always adopted such a placatory, patient manner towards her, as if she must be humoured at all costs. It was almost as if she were afraid of her own daughter, but that couldn't be so; after all, what had Thelma ever done that had harmed her? The only person who ever got hurt was Thelma herself.

This thought, which came to Thelma as she tried to enjoy Edward's bony embrace, was not welcome. She pushed it from her mind, concentrating on her present activity, but once again she found no pleasure in it.

'Why do you bother?' asked Edward at last, sitting up in bed when their transports were concluded. 'I don't turn you on, do I?' He spoke sadly, regarding the failure as his.

'No,' she admitted, and then, with sudden candour, added, 'It's not just you, it's everyone. That is, everyone I've tried until now.'

Edward stared at her.

'Even your husbands?' He knew now that there had been two.

'Mm.'

'You've not got the knack,' he told her, after a pause for reflection. 'It's a gift, you know.'

'I suppose it is. Either you have it or you don't,' she said.

'Though why shouldn't I? I can do most things.'

'I didn't mean that,' said Edward. 'It's the gift of your-self.'

'Well, I did give you myself,' Thelma pointed out, swinging her legs over the side of the bed.

She still had a lovely body, her ribs tapering to a narrow waist and then swelling out into the soft curve of her hips. She might be too plump for some tastes, but Edward ad-mired her generous charms and they had led him to expect a nature to match.

'We're not going on together, you and me,' he told her. 'Like this, I mean.' He gestured at the crumpled sheets. 'Not in your mother's house. It isn't right – she wouldn't approve, not a lady like her, at her age. She's one that'd have old-fashioned ideas about things and I don't want to upset her.'

'What about upsetting me?' Thelma demanded. 'Don't you care about that?'

'Not as much as her,' said Edward. 'Anyway, you do plenty of caring about yourself, so no more is needed.' As he finished speaking, he snatched up his clothes and, holding them against his nakedness, left the room.

Thelma's instant pique turned to anger. They were all against her, every one of them trying to put her in the wrong, dumping her for their own selfish reasons, no one caring what became of her. Even her mother's welcome had been lukewarm and she hadn't asked how badly Thelma had been hurt by Lucian. For all her mother knew, he might have damaged her physically, instead of merely wanting her to leave. For some minutes she shed tears of fury; then – for there was no witness, no one to offer sympathy and her eyes would get all red – she began to simmer down. She blew her nose hard, went into the bathroom, turned on the taps and ran a deep bath. There was no bath oil, which annoyed her; her mother indulged no hedonistic weak-nesses and used only Imperial Leather soap and Pond's cold cream, with a little compressed powder to mask the worst of the shine on her face. Funny, that; when Daddy was alive, she used a little lipstick. She'd always worn her hair in that curious Edwardian style; perhaps it was better than some ill-fitting, badly chosen wig.

She scrubbed herself hard, wanting to remove every trace of Edward from her body; then she dressed in clean clothes and made up her face carefully; outlining her eyes and applying deep pink shadow to the lids. Downstairs, the Metro's keys hung on a peg on the dresser: her mother, out with Gerald in his swanky BMW, could not possibly require it. Thelma drove off in search of diversion from yet another disappointment.

There was no sign of Edward. By the time she had left the village she had successfully forgotten him.

Never one to dawdle, Thelma pushed the little car along the twisting lane. Going round a bend too fast on the wrong side of the road, she narrowly missed an oncoming car whose driver stood on his brakes before reversing to let her pass.

'Silly fool,' she said, aloud.

She drove on, not showing any caution until, when she reached Heronsmouth, increased traffic forced her to slow down and begin to concentrate.

Where now? Why, to the Swan, of course, where Daddy had so often taken her for their little treats together. It was past one o'clock and she was hungry.

Thelma turned into the hotel yard, which bordered the estuary, and parked the car. Gulls cawed and some pecked in the mud below the tideline as she walked towards the hotel's side entrance, so convenient for access from the water. She went into the saloon bar, ordered a crab salad and a glass of lager, and sat down at a window table to enjoy them. Food was a great solace, and if it were not for the fact that she often felt compelled to take violent physical exercise, Thelma would have had a serious weight problem. Now, she felt a warm glow deep within her as she drank down half the glass of beer. Then she looked around her, waiting for her salad to arrive.

Thelma was used to going into bars on her own, and she had often, in her restless search for company, found adventure there.

She hated to be alone. For an honest instant, she admitted that to herself as she sat in the respectable panelled and leather surroundings of the Swan's bar. When you were by yourself, thoughts crowded in, many of them unwelcome and upsetting. In company, you could forget everything except the moment; there was always the chance that just around the corner was the cure to misery. It was like acting, when even if the character you portrayed was wretched and despairing, you knew that all her troubles were imaginary and would go at curtain fall.

Sitting there, Thelma told herself that she was a great actress, as talented as Peggy Ashcroft but as beautiful as Gladys Cooper in her youth. She had stayed beautiful all her life, Thelma remembered, and had not both these great ladies of the theatre been married more than once? All she need do was wait for the present clouds to pass and her life would blossom: some famous director would, by chance, be staying in the district when *The Seagull* was performed and would see her, deciding she was just the person he was seeking for his next production, and another man would come along to love her and take care of her, and turn her once again into one of a pair.

Her salad arrived while she sailed on this pleasant sea of fantasy; the comfort of the food and drink and her own invention wrought a transformation in Thelma's appearance as her low mood was dispersed. Her face filled with colour, and her body, which had drooped with dejection as she entered the hotel, grew tense and taut. Her pulse speeded up and she looked about her in a subtle way, avoiding any eyes which might be turned towards her, as some celebrity, aware of being stared at but evasive in her modesty, might do.

In fact, several people had looked up when Thelma took her seat. Most of them were middle-aged or elderly couples enjoying a Saturday drink, local residents pleased to have their town and their hotel returned to them as the season ended, and a few late tourists. One man, however, had seen Thelma before, and he remembered that occasion clearly for she had been wearing not a stitch. It was the elderly man who had witnessed her swim in the pool at Milton St Gabriel.

Thelma saw two women sitting together at one table; at another were three more; over in a corner, a quartet of what looked to her like aged crones talked animatedly about a golf foursome they had played the day before. The thought that she might continue through her life unpartnered, ending up like them, frightened Thelma badly. She reminded herself that she still had the power to attract and thrust away the knowledge that what came next was what she lacked.

Arthur Morrison had noticed Thelma's quick, assessing glance about the room. Nowadays, you couldn't tell just by looking at her whether a woman was available or not, but he already knew that this one was unhampered by inhibition. He watched her covertly as she ate her salad. She had a second glass of lager, and as she fetched it from the counter, she saw him looking at her. Each held the other's gaze for just a moment, and Arthur smiled. He looked a nice old boy, thought Thelma, smiling back. It was encouraging to see a man alone, even though he was quite old.

Arthur had finished his veal and ham pie. He toyed with the dregs of his pint of bitter as she ate up her salad and slowly drank her beer. She left the bar first and he followed her. She returned to the car-park, but she did not get into her car; he saw her leaning over the wall looking at the water where the moored boats moved gently on the incoming tide. A customs launch puttered down towards the sea, and some people in a dinghy rowed out to a tall-masted yacht, their oilskins yellow against the blurred greys and browns of the dull day. Further up the river, the ferry chuntered across to the other side where small houses rose in stepped layers among the yellowing trees to the skyline.

Arthur Morrison moved to a spot by the wall away to her right. He did not speak to her for several minutes, for it was many years since he had attempted this manoeuvre.

10

Arthur Morrison was a widower. Soon after they had moved to Heronsmouth, when he retired, his wife had fallen ill and within three months was dead. They had come to the West Country to be near their son, but within a year Nicholas was moved by his firm to Leeds. This was promotion which he could not turn down. Arthur decided to remain in the solid, comfortable house above the estuary; there was no guarantee that Nicholas would not be moved again, and the notion of retirement spent in Leeds was less appealing than life here, where the pace and the climate were gentler. He had made some friends, mainly through the bridge club he had joined. Most of the members were elderly widows but there were some couples, a few of whom were also new to the area.

Arthur enjoyed the company of women and sadly missed his wife, whom he had loved with faithfulness for more than forty years, but he sometimes grew depressed by the white heads and arthritis common to the members of the bridge club.

This girl in the boiler suit, with her mass of springy golden curls was not conventional. If he spoke to her, she was unlikely to be shocked, Arthur thought, composing and discarding various opening sentences in his mind. Foolish old man, he told himself: of course you want to pick her up, to talk to her, because you're intrigued by her and because you're bored. She's alone. She may be bored, too. You can drop her, sharpish, if you've miscalculated, and she won't scream and cry rape if you simply speak about the weather. At the worst, she'll walk away.

But she wouldn't; he knew that; not after that smile.

Aloud, Arthur regretted the grey skies and damp air.

'Yes.' Thelma said, and added, tritely, 'Winter won't be

long.' She turned on him the radiant look which had captivated more sophisticated men than he. 'But it's lovely to be back in England. Everything's so green. Oh – not here – ' she waved at the grey water and the leaden skies, ' – but in the countryside.'

'Oh – have you been away?' For she was a native Briton, that was certain from her voice.

'I've just got back from Los Angeles,' Thelma said.

'And what were you doing there?'

For some reason that she couldn't understand, Thelma immediately told him the truth.

'Shall we go for a walk?' Arthur suggested. 'I often stroll along here by the water.'

'All right,' agreed Thelma, who now felt embarrassed by her frankness.

But Arthur had seen, as her bleak words fell quietly between them, that her spirit was bruised, and he knew that it was often easier to confide in a stranger than someone closer.

'You were well out of it,' he told her.

'Yes, but what am I going to do now?' Thelma appealed to him.

'Have you made no plans?' Poor dear, how sad she looked with her beguiling blue eyes brimming full of tears and her pretty fair curls misted with damp from the moist air around them.

'Not really,' said Thelma. 'Only the play.'

She told him about it, forgetting her self-pity in her enthusiasm.

'But that's good,' he enthused. 'I used to like acting.' Long ago, he and his wife had been members of a dramatic society.

'Why don't you join us?' she suggested.

'I'm too old,' he said.

'No, you're not,' she said. 'But Shamrayev's been cast. What a pity. Do you know the play?'

He did, and was sorry she had not seen him as the doctor rather than the wheelchair-bound old soldier.

'I'll come to the performance,' he promised.

'Do you live in Heronsmouth?' she asked.

'Yes. Up there.' He pointed in the direction they were going, up the hill out of the town. 'You can't see the house from here. It's beyond the headland, before you reach the Cliff Hotel. It's called The Shieling.' He paused to glance sideways at her, not averse to being seen out in the town with so attractive a woman. He liked her pretty, petulant face, her provocative walk, the sudden flashing smile which turned her into a beauty. 'A most inappropriate name,' he added.

'Why?'

'A shieling's a hut. Mine's a comfortable Edwardian villa,' he told her.

'You could change the name.'

'There's a superstition that it's unlucky if you do,' he said.

'Oh, is there? I didn't know that,' said Thelma.

'What are you going to do now?' he asked. 'After our stroll, I mean? Go back to your mother's house?' She had told him that her mother lived in a village some six miles away. Did she make a habit of going round the local hotels for her lunch?

'I don't know,' she replied.

'I'd love to ask you to tea,' he said. 'But at four o'clock I'm due to play bridge with three charming elderly ladies.' He laughed as he spoke. 'I'd much rather play truant, but there we are, I'd spoil the four.'

'My mother doesn't really want me at home,' Thelma said, and now she sounded like a sulky schoolgirl.

'I'm sure you're wrong,' said Arthur. 'Were you very attached to this man in Los Angeles, or did he just answer your problem about what to do next?'

'I thought I was,' said Thelma. 'But I was wrong.'

'You don't often admit that, do you?' he asked her.

How did he know?

'I suppose not,' she said grudgingly. 'You're a mind reader,' she added.

'Not really,' he said. 'I've just been about longer than you have and I know how stubborn one can be.'

'I'm not exactly young,' said Thelma. 'And I've been married twice.'

'You seem young to me,' he said. 'What happened?'

'My first husband was killed in an accident,' she said.

'And I split from the second.' That was a better way to put it than to say he had left her.

'I'm sorry about that,' he said. They had reached the end of the harbour walk, where the path now became a track approaching the headland. 'Look, you can see my house now,' he added and lifted his walking stick to point it out to her. 'There – the white one with the gables. The window frames are blue, but you can't see that from here.'

Thelma looked across at the row of solidly built houses, once the homes of tradesmen, Merchant Navy officers and other worthy citizens of Heronsmouth, most now converted into holiday flats or boarding houses.

'Isn't it rather big for you, on your own?' she asked. He must be unpartnered, like her, or perhaps his wife was away.

'My wife died after we'd moved here when I retired,' he said. 'I like the house and I don't want to move again.'

'I see.'

He did not want her to go, but the afternoon was passing and soon he must prepare for his bridge.

'Have you a car?' he asked.

She nodded.

'Yes – in the Swan yard.'

'I'll walk back with you, then,' he said.

'Won't that make you late?' Thelma glanced at her watch.

'I think there's just time,' he said.

She wondered what was wrong with his leg; he had quite a pronounced limp although he could walk quite fast. She did not like to ask, but when they returned to her car, she offered to drive him up the hill to his house.

'Otherwise you may be too tired for your game,' she said, smiling.

He accepted, inserting himself into the Metro's seat, then pulling his stiff leg in after him.

'How nice of you,' said Arthur. Then he plunged. 'Will you have lunch with me on Monday? Perhaps you'll have made some plans by then. You'll be staying in the area, won't you, because of the play?' He wondered how she was placed financially. Nowadays, appearances told you nothing. He was unsure if young widows received pensions; anyway, the remarriage would have cancelled that out. She obviously had means enough to run a car and take herself out to lunch, and to fly the Atlantic, but perhaps the American suitor had financed her trip.

'I'd like that. Thanks,' she said.

Both of them were pleased to have something to look forward to.

'Shall we make it the Swan?' he said. 'Quarter to one?'

It was agreed. She dropped him at his door, turning in the driveway, and he stood and waved her off.

Thelma drove down the hill again, past the narrow pavements where shops and houses leaned against one another, huddling into the lee of the hill. At the bottom, as she turned inland, there was a new block of holiday flats on the site of a former hotel. There had been an outcry because it had been totally gutted, but it had not been pulled down and the so-called renovation fell within planning regulations. There were To Let signs in a window, she noticed as she stopped at a pedestrian crossing nearby.

She could rent one.

She was elated when she returned to the lodge.

What had she been up to? Lydia's heart sank as she saw her daughter's shining eyes and heightened colour; she had learned that these were signs that Thelma had found a new interest which very often turned out to be masculine, and had embarked on a fresh path to disaster. Thus had she looked when she married Charles, radiant in cream satin to match the family Honiton lace; thus had she looked at her second wedding, in a register office, when she wore a white wool dress with a flower in her hair. Thus had she been before setting off for the States, and on countless occasions in between. Still, at least her sunny mood would probably last through the evening, and that was something.

They dressed for dinner according to their resources. For Thelma, this meant a white crepe off-the-shoulder dress with loose billowing sleeves which began at her upper arms, a gold necklace, bracelet and drop earrings to match, and a lot of eye make-up. Edward whistled when she appeared in this garb five minutes after they were due to meet Gerald in the bar at the Manor.

'We'd better take you in the car, Princess,' he said. 'It's

damp out. What do you say, Mrs Cunningham?'

'That won't be necessary,' said Lydia. 'We've all got the use of our legs and the distance is only a few hundred yards.' But though her words and her tone were wintry, she was almost smiling.

'You're very smart, if I may say so,' Edward told her, deciding not to call Mrs Cunningham Duchess, which had occurred to him. He felt excited, stimulated by the prospect of dining in such style. His lifestyle had certainly undergone a fundamental change within a week.

'You may,' Lydia allowed, graciously. Tonight, her hair was secured by a purple velvet band, and she wore a plainly cut dress in shades of purple and maroon. It offset her high colouring and in it she looked almost handsome. The dress was one she had had for years and it had originally been expensive; it was too short, though: Edward noticed that as the two women put on their coats. Styles had changed. It displayed, however, Mrs Cunningham's thin and still shapely legs; on her long, narrow feet she wore black leather court shoes with a medium heel.

Edward had bought himself a pair of white cotton trousers for this engagement, deeming jeans in the evening unsuitable. Karen White from next door, hearing where he was going, had lent him one of her father's ties and a blue and white striped shirt with a white attached collar which was much too big but which looked good with the trousers. Edward was sorry that Karen could not be included in the party and had promised to take her to the Blue Dragon in Cheverton if he could borrow Mrs Cunningham's car some night.

They caused quite a stir as they entered the bar. Gerald had to admit that Thelma looked stunning, her bright hair set off by the costume jewellery, her fair skin emphasized by the white of her dress, her blue eyes shining. His face creased into a welcoming smile as he settled them round a table near the log fire which, on this chilly evening, was burning in the hearth. Edward hovered, at first ill at ease but soon reassured by Gerald's friendly greeting.

'Now – what will everyone have? Mother?' Gerald rested his hand on the back of his mother's chair, standing beside her, catching the eye of Ferdy who immediately came round from behind the bar to take the order.

Thelma, who wanted a Bloody Mary, might have been drinking already, thought her brother: the flush on her cheeks could very well have been caused by alcohol. She seemed to be in a good mood, whatever the reason.

Edward would have liked a beer but was not sure if that would be in order here. Mrs Cunningham had chosen sherry, so he did the same. When it came, it was so pale and dry that it made him wince. He sipped carefully, copying her.

Gerald ordered another double gin and tonic for himself. Somehow he felt a long evening lay ahead, and he had so far done nothing to solve the problem of Thelma's future. Perhaps her improved humour would endure until the next day and they might be able to have a constructive talk. This evening should be devoted to having a good time – not always easy in any family, and especially this one.

But one person was enjoying himself without any doubt. Edward, once the sherry took effect – which it did quite quickly – relaxed. If his companions of only a week ago could see him now, he thought, sitting back in the deep leather-upholstered armchair. Here he was, living it up like a lord, accepted simply because Thelma had introduced him into the family.

If they knew the truth, they'd all have shown him the door.

He thrust the thought away and spoke to Gerald.

'Must have been nice when you lived here,' he said. 'Don't you wish you still did?' He wasn't quite clear why Gerald hadn't been able to keep the place on; he wasn't short of a bob or two, after all. Something to do with his marriage breaking up, Thelma had said, and she felt bitter about it.

'It was lovely when we were children,' Gerald side-stepped the question. 'Wasn't it, Thelma? We had space – which we took for granted, of course – room to play, trees to climb.'

'Ponies and that?' Edward suggested.

'Thelma did. I never took to riding,' said Gerald. He grinned, not choosing to recall being forced to ride a small bad-tempered pony called Brownie with a mouth like iron and a perverse nature. Only after Gerald had broken his collar-bone and an ankle after his umpteenth fall from the animal had he been reprieved. It was a waste to keep a pony no one was using, his father had said, and Brownie had gone. Gerald never asked where; he didn't mind if the little brute had been turned into meat. 'I preferred my bike,' he told Edward. 'Where do you come from?'

'Birmingham,' Edward said. 'My dad worked in a car factory – still does.' He'd had spells out of work and spells on strike, but there had been prosperous periods too. He and Julie had always had plenty to eat and good clothes to wear.

Before Gerald could ask him any more questions, the head waiter arrived to take their order. Thelma took a long time to make her choice. She changed her mind several times, drawn variously to venison, roast duck, or veal in an elaborate wine sauce, finally settling for the venison. Edward chose it, too; he'd never eaten it and might not get another chance. Mrs Cunningham chose veal.

'Think of all those poor little calves,' said Thelma. 'How could you?'

'They're dead anyway. Not eating them won't resurrect them,' said Gerald, who had chosen duck.

He had suggested that everyone should select their main dish first, then a starter that would go with it. Edward longed to ask for smoked salmon, but saw that it cost extra.

'It's dear, isn't it?' he murmured to Lydia, who had decided on chilled cucumber soup.

'Thelma will choose it,' Lydia answered softly. 'You'll see.'

She was right. After deciding against crab mousse because she'd had crab for lunch, Thelma did so.

'Wouldn't you like that, too, Edward?' asked Gerald, who had caught his mother's eye and for once not misread its message.

'Yes, please,' Edward replied, eagerly.

Gerald was reminded of taking Fiona and Christopher out to meals, and their undisguised greed. Gluttony, although allegedly a deadly sin, was not as damaging to others as some of the remaining six, he thought: or not as practised at this level.

During the meal, Thelma began to talk about *The Seagull* and how she would interpret her role. Edward had no idea what the play was about, and so the story was related, everyone chipping in to make sure he missed none of the points.

'I was in it before,' Thelma told him. 'I was Nina, the young girl, then.'

No one mentioned that she had only been the understudy, called on because of the illness of the principal.

'She has a hard time, doesn't she? This old writer guy leading her up the garden, I mean,' said Edward.

'He's not so old,' said Thelma. 'But he and Arkadina had been together for years.'

'I've always disliked that woman,' said Lydia, setting down her glass. The waiter had topped it up three times without her noticing.

'Who?'

'Arkadina, of course. A very vain creature,' said Lydia firmly.

Gerald hid a smile. He was pleased to hear his mother speak so positively, and he resisted the temptation to say that Thelma had been perfectly cast.

'It's a classic role,' Thelma told Edward, ignoring her mother's remark.

'It's a classic play,' said Gerald. 'We must all go to see it. You must get us tickets, Thelma.'

'All right,' said Thelma. 'It'll cost you, though. It isn't free to members of the cast.'

'Relax. I'll pay,' said Gerald.

'Dorothy went to Russia in June,' said Lydia, breaking in. Thelma could be very tiresome.

'Dorothy is your friend you were going to have supper with when Thelma kept the car?' said Edward, wanting to make sure he'd got it sorted out.

'Yes,' said Lydia.

Gerald managed to bite back a comment on this revelation of his sister's behaviour.

'Tell us about Dorothy's trip,' he said quickly.

'You'll have to ask her yourself, really,' said Lydia. 'It seems to have been most interesting. Of course, she'd read it all up, as you'd expect, and knew what she was seeing.

They were filming in Red Square, she said – Boris Godunov, it was – horses and actors everywhere. She went to Leningrad as well as Moscow. A land of contrasts – that was what she said. Magnificent palaces full of gilt and colour, and the people looking drab.' Lydia had grown quite animated, telling them about it.

'You should have gone with her,' Gerald said.

Lydia did not answer. Her friend had gone with an up-market cultural group and Lydia could not have found the money, even if Dorothy had been prepared for her to join the tour.

Gerald resolved to sound Dorothy out about her future plans; he would gladly pay for his mother to join her on another trip. It was time she made up for all those years immured at the Manor with his father, going nowhere; it was not too late for her to see the world.

At this moment Lydia's cucumber soup arrived and Thelma decided to tell them all how it should be made. The head waiter, overhearing, said the chef had prepared it just as she described but with the addition of a secret ingredient.

'It's excellent, I'm sure,' said Lydia.

'You can't argue about smoked salmon, anyway,' said Gerald. 'It either is, or it isn't. How's yours, Edward?'

'Very tasty,' said Edward, who in fact found it rather disappointing. Still, you couldn't know unless you tried a thing.

He enjoyed the venison, though, savouring every morsel of the rich dish, shovelling it into his mouth as though he feared his plate might be snatched away before he had finished. Across the table, Gerald noticed this, and Lydia too, but Edward was not aware of their critical observation. He sensed interest from another area, however, and glanced up. A waitress standing beside the sweet trolley nearby was staring at him, and he saw that it was Julie, all tricked out in a black dress and frilly apron.

She was a chambermaid. What was she doing in the restaurant?

At this moment she was frowning at him severely and gesturing as if using a knife and fork, and he realized she was commenting on his table manners.

He glanced round and saw that the others had rested

their knives and forks on their plates whilst they were speaking. Lydia, anxious to mask his uncouth lapse, had begun a discussion with Gerald about Christopher, his son, who was working with a wine producer in Bordeaux, learning both the French language and the trade. Gerald said he seemed to be enjoying himself, though all he had received were several postcards. Lydia had had one too.

Thelma, not remotely interested in her nephew's career prospects, interrupted.

'I wonder how well the Heronsmouth Players will dress their production,' she said. 'I want some good costumes.'

'I'm sure you'll get them, Thelma,' said Lydia, unwilling to let this become a problem so far ahead of time.

'I suppose they'll hire them,' said the star.

'Maybe they've got a clever little woman who'll run them up out of old curtains, like Scarlett O'Hara,' said Gerald, who had been much taken with Vivien Leigh's striking appearance in her green velvet outfit.

'I don't like wearing things other people have used,' said Thelma, wrinkling her nose.

'I'm sure you won't have to do that, Thelma,' said Gerald. 'You very rarely do anything you don't want to, do you?' He leaned across the table to pour more wine for his mother, and Edward decided to draw the flak away by offering an excuse for his poor manners.

'I got rather hungry today,' he said. 'Sorry if I was eating too fast.' His plate was nearly empty.

'What were you doing, to give yourself such an appetite?' Lydia asked, looking kindly at him.

I was in bed with your daughter, trying to make the earth move for her, Edward thought of saying, but instead informed her that he had taken out the row of runner beans that was over – another row was still cropping – and had burned them since he had the bonfire going so well.

'It has died down now, hasn't it?' Lydia asked anxiously.

'Yes. I made sure it was out,' said Edward. 'It hadn't all burnt up, but I can always light it again.' He liked that thought.

When Julie wheeled the sweet trolley to their table, she looked very demure, her mouth primly arranged in a straight line, happier now that Eddie seemed to have remembered where he was. They all chose raspberries and cream, with Thelma wanting meringue as well.

'And you, sir?' she asked Edward. 'Would you like trifle with yours?' She knew that he loved it.

'Yes, please,' said Edward, trying not to giggle as Julie served him generously, the cream washing dangerously close to the lip of his plate as she set it before him.

'She's taken a fancy to you,' remarked Thelma.

'I'm sure I can't think why,' said Edward, who was on the brink of dissolving into hysterical laughter.

The head waiter had noticed a certain amateur approach on the part of Julie Fletcher, the stand-in waitress. Victor had bribed one of the regular waitresses to feign toothache so that, as a dare, Julie could take her place and enjoy the spectacle of Edward dining in style.

Julie had been in two minds about accepting the challenge; she was so uneasy about Edward's presence, a cuckoo in the Cunningham nest, that part of her would prefer to ignore the whole thing; the other, less anxious part, thought it might all be rather fun, and she was reassured by seeing how easy the quartet seemed together; the Cunninghams could be a good influence on Eddie if only he didn't step out of line. As she finished serving the table, the head waiter swam up to Gerald.

'Everything all right, sir?' he inquired. 'Madam?' He inclined his head towards Lydia. He had spent a year at a big hotel in Lucerne and aspired to higher things than his present position; here, it was all too informal.

'Yes – excellent, thank you,' said Gerald.

'Very nice indeed,' affirmed Lydia. 'The raspberries are delicious. Are they from the garden?' In the old days, hers were long over by now but there were some new late-fruiting strains.

'They come from Scotland, madam,' said the head waiter, and he moved away in response to a call from another table.

Here was Edward's chance to introduce Julie, acknowledge his sister's identity and at the same time pay her out for her trick.

But Gerald was looking at her intently.

'Are you one of twins?' he asked. 'I could have sworn you

brought me my tea this morning.'

'I did, sir,' said Julie. 'One of the proper waitresses is ill and I'm standing in for her.'

'I see,' said Gerald. 'You've worked a long day, then.'

Edward knew it was all a set-up; the illness was faked so that Julie could keep an eye on him. Gerald would take the deception in good part, he was sure, but the old girl and Thelma were different; there was no knowing how they would react.

He kept quiet.

Gerald walked back with them down the drive after they had all had coffee and liqueurs. Even Lydia had accepted a Cointreau.

'Just to settle the meal,' she excused her indulgence.

Why could she never enjoy something for its own sake, wondered her son.

'Are you coming in?' she asked him, when they reached the lodge.

What for, he wondered bleakly. There had already been longueurs in the conversation while they drank their coffee and sipped their drinks. If he went into the lodge with them now, what would follow? Would he and Thelma embark on another spat? He longed for his mother to press him, but she merely stood by the door waiting neutrally for his response.

'I'm sure you're tired, Mother,' he said. 'Goodnight. I'll come down again in the morning.'

'Goodnight, Gerald. Thank you for an excellent evening,' said Lydia.

'Yes – thanks – er.' Edward felt inhibited about calling Gerald by his first name. The word 'sir' kept springing to the tip of his tongue. Gerald was definitely one of 'them'. 'It was great,' he added.

Thelma had entered the house without a word. Gerald turned back feeling as forlorn as when he was a small boy returning to school. Well, on Monday he would be safely in the bank again, with the hum of computers and the ordered bustle of high finance to protect him from family life.

Back in the hotel, he ordered a brandy. An elderly couple touring the district began telling him how they had spent the day and he passed a pleasant half-hour with them.

Was this his future? Anxious visits to his mother, always

tinged with guilt because his father had made her depen-
dent upon him, interspersed with sexual encounters that
were often furtive and too fleeting to merit any better description? Was there never to be more?

He went for a stroll in the grounds before going to bed,
passing the stable block where his mother had hoped to
live. Part of it had been converted into accommodation for
resident male staff; the women workers were housed in the
attics where Mrs Thomson had her flat. Several windows
showed lights, and Gerald, glancing up from the shadows,
saw a girl reach out to draw a curtain. He had time to
recognize the maid who had brought his tea that morning
and who had waited on them at dinner. A man stood beside
her, and Gerald saw that it was Edward.

Well, he had not wasted much time, Gerald thought, and
smiled to himself. How would Thelma react to this, if she
discovered the dereliction?

He had not seen Victor, who had just handed Julie the ten
pounds she had won by deputizing for Mavis and who was
also in the room. The four stayed together for some time,
listening to music and innocently drinking coffee.

Lydia had let Boris out for a final run. She walked down the
garden behind him, inhaling the damp night air. People
had been smoking in the hotel; not many, it was true, but
enough to remind her of how the smell of Henry's tobacco
had clung to the curtains and lingered about the place.

Boris, who rarely barked, lolloped up to the boundary
fence uttering restrained yaps. From beyond came the
strains of pop music as the Dennises' barbecue party continued. Lydia admonished Boris, wondering how long the
noise would go on, and whether anyone besides herself
would find it irksome. If she opened her bedroom window,
she would hear it. Why must they play it so loudly? The
Dennises, surely, both embarked on a second marriage,
were too old for such juvenile conduct and lack of con-
sideration for other people.

But people of any age jostled against you on pavements,
pushed into you in shops, thrust you aside if you got in
their way. She collected up Boris and returned to the house
where Thelma was sitting looking at television.

'That party's still going on at the Dennises,' Lydia said.

'I know. I can hear it,' said Thelma. 'It's early yet. It'll last a lot longer, I expect.'

'Where's Edward?' asked Lydia.

'Gone to see his sister,' said Thelma.

'Isn't it rather late for that?'

'Not really. We don't all go to bed at ten,' said Thelma.

'It's almost eleven,' Lydia pointed out. 'And I'm going up. Goodnight, dear.'

She glanced round the room, plumped up a cushion, paused at the jigsaw but, without her glasses, saw no likely piece to insert, and went out of the room. Thelma heard her moving about in the kitchen settling Boris and no doubt finicking about with her obsessional tidying. At last she went upstairs.

Thelma lit a cigarette and puffed smoke defiantly round the room. She rarely smoked, believing it to be unhealthy but as a girl she had done it to annoy her mother and demonstrate rebellion; it was in the same spirit that she now inhaled deeply, but almost at once she began to cough so she stubbed out the cigarette, leaving it in an ashtray where her mother would find it and take the point.

It was too early to go to bed. If she went down into the village she might meet Edward returning from his visit, except that she did not know where his sister lived.

She went out of the house, leaving the door unlatched, and took off her high-heeled sandals so that she could run lightly on her bare feet down the road and round the corner to the new estate from whence came the sounds of the Dennises' party. When the tarmac hurt her soles, she moved on to the grass verge, which was damp and springy with autumn growth. A street light on the corner showed her the way, and as she went on the clouds divided to allow a sliver of moon to lighten the scene.

The gate of Mauden, the Dennises' bungalow, was open. Thelma drifted through it and up the path.

A man stood in the front porch smoking a cigar, whose strong scent came wafting towards her as she briefly paused.

'Hail unto thee, fair sprite,' he addressed her. 'What fortunate wind blows you to these shores?'

'Oh, I was just drifting,' said Thelma airily, waving one pale arm on which her gold bracelets jangled. 'Sounds like fun here.'

'Float this way, lovely wanderer,' said the man, moving towards her. He was tall, brown-haired, with a little beard. 'Come and join us.'

'Why not?' Thelma said, shoes in hand, stepping on.

Lydia sat propped up in her high old bed, spectacles on, trying to concentrate on Florence Nightingale. She read no fiction, choosing to immerse herself in dense biographies of the long-dead who had been achievers, as an escape from what seemed to her the ugliness and licence of contemporary life.

This year she had desperately needed diversion from the continuing celebrations of the ending, forty years ago, of the Second World War, an event that had been cataclysmic to her generation. For what better world had so much been sacrificed? Every day there was news of violent disorder of one kind or another; men still killed; children starved. Lydia was weary of seeing films of old soldiers parading at the sites of their victories. What were their thoughts and hidden griefs? It was right that succeeding generations should be made aware of the past, especially when patriotism seemed to be out of fashion, but she could no longer bear to remember those bright youthful hopes and illusions which had been cast into ruin. At least, though, she could turn off the television and ignore the papers. Henry, if he were alive, would have missed none of it; out would have come his medals and off they'd have gone to Caen or some other place where his regiment had covered themselves with glory. VE day had come and gone, but VJ day still lay ahead and no doubt would receive the same treatment.

Resolutely, Lydia read about Florence Nightingale's busy correspondence from her chaise longue, but she was unable to absorb it. At last she snapped the book shut, took off her glasses, turned out the light and tried to compose herself for sleep, but the stresses of the evening combined with the rich meal and alcohol had over-stimulated her and she could not relax. Images chased one another in her mind:

Henry back from the war for good, presiding over guests at their dinner table, port circulating; herself gathering up the dull wives, trying hard to make conversation but aware all the while that later there would be reprimand from Henry for the slightest fault or imperfection in either the meal or her conduct – and there were always some he could find. She had learned, in time, to discuss gardens, schools, and lack of help in the house as if nothing else was important. Now she need do it no longer; now, if things went wrong, she had only herself to please. Henry was not waiting to pounce on her slightest mistake.

It had been a very long punishment.

Unable to settle, Lydia got out of bed and went to the window. She could hear the sound of the Dennises' stereo. Surely it was too cold by now to be outside in the garden, and if they were in the house, wasn't the noise too loud to permit conversation?

She put on her dressing gown and stepped out of her room on to the landing. The house was still and silent; she knew she was alone in it before she glanced at the other bedroom doors, both ajar. It was odd how different it felt from when she was really alone; there was a tension now, a sense of something about to happen as the house waited for its occupants to return.

How fanciful she was! Lydia reproved herself for allowing her mind to stray in so foolish a manner. Slowly she went downstairs, unlocked the french window and walked across the garden. How could the Dennises endure such a noise so late? They must be both in their forties. Sometimes the teenage children from their previous marriages were at the bungalow and perhaps the party in progress was for them. Shadowy in the darkness, the mass of the bungalow roof rose up against the lighter night sky. She couldn't throw moss at it now, though to do so would relieve her feelings.

Suddenly she heard a woman's high, excited laugh. It was Thelma's laugh; unmistakable to her mother. Well, that answered the puzzle of where she had gone, since she was not with Edward. Why had she not said she was going on to their party? Lydia was not aware that she knew them well enough to be invited.

Shivering now, partly with annoyance, Lydia went back to the house and turned on the electric fire in the sitting-room. She was still there, doing her jigsaw, when Edward came in half an hour later.

'What, still up?' he said. He had seen the light as he walked down the drive from the Manor and had come in expecting to see Thelma waiting for him in either an angry or a voracious mood: maybe both. Instead, he saw the thin figure of his hostess, in a blue wool dressing-gown, sitting intent at her puzzle.

'I couldn't sleep,' Lydia told him. 'Too much excitement, I suppose. I don't often eat such a meal, especially at night, unless Gerald takes me out.'

'He's a nice guy,' Edward said, pulling up a chair so that he could sit beside her and look at the puzzle. He picked up a piece, held it poised for an instant, then fitted it in.

'Yes,' said Lydia. 'He was always a good boy. He never gave any trouble.'

'Not like Thelma, eh? I bet she's kept you on the hop,' Edward said. 'I expect you miss him, now he doesn't live up at the big house any more.'

'Yes,' said Lydia.

'Sad, that, folk splitting up,' said Edward. 'My mum walked out on my dad when I was a kid. Funny, I thought it was my fault.'

'What gave you that idea?'

'Well, I was quite naughty. Used to be cheeky and that, and I kept tearing my clothes and getting told off at school for not paying attention,' said Edward. 'But I know now that wasn't why she left.'

'What was the reason?'

'Fancied another bloke more than my dad,' said Edward. He put in another piece. 'I never saw her again. Don't know where she is now.'

'How dreadful,' said Lydia.

Edward shrugged.

'It was OK until my dad married again,' he said. 'We got on well, the three of us. Julie, my sister, was like a little mother to me. Then Dad remarried.'

'And you didn't get on with your step-mother?'

'She didn't like me. Said I was just like my mum,' said

Edward. 'I am, to look at. Julie looks like dad.'

'She was jealous,' said Lydia.

'Maybe. Anyway, it didn't work out and I left home as soon as I could,' said Edward. 'Stayed with an uncle for a bit, until I left school.'

'Don't you see your father?'

'No. We kind of lost touch. Julie sees him, though, sometimes.'

'What a pity,' said Lydia.

'Doesn't bother me,' Edward declared.

'You must find a new job,' Lydia told him. 'A proper one – not just bits of gardening and so on. Can't the Job Centre in Cheverton help?'

'I guess it's mostly seasonal down here, with the tourist trade and that,' Edward said. He had heard the staff at the hotel talking about it.

'You must take the car on Monday,' Lydia said. 'Haven't you got to sign on?' He'd be eligible for the dole, even if he was doing odd jobs in the village; moonlighting, wasn't it?

'Oh thanks,' Edward said. 'I'll do that.' He reached into his pocket and pulled out the ten-pound note Julie had given him; with typical generosity she had passed on the proceeds of her wager. 'Here's something towards my keep in the meantime,' he said. 'I'll give you some more as soon as I draw my social security.'

Lydia hesitated. She did not want to take money from a young man in straits, but on the other hand he must be allowed to retain his self-respect. Charity was not beneficial when it sapped initiative.

'Thank you,' she said, accepting the note.

They stayed up until they had finished the puzzle. Then Edward made some tea and Lydia took her cup up to bed where she soon fell asleep.

Neither of them mentioned that Thelma had not come home, but Lydia left the front door on the latch.

Thelma and her new companions had been sitting under a tree, once part of her father's estate and spared by the bulldozers, in the small garden of Mauden. They were drinking a potent wine cup.

The assembled guests were several assorted couples,

some married, others paired one way or another, all celebrating Roger Dennis's birthday. By the time Thelma arrived, surface inhibitions had gone and undercurrents of different emotions had risen with various effects. Maureen Dennis was in the kitchen, in earnest conversation with the boyfriend of one of her colleagues at work. Other minglings had caused new pairs to coalesce. Giggles and shrieks came from one shadowed corner of the patio; a couple had gone into a bedroom. Thelma's arrival produced a diversion and a chance for those who had so far drawn unlucky to re-group.

She felt at home at once. This was what she enjoyed – light, meaningless chatter, superficial flirting; and she was always full of confidence at such a time. She told the man who had greeted her that her name was Guinevere and that she had emerged from the lake on the marshes beyond the golf course. He promptly said that she must call him Lancelot.

After a while they moved indoors because it was getting chilly outside, and she sat with him on a sofa in the large living-room with its dining recess at one side. They talked frivolously, he pretending to be off to the jousts wearing her favour on his helmet. Something was wrong somewhere in this, Thelma thought: surely Lancelot didn't go jousting? But quite soon, sitting there, she began to wheeze and her eyes started to run.

'Oh damn,' she cursed, moving away from his encircling arm, pushing aside the hand that was resting on her thigh. She sat up, gasping for breath.

'What's wrong?' he asked. This wasn't a normal brush-off.

'There's a cat here. There must be,' she said.

'I've not seen one,' said Lancelot.

'There is a cat in this house,' Thelma insisted. She tried to breathe evenly, forcing the air out of her lungs so that they would reflate by reflex, trying to use her diaphragm and stomach muscles as she had been taught, but already she was panting.

'Roger – got a cat anywhere? The lady doesn't like them,' said Lancelot.

'We've got two,' Roger answered. 'But they're nowhere

108

about. Off looking for fieldmice, most probably.'

'They don't have to be in the room.' Thelma's voice was already a croak. 'Their hair or their dust – it's enough to set me off. I'll have to go.'

She didn't look fit to depart the way she had come, mysteriously out of the air.

'Let me take you for a drive in the car,' suggested Lancelot. 'There's no cat in my Porsche.'

'All right.' She would probably get over her asthma attack quite quickly if she left the source of the trouble. Thelma went with him out of the room and he handed her into the low black car which was parked outside in the road.

'My shoes!' she remembered.

He went back for them and had quite a job to find them. They were out in the garden beside the goldfish pool. She was still wheezing when he returned. The noise was mildly irritating so he hoped that she would soon recover.

'Can't you take something for it?' he asked.

'I've got an inhaler, but I came out without it,' she said.

'Shall we pick it up?' She was really in distress, he could see. 'Where do you live?'

'No – don't worry. I'll be all right in a few minutes,' Thelma said. But she should have washed her hands. Cat dust transferred easily from upholstery to hands and that was probably how the attack had started. She kept her hands locked in her lap, and eventually the spasms decreased, but they did not cease, and she knew she was in for a prolonged attack that might last for hours unless she used her medication.

Lancelot was sympathetic and forgiving when she refused his overtures, made after he parked in a gateway in a quiet lane not far from the village. Her gasps were rather a turn-off.

Thelma began to feel better as he drove her back to Milton St Gabriel and dropped her, as she had asked, at the entrance to the Manor Hotel. He supposed that she worked there; she might be a receptionist; Roger had seemed to know her and had called her Thelma.

Letting him go, Thelma told herself that such was her luck, he was the one who might have made all the difference.

12

Gerald was again called by Julie in the morning. She brought him the *Sunday Times* with his early tea.

'Oh good,' he said. 'I didn't expect it to arrive until later.' An irritation during weekends in Milton St Gabriel was the late delivery of the papers.

'One of the staff brings them from Heronsmouth,' Julie said. 'On his way in to work, I mean.'

'Oh.' Gerald had laid down his book and he looked at her over his glasses. 'Do you like working here?'

'Yes,' said Julie. 'It's nice being in the country and there's a friendly crowd here. We all help each other out.'

'Like you did last night,' he observed.

'Yes,' agreed Julie, turning quickly away so that he should not see her guilty blush. She hurried off, with, he supposed, other trays to deliver. Certainly, as a guest, he had no complaints about how the hotel was run; rather the reverse; and as an investor, this pleased him.

When he walked down to the lodge later on, the dull clouds were lifting and a hint of sunlight to come lightened the distant hills. His mother was already out in the garden snipping dead blooms from the rose bushes.

'Ah – there you are, Gerald,' she said.

Hypersensitive to her tone, he inferred that she had expected him sooner.

'Did you sleep well?' he asked her.

'Yes – after the noise from the Dennises' stopped,' she said.

'Their party went on a bit, did it?' He suffered from this in his block of flats, where one set of neighbours tended to live by night and sleep by day, and others overhead tramped about in what sounded like seven-leagued boots.

'They don't do it very often,' she allowed.

She wondered whether to tell him that Thelma had gone to the Dennises' party, then decided not to; his disapproval might fuel the friction between brother and sister. It did not occur to her that he might see no reason why Thelma should not be the Dennises' guest.

'I wish we could put the financial skids under Thelma,' he said, as if he had tuned in to the subject of her thoughts. 'If she was forced to earn her living, she might knuckle down to something specific instead of flitting from thing to thing.' And man to man, he silently added.

'The same could be said of your daughter, Gerald,' Lydia told him, her voice grim. 'You must remember that Thelma was widowed so young. If Charles hadn't died, things would have been entirely different.'

Gerald decided to ignore the bull's eye about Fiona.

'Yes, and she'd still have been bored,' he said. 'She was bored then. Mother, we can't go on making excuses for Thelma because of that tragedy. Plenty of women have been left alone in far worse circumstances and made good lives.'

While he was speaking, he made a snap decision: it was useless to stay and provoke more hostility. He rushed on before she could spring to Thelma's defence.

'I'm going to start back to London before lunch, if you don't mind. I want to call on some friends on the way. I haven't got anything positive out of Thelma about her plans and perhaps it's too soon to expect her to have any,' he said.

'Oh – very well, Gerald.' His mother's back stiffened. She must not let him see she was disappointed because he was leaving so soon; she had hoped he might suggest they should go for another walk; they might even have talked properly again. But she would not plead with him to linger; he had his own life to live and it was her strict rule never to make demands. She had planned to discuss Edward's position with him; now she must make her own decision about that. She told him what it was. 'I'll let Edward stay for a while,' she said. 'As long as it fits in with Thelma's plans and doesn't make anything awkward for her.'

'I think he may have other fish to fry,' Gerald said.

Lydia ignored this.

'He's quite a help,' she said. 'A thoughtful boy, and he

seems to have no settled home, so it may do him good to stay here for a week or two while he looks for work, and until he can move to his sister's. He's already given me some money towards his keep.'

'Oh, has he?' So the young man had meant what he said. 'Well, keep him to that,' Gerald advised. 'Don't soften him up with acts of charity.' He hesitated, as unhappy about leaving as she was to see him go. 'I'll be off now, Mother, and let you get on.'

With what, she thought sadly.

'Well, goodbye,' he said.

He would have been amazed if he could have seen his mother, after he had gone, walking down the garden to the bonfire spot with her pile of dead roses, her face contorted with tears. It took her several minutes to compose herself enough to return to the house.

No one else, however, was up yet. Discipline directed Lydia's next actions: the meat must be prepared for the oven; potatoes must be scrubbed; there were runner beans and courgettes in the garden.

Why bother? Why spend the morning cooking the meal for Thelma and Edward? Why wasn't Thelma up now, undertaking this task herself? Daughters were often compelled to look after their elderly mothers. Lydia supposed that she was, by now, elderly, although she felt she had changed very little in recent years.

She was not obliged to cook lunch for Thelma and Edward.

Lydia took a sheet of paper and wrote a note, which she put on the kitchen table. *Gone out. Back tonight. Meat in larder, vegetables in garden.*

Then she went upstairs, washed her hands and powdered her nose, checked that her hair was securely latched under her snood and slipped on a jacket. She left the house very quietly, not wanting to be detected in the act of playing truant. Boris followed her out to the car and hopped into it more alertly than usual, as if catching her own excitement at running away.

'Damn it, she's taken the car!'

Thelma had come downstairs and found her mother's

message. Edward, who had already seen it, was sitting at the kitchen table eating toast thickly spread with butter and marmalade. In his new freedom, he still appreciated hot toast soaked with melting butter.

'Why shouldn't she?' he asked. 'It's hers, after all.'

Thelma tossed the note aside.

'Make me some coffee, Edward, there's a dear,' she said. She slumped on to a chair, her hands to her head. 'I've got a cracking hangover.'

'Where'd you go last night, then?' He had not heard her come in.

'To the Dennises.' Thelma waved towards the garden.

Edward had switched on the kettle. He heaped two large teaspoonsful if instant coffee into a mug and waited for the water to boil.

'Good, was it?' he asked her.

'All right, but I got an asthma attack,' said Thelma. 'They've got cats there. They affect me.'

'Oh. That's rough.' There had been a man in prison with Edward who had suffered from asthma; it was alarming to see him in the throes of an attack.

'It's a nuisance,' Thelma said. 'It's funny, horses don't bring it on, and they're very dusty.'

'Julie can't eat cheese,' Edward volunteered.

'Julie?'

'My sister.'

'What happens to her if she does?'

'She gets terrible headaches. Chocolate, too. Makes her ever so sick and rotten,' said Edward.

'Poor thing,' said Thelma. She took the mug Edward gave here. It was too hot to drink straight away. 'Fancy mother going off like that without a word,' she marvelled.

'There is a word. She left a note,' Edward pointed out.

'But not to mention it yesterday,' Thelma insisted. 'That's unlike her.'

'You didn't mention where you were going last night, did you?' Edward said.

'That's different.'

'Why? Your mum's entitled to make her own arrangements. She doesn't have to consult you just because you've turned up – unexpectedly, as I remember.'

'It's not the same,' said Thelma sulkily, sipping her coffee. 'I want to know where she is. She never goes anywhere, apart from to Dorothy's.'

'More's the pity, then,' said Edward. 'You'd think she'd have lots of friends here.' Edward had noticed plenty of grey heads among the residents; he counted on them as his prospective employers.

'She thinks herself too grand to mix with the new people,' Thelma said dismissively. 'Because she was the lady of the manor, I mean,' she added, as Edward looked uncomprehending.

'Is that right?' She hadn't seemed the least bit toffee-nosed towards him. 'What was your dad like?' Edward asked, spreading more toast. 'A proper blimp, I bet.'

'In your terms, perhaps,' Thelma said. Out of deference to her father's views, she had not obeyed her impulse to demonstrate at Greenham Common. Now that he was no longer about to be upset by her actions, she might join the Peace Movement. 'He had high standards,' she told Edward. 'And he set a good example.'

'Like your mum does.'

Thelma was silent. She had never seen her mother's conduct in this light.

'She might have said where she was going,' she repeated. 'And what about Gerald? Where's he, I'd like to know?'

'He was here,' Edward said. 'I saw him talking to your mum in the garden. He went away.' Edward himself had gone back to bed after seeing them out of the bathroom window.

'I suppose he's got bored and gone back to London,' said Thelma, 'He'd done his bit, after all. Squared his conscience.'

'You are a cow,' Edward told her. 'He's really nice, your brother. Cost him a pretty penny last night, I'll bet. He didn't have to include me, and he even asked if I'd like to bring Julie.'

'Oh, Gerald always does the right thing,' Thelma said.

Edward was afraid that perhaps he had gone too far. To improve things, he said, 'Your mother's left us a lovely piece of meat. A whole leg of lamb – too much for just us two.'

With no other ally to hand, Thelma was not inclined to quarrel with Edward. She decided to overlook his insult.

'We could have a party,' she said. The coffee was beginning to take effect and the pulse in her head was easing.

'I suppose we could. Who shall we ask?' Edward had been wondering how he could avoid being alone with Thelma. Who knew what would happen once she got over her hangover?

'Why not your sister?' Thelma suggested. 'Could she get away? And I could ask the Dennises.' Then she would be able to find out who Lancelot was, and where he lived.

'Julie might be able to come,' Edward said. It was a daring idea.

'She lets rooms, doesn't she?' Thelma said carelessly. 'I wondered if she had to give lunch to her lodgers.'

'Not exactly,' Edward said. He ought to tell her, now, about Julie; still, it would be rather fun to surprise her. Thelma was recovering as he watched her; her pallor had gone and the pretty colour was returning to her cheeks. 'You certainly do snap back fast,' he said.

'I've had plenty of practice,' said Thelma.

She sent him off to issue the invitations in person while she set to work to roast the lamb and prepare the rest of the meal. He was gone so long that she had to pick the beans herself, a task she had planned to give him. She set him to slice them; they were so young that they barely needed stringing.

'They're all coming, I suppose,' Thelma said.

'Not Julie.' He had had second thoughts about inviting her; shades of Daddy might cause Thelma to issue a snub and he would not expose Julie to such a risk. Instead, he'd asked Karen. The girl was alone; her father had left to pick up a new load and her mother was working. She was delighted.

Thelma had quite recovered. She was at her best when entertaining, knowing that she did it well. Karen was the first to arrive, having spiked her short hair into a jagged halo that made her look like Puck, Thelma thought: there was a muted rose streak across the front and a hint of blue, and Thelma thought it attractive. She said so, and Karen, used to complaints from her father, beamed with pleasure.

The Dennises were late; they had had a tough morning clearing up after their party.

Now Thelma sparkled. She had made a chilled tomato soup to start the meal and had sent Edward to the Bell as soon as it opened to buy two bottles of wine, since her mother had no two alike and only three altogether. Everyone seemed to have plenty to say and even Karen relaxed. The Dennises had only agreed to come when they learned that Mrs Cuningham would be absent. They found her formidable.

They soon told Thelma that Lancelot, whose name was really Jim, was sales director at a big garage in Cheverton.

After lunch Thelma found some brandy, and as the sun had come out they all strolled, glass in hand, round the garden.

'Our roof looks pretty dreadful from here,' Roger Dennis said. 'I hadn't realized how it cut off your mother's view. She must mind about it.'

'She's used to it now,' said Thelma.

Edward and Karen, both so much younger than all the others, soon grew bored, and although they both drank some, neither appreciated brandy at that time of day. He went with her back to her house to listen to her new tapes, and soon the voice of Michael Jackson floating towards them showed the Dennises how noisy a neighbour could be. But they and Thelma quite liked the choice of music now relayed across the space between the two houses.

Edward did not return to the lodge until after dark.

13

When she drove away that morning, Lydia had no goal in mind. Automatically, she took the Heronsmouth road, but as she approached the junction for Cheverton she slowed down. She knew no one in Heronsmouth now, apart from Betty. She must go further, stay out the whole day, give them all a breathing space.

Dorothy Butler was the only living person whom Lydia would contemplate visiting unannounced, though she could never remember doing so. The two had been at school together, before the war, and later, when Dorothy was in the WRNS and stationed in Dartmouth, she had spent some of her leaves at Milton St Gabriel. Dorothy, too, had made a swift wartime marriage; after her husband was killed, she had spent a short compassionate leave with Lydia at the lodge and there she had done her overt grieving. After that, she had continued her service, and when the war ended she trained as a teacher. The last years of her career were spent as headmistress of a girls' school in Kent. Now, she had taken up painting and foreign travel, sometimes combining the two. Some years ago, she had bought a holiday cottage in Wilcombe in preparation for retirement. In the winter, she attended various adult education classes and she had joined an association of local artists who exhibited their work and sold it to tourists. This kept her occupied and had brought her a new circle of friends, but she reserved space in her life for Lydia, kept in touch by telephone, and the two met at least once a month.

Dorothy had been annoyed when Lydia, at the last moment, cancelled their arrangement for supper because of Thelma's sudden homecoming. According to Lydia, she had not made it clear to her daughter that she needed the car. Dorothy saw the incident differently; it was another example of Lydia's failure to stake a claim to rights of her own. Thelma had been indulged by both parents throughout her childhood, and the pattern remained. Dorothy had been widowed at a younger age than Thelma; she was in the early stages of pregnancy, and had miscarried while at the lodge. Lydia's unemotional kindness and practical help had seen her through the worst days of her life, although now she found it difficult to remember Alan's features or the sound of his voice. Photographs showed a smooth, unformed face with a gentle expression. How would they have fared together if he had survived? She had never known if he had even received her letter containing the news of the forthcoming child.

As girls, she had been more academically minded than Lydia, who was good at games and had played both lacrosse and tennis for the school, where she had gone on a bursary available to the daughters of the clergy. Their friendship had continued because of the accident of geography and Dorothy's wartime presence nearby. Now, they were bound by the tie of the years.

As a teacher, Dorothy had encouraged her girls to pursue careers first and to think of marriage as a step for later, not as a means of escape. Many of her girls had built successful lives, but there were failures too, and sometimes unhappy young women sought her advice. On that Sunday, as Lydia drove towards Wilcombe, Dorothy was meeting such a one.

Because she had been a frequent visitor to the Manor, Dorothy had seen beneath the surface of Lydia's marriage. Henry tolerated her because she was Thelma's godmother, and because he found her attitude towards him a challenge. Dorothy's views differed from his on almost every subject; she was more stimulating company than Lydia, who would never be goaded into argument. As the years passed, Dorothy had seen Lydia, who had always been shy and reserved, lose the small spark of irony that had once made her good company. Henry had killed some vital part of her nature, and in time Dorothy learned enough about him to make her pity Lydia.

In the end, his death had been sudden, although he had creaked along with a bad heart for some time, his condition not helped by his fondness for whisky and tobacco.

Dorothy had hoped that Lydia would spring back into life herself, once she had had time to adjust to her new situation, but this had not happened. More than forty years of attrition had been too much for her.

Now, as Lydia drew up outside Honeysuckle Cottage, she could see there was no one at home. The small windows beneath the steep thatch were shut. She rang the bell, then peered into the garage, which was empty. Dorothy's garden was like a small jungle, untamed and lush; a rampant honeysuckle, no longer in bloom, smothered a rustic arch; clematis cascaded over the dead stump of a tree; vivid dahlias with huge faces formed bold blobs of colour in the beds. It made Lydia uncomfortable; she preferred her own plot with its barbered lawn and straight rows of vegetables marching in echelon across the red earth like soldiers on parade.

She returned to the car. What now? She couldn't go home until at least three o'clock or her gesture would be useless.

Driving out of the village, she saw that there was not much petrol left in the car. It never occurred to Thelma to fill the tank. Keeping a vague lookout for a filling station, Lydia turned away from home. She'd stop somewhere and give Boris a good walk. After a while, beside a lay-by, she saw a fingerpost indicating a footpath and parked the car. She and the dog set off together, climbing a stile over a low stone wall, following the trail. They walked for several miles, the path taking them through woodland and across a stream. She lost all sense of time, as often happened when she walked like this. She had learned to make her mind a blank, noticing only plants and wild life as she passed. Eventually, because the weather was uncertain, she turned back.

When she reached the car, Boris displayed fatigue and Lydia, too, felt tired and hungry. She always carried a bowl and a bottle of water in the car, for such long expeditions were quite usual, and she gave him a drink before setting off again. When she was in no hurry, Lydia chose to drive along the lanes rather than on the busy main roads, but now she was aware of the need to pick up petrol, so she took the major road at the next opportunity. This brought her close to the motorway service station, and because she was now afraid of running out of petrol, Lydia followed the signs towards it. The needle was showing empty when she stopped at the pumps. She felt relieved, filling up the tank.

Since she was here, she might as well deal with the wants of nature for herself, and buy a sandwich.

She drove on into the parking area and locked Boris into the car, telling him she would not be many minutes. After so much exercise, he was feeling sleepy and merely blinked an eye at her.

Because it was Sunday, the place was very busy. Lydia, who had seldom used a motorway service area, felt confused by having to buy her sandwich from one counter and her coffee from another, then queue to pay at a third. She found a place to sit and eat her meal, swallowing it quickly. People milled about with trays. How young they all looked, Lydia thought, and so many of them were so overweight. She saw heavy, fleshy faces, beer bellies, broad chests straining against taut shirts, huge buttocks and round stomachs swelling out tight jeans or wobbling under baggy cotton pants.

She had just finished her coffee when the little girl came past her table. She was about two years old and she was wandering along with her face already puckered, ready to cry.

Lydia did not reason for an instant. She swooped upon the child, said in her ear, 'We'll soon find your mummy,' and led her out of the cafeteria. It was time someone learned a lesson.

The child was already bemused, stunned because among a forest of knees and thighs she saw no familiar face. The seizure of her hand and the swift movement deprived her, for a moment, of the ability to yell although she drew in a preparatory breath. Lydia picked her up and carried her out to the car. Held on high, hearing a friendly voice telling her what a nice little girl she was and that she was going to see a lovely dog, she still held back her tears. Lydia found her very heavy. She set her down before they reached the car and held her hand. The child trotted along beside her, to anyone who cared to notice them, apparently her grandchild. Lydia let Boris out to stretch his legs and they went for a stroll among the cars. There was a play area for children, but Lydia decided not to take her there because that action could be challenged if the parents came along before she was ready to return her.

As it was, a police car had just drawn up outside the main building when Lydia and her charge reached it again.

'This little girl's lost,' Lydia told the constable, coming up beside him before he could get out of his vehicle. 'I found her wandering about.'

The constable, despatched to the scene because a small girl had been reported missing, saw that this one matched the issued description, even to her red shoes. It was not often that a search ended before it had started.

'Ah,' he began, getting out of the car.

'It was lucky I found her. It could have been anyone,' said Lydia sternly. 'Her parents had let her stray.'

'Well, kids are little devils sometimes,' said the constable. 'Move like eels, they do. Give you the slip as soon as you let go their hands to pay.'

By this time Lydia had transferred the child's hand to the policeman's grasp. She left before the officer could ask her name.

A teenage couple, the girl with cropped purple hair, the boy with three earrings in one ear, both his arms tattooed, had come forward when, over the intercom in the refreshment area, the child had been reported missing. They had seen a little girl wearing the clothes described going off with an old lady. No one paid attention to their information. Old ladies did not abduct children and there were plenty of grandmothers legitimately about the place with their families. In vain did Sandra insist she had seen the old woman carry the child away. She'd not taken any notice at the time, not until she heard the broadcast, when she realized that there was something wrong.

When the child had been safely restored to her distraught parents, Sandra heard that an old lady had found her outside. She told the policeman about her doubts but he was not the least bit interested.

Sandra, however, didn't like it at all.

That evening, when Thelma had grown bored with

watching television, she told her mother she wanted the car the next day.

'Is that all right?' She made an effort. 'Do you need it?'

'I told Edward he could have it,' Lydia said. 'He must go to the Job Centre.'

'And sign on,' said Edward practically.

'Where do you have to go for that?' asked Thelma.

'To Cheverton,' said Edward.

'Well, you can drop me in Heronsmouth on the way,' said Thelma. 'I'm meeting a friend for lunch but I don't mind going early. I've one or two things to do in the town.' Like go to an estate agent about a flat.

'Is it really all right if we take the car?' asked Edward. 'Don't you really need it, Mrs Cunningham?'

'No,' she answered.

'OK, then,' said Edward. 'I'll pick you up on the way back, Thelma.' He wouldn't mind whiling time away in Cheverton.

Lydia hugged to herself the knowledge that if they were out for most of the day, she would be peacefully alone.

They had been gone for only a very short time the following morning when the police arrived.

14

The sight of a uniformed woman police officer standing on the doorstep made Lydia's heart lurch. One of them had had an accident. Which was it? Thelma, on the way to Heronsmouth, or had something happened to Gerald?

While she braced herself to receive bad news, the young woman made certain that she was, in fact, Mrs Lydia Cunningham.

'Yes – yes. What is it? What's happened?' Lydia asked testily.

'May I come in?' requested WPC Cotton, who was a sturdy girl with fresh pink cheeks and straight brown hair cut short beneath her cap.

Lydia motioned her to enter, then led the way to the sitting-room.

'What's happened?' she repeated.

'Shall we sit down?' suggested WPC Cotton.

She's saying that in case I faint, thought Lydia, smoothing her skirt and sitting in her usual highbacked wing chair. WPC Cotton took another chair, pulled out her notebook and consulted it.

'Your car is a blue Metro, registration number – ' and she quoted it.

'Yes,' Oh God! Thelma had driven too fast down the lane and killed herself and the boy.

Lydia took a deep breath and waited, her mind already flying to mortuaries and funerals, the paraphernalia of death.

The policewoman asked her if she had stopped at the service station near the motorway the previous afternoon.

'Yes, I did.' What had this to do with Thelma? Oh, couldn't she get on – tell her the worst?

At least Mrs Cunningham had not denied the facts so far.

WPC Cotton plodded routinely on. This old woman certainly did not look remotely like a kidnapper.

'A little girl, Melanie Smith, aged two, went missing,' WPC Cotton pursued.

'I found her straying,' Lydia said. Was that the reason for the visit? Colour began returning to her face and her heartbeat steadied as she realized that there had been no accident. 'I took her to a policeman.'

'You left before the constable could take your name,' said WPC Cotton.

'There was no need,' said Lydia. 'The child had come to no harm.'

'Where did you find her, Mrs Cunningham?' asked WPC Cotton.

'Wandering about,' said Lydia.

'You approached the police officer from outside – from the car park area,' said the girl.

'This is correct. I had hoped her parents would appear. Meanwhile, I amused her by showing her my dog. We gave him a little run – he'd been shut in the car,' said Lydia. She glanced across to Boris, lying nearby.

'Where was she wandering, Mrs Cunningham?' WPC Cotton persisted.

'Oh, just about,' said Lydia. 'She was frightened. It must be terrifying for a child to lose its parents in a crowd.'

'It's easily done,' said the policewoman. 'Children slip away.'

'Yes – and then they get run over, or worse,' said Lydia. 'Someone else might have come across that little girl. Some pervert.'

'Well – that can happen,' allowed the girl.

'The parents should have taken better care of her,' said Lydia.

'No one's perfect, Mrs Cunningham. A moment's inattention – that's all it takes,' said WPC Cotton.

'I don't understand why you're here. I want no thanks for stopping her from wandering away or going off with someone who might have hurt her,' Lydia said.

'Mrs Cunningham, it's been alleged that you abducted the child, then thought better of it,' said WPC Cotton. 'Two witnesses saw you take her out of the cafeteria and go outside with her. They thought at first that you must be her grandmother, but when she was reported missing over the loudspeaker system, they came forward. They recognized Melanie when the constable reunited her with her parents.'

Barry and Sandra, riding home on Barry's motorbike, had passed Lydia as she drove sedately home. Sandra, glancing back, had recognized her. They'd pulled into a lay-by, let her pass, checked again and noted down the number of her car. Then they had reported her.

'But that's ridiculous,' said Lydia. 'At least – ' she floundered briefly, then pulled herself together. 'I did take her into the open, away from the crowds, to give her parents the opportunity to see her with me when they searched for her. They would not have easily seen her in the cafeteria, it was so busy.'

'It's very well staffed, Mrs Cunningham. An assistant would soon have noticed a lost child.'

'Well, they hadn't by the time I saw her,' said Lydia, truthfully enough. 'I hope you're not seriously accusing me of stealing her?'

'No, certainly not.' If she'd meant to abduct the child, she'd have driven off with her. Obviously the informants had made a mistake, or for some reason had a grudge against Mrs Cunningham, who was of a type to rouse ire in certain kinds of people. You got all sorts at service stations. 'It was just to keep the record straight, to tidy up the files,' said WPC Cotton, now smiling. 'It had been reported, you see, entered in the book. We had to look into it.'

'Hm,' said Lydia.

'What would you have done if the police officer hadn't come along, Mrs Cunningham?' asked the girl, closing her notebook.

'Why – looked for someone in authority at the place and got them to telephone the police,' said Lydia. 'The child could have been abandoned, officer. It happens.'

'Yes, I know.'

'The parents ought to be more careful,' Lydia repeated. 'Careless parents don't deserve the blessing of a child.'

'Cruel parents don't. Careless ones should learn better ways,' said WPC Cotton. 'I'm sure Melanie's will take more care of her in future.'

'Good.'

Lydia stood up. The interview was over.

'I was afraid you had bad news for me,' she confessed, leading the way out to the hall. 'My daughter is out just now, in my car. I was afraid she might have had an accident.'

'Oh no. I'm sorry if you were alarmed,' said WPC Cotton.

'Well – no harm done,' Lydia said.

That was soon tidied up, thought WPC Cotton, driving off. The only odd thing about it was that the old woman had clearly taken the child outside instead of immediately trying to locate the parents through the administration of the building. Younger women, frustrated mothers, sometimes stole babies out of prams; was there a similar grandmother syndrome?

She'd make a full report, of course; that was routine; but Mrs Cunningham was no criminal.

The policewoman's visit had unsettled Lydia, not that she was in a calm state of mind in any case. It was horrible to think that someone had been spying on her, had described her to the police, perhaps noted down the number of her car, for that must be how they had traced her. Even Lydia had heard of the police computer. She shivered. Suddenly, she felt quite ill.

She sat down in her armchair to allow the dizzy, disoriented feeling to pass, then, with an effort, got up and called Boris. Exercise was a good antidote to worry so she would go for a nice long walk. She set out, forcing her mind away from her anxieties, concentrating on her surroundings, the bracken by the roadside with its curious, musty smell, the fuchsias in the gardens. Boris waddled along, keeping pace with her; sometimes he paused to investigate a seductive odour, sometimes he lolloped clumsily ahead, but he always kept close to the verge, an obedient dog who came to heel immediately when she called him, as she did each time a car went by. There were few today, but in high summer this lane was perilous with traffic.

There were large, dark storm clouds in the sky but the sun shafted down between them and there was a breeze. Lydia walked for over two hours and was so tired when she reached home again that, after drinking some fresh orange juice and changing from her walking shoes into low-heeled pumps, she sank down in her chair and found her eyelids closing.

She woke to hear a female voice.

'Lydia – are you asleep? Goodness, are you ill?'

Dorothy Butler had expected Lydia to be working in the garden on this sunny afternoon and had walked round the back way, leaving the car outside the garage, which Edward had closed when he and Thelma left that morning. Lydia was nowhere to be seen, but the french window was open and Dorothy was startled by the unlikely sight of her friend's surrender to physical fatigue.

'What? Oh – !' Lydia sat up, blinking. She had been having that dream again, the one where she was forced to move to some other house. Dorothy's bulk obscured the light from the french window and it took Lydia a moment or two to recognize her visitor. 'Whatever is the time?' she said. 'I must have just dropped off.'

'It's nearly four o'clock,' said Dorothy.

Lydia had been asleep for over an hour.

'Oh dear!' She struggled to her feet, blinking. 'Goodness, I'd no idea it was so late,' she said.

'Well, you aren't going anywhere, are you?' Dorothy said mildly. 'I expect you needed forty winks. I'll go and put the kettle on. A cup of tea will wake you up, and I could use one too.'

That morning her neighbour had come hurrying round to tell her that someone had called while she was out the previous day.

'That friend of yours in the blue car who sometimes comes,' she'd said. 'She looked quite put out when she found you weren't at home. Didn't she leave a note?' The inquisitive neighbour hadn't seen Lydia writing one, but she had observed her air of indecision.

After this conversation, Dorothy had telephoned Lydia but had got no reply. She had tried again at lunch-time, then at intervals during the afternoon, still with no result. It was so much out of character for Lydia to come over un-announced that Dorothy had felt uneasy; Thelma was staying with her mother and Thelma spelled trouble. Unable to settle to the still-life on her easel which needed only final touches, Dorothy had decided to make a surprise call herself and if Lydia were still out, she would put a note through the door asking her to telephone when she returned.

Dorothy headed for the kitchen while Lydia went into the cloakroom, emerging after she had sponged her face and settled some straying wisps of hair under her snood. She still felt heavy and slow when she joined Dorothy, who meanwhile had laid a tray and found two cups and saucers and the china teapot. The silver one, by Henry's decree always used at the Manor, had vanished when Lydia moved; perhaps it had been sold in the hotch-potch of the estate, or maybe Iris had collared it among her spoils.

'There isn't any cake,' said Lydia. 'Would you like a biscuit?' There were some custard creams in a tin; she had discovered that Edward was very fond of them. Lydia put five on a plate and took the tray which Dorothy had prepared back to the sitting-room. She now seemed perfectly composed.

'I'm sorry I missed you yesterday,' said Dorothy. 'I went to see a former pupil who's in trouble.'

'How did you know I'd been over?' Lydia snapped the words at her, quite fiercely.

'A neighbour noticed – Madge Green from opposite. I think you've met her,' said Dorothy.

'People are much too keen on minding what's not their business,' Lydia muttered crossly.

'True, true, but I'm glad she mentioned it,' said Dorothy. Lydia was getting very difficult these days.

'I was just passing by and thought I'd drop in,' said Lydia, making an effort to speak more calmly. 'I should have telephoned first, as I usually do.'

'It's quite all right by me if you don't,' said Dorothy.

'You might have found me out this afternoon,' said Lydia, ungraciously. 'Or were you passing too?'

Dorothy decided to embroider the truth.

'I felt like going for a drive and so I came this way,' she said. Honours were even.

The tea had drawn. Lydia poured it out, two cups of pale clear fluid with a slice of lemon; one of her few luxuries was her Lapsang Souchong. She had never acquired a nurse's taste for strong dark tea.

'A biscuit?' she suggested.

Dorothy took one, then watched in surprise as Lydia ate her own up quickly and started on another.

'Didn't you have any lunch?' she asked, not really seriously; Lydia's strict timetable, structuring her life, was well known to her.

'No – now that you mention it, I forgot,' said Lydia. 'Boris and I went for a very long walk and I must have fallen asleep straight away when we got back.'

This was not like Lydia at all: even if she had no appetite, a bowl of soup, an apple, or some cheese would be consumed while listening to *The World at One*, especially when it was Sir Robin Day in charge.

Though she looked her normal self now, her hand shook slightly as she drank her tea.

'What's upset you?' Dorothy asked.

'Nothing – there's nothing wrong,' said Lydia brusquely.

Dorothy sighed. How easy it would be to walk away, accept this statement at its face value and go home. But she owed Lydia more than that.

'You don't deceive me,' she said gently. 'Come on. Out with it. Is it Thelma?'

'No, not really. Not more than usual,' said Lydia. 'It's something so ridiculous. The police came to question me this morning.'

'Oh Lydia! Whatever have you done?' For a wild moment the thought that Lydia might have started shoplifting ran through Dorothy's mind.

'Nothing. Nothing at all,' said Lydia. I let a man die once, she thought, but no one now will ever find that out.

'They must have had a reason. Did you witness an accident?'

'No. It was about a little girl – a toddler,' Lydia said. 'Her parents let her wander off at the big motorway service area yesterday. I called there for petrol and found her wandering about. I handed her over to a policeman who arrived in a car.'

What on earth had she been doing, driving all that way?

'I see,' Dorothy replied. 'Why should that upset you?'

Weren't they just tidying up their records?'

'They seemed to think I'd kidnapped her,' said Lydia.

'Oh, what nonsense! It was lucky you found her and not some suspicious character,' said Dorothy.

This robust reaction cheered Lydia.

'I told them that,' she said.

'Good for you. I don't know why you're fussing,' Dorothy declared. 'Anyway, as soon as the policeman saw you, he must have known it was rubbish.'

'It was a policewoman.'

'Well, she was satisfied, wasn't she?'

'I think so. Yes, she seemed to be,' said Lydia.

'I expect it was just a formality,' said Dorothy. 'Suppose you had been some sort of baby farmer and they hadn't checked, there'd have been an awful song and dance.'

'That's true,' said Lydia.

'Now tell me about Thelma,' Dorothy instructed. That was really the trouble, the reason for Lydia's unheralded visit, she was sure: this other thing, the alleged baby snatching, had happened after that abortive call. 'What state is she in this time?'

'She seems all right,' said Lydia carefully. 'It's as well this American dream of hers didn't work out, I suppose.'

Dorothy didn't agree. She had hoped that Thelma would settle down far enough away to let her mother have some peace.

'Is she heartbroken again?' she asked.

'Not really. She's mended very quickly,' said Lydia. As she spoke, she heard a car draw up outside. 'Here she is,' she added, and went on quickly, 'There's someone else staying here. Edward Fletcher is his name.'

Thelma came in looking beautiful. She seemed pleased to see her godmother, greeting her warmly with a kiss. Her face was smooth and cool. Dorothy, when Edward was introduced, held out her hand as she had taught her girls, and, awkwardly, he shook it. His palm was slightly damp. Now, why should he be nervous?

'No need to ask you how you are,' Dorothy remarked to Thelma. 'You look marvellous.'

'She had a real good lunch with this old guy,' said Edward eagerly. 'And he's offered her a job. She's going to be his housekeeper. How about that?' This news had been a big relief to him.

Lydia would not allow herself to share that feeling. She needed to know more.

'Living in?' asked Dorothy practically.

'Not at first,' said Thelma. 'In case it doesn't work. We're both agreed on that. I'd already decided to rent a flat in Heronsmouth – there are plenty going, now the season's over, and I've got one down by the harbour below the Swan. It'll be handy for rehearsals.'

'And who is your employer?' Dorothy pursued.

'He's a widower who needs looking after. Gerald suggested I should get a job like that. Aren't you pleased?' She looked at the two women defiantly. Both had seen her with that expression so many times before, beginning at the age of four or five; she had something to conceal.

'He's really nice,' said Edward. 'I met him when I picked Thelma up. We had tea with him. He wants a few things doing round the place and I said I'd help him out. Painting and that.'

'Are you moving out too?' asked Lydia faintly. Perhaps he planned to share the flat with Thelma.

'Not right away – unless you want me to,' said Edward.

How did he fit in here, wondered Dorothy.

'I'm glad you've got something satisfactory settled,' she told Thelma.

The whole atmosphere had lightened and Lydia looked quite different, her torpor gone.

'Will you stay to supper, Dorothy?' she asked. There should be plenty of cold meat left from yesterday.

Dorothy accepted, but Lydia had a shock when she went to take it from the fridge. Very little remained beneath the foil which Thelma had carefully wrapped round what was mostly bone. Lydia had to eke it out with a tin of ham.

They spent an animated evening, with Lydia controlling the conversation in the manner Dorothy had watched her painfully acquire over the years. She told Dorothy that Edward had a sister in the village who let rooms and that he was moving there when she had space. Thelma must have given her this idea, Edward supposed; he felt worried by their continuing wrong assumption but told himself that this was not the time to put it right. He was relieved when the talk turned towards *The Seagull*, then the state of the theatre in general, which interested Dorothy. Edward fed in questions to keep the conversation safe.

When Dorothy left, she realized that she had learned nothing about the young man except that he had a sister in the village. Lydia must have taken him in from the kindness of her heart.

15

Things moved fast the next week. Thelma borrowed the car again to go over to Heronsmouth to take possession of the flat. Edward went with her to help with any tasks that had to be done. Thelma had filled the washing machine before they left. The girl was forever laundering her clothes; no wonder they soon wore out, Lydia thought, pegging them on the rotary line.

When the pair came home in the late afternoon they were in high spirits. They had cleaned up the flat and stocked the store cupboard in preparation for Thelma's removal.

'The old guy came down with some wine and stuff for lunch,' Edward said. 'He's taken a fancy to Thelma. I reckon she'll have to watch out. He's still got a twinkle in his eye, for all he's so old. What do you say, Thelma?'

She shrugged.

'Who can tell?' she replied, but she was laughing.

Edward found that this line of thought eased his guilt about Thelma.

'He's bald,' he said in a more critical tone.

'I like bald men,' said Thelma staunchly. 'Think of Yul Brynner.'

Edward couldn't remember him.

'What nonsense you both talk.' Lydia spoke tolerantly. Thelma might be bored again before long, but for now she had an aim.

'I need some linen – sheets and things,' Thelma said. 'They're not provided.'

'I'll find you some,' her mother said.

The following day, Edward helped Thelma move and he returned to the lodge alone.

'Well, she's settled,' he told Lydia. 'And I've made a start up at the old guy's house. He's having a second bathroom put in just for her – imagine! I'm to do that up, to madam's taste, when the plumber's finished. It'll be like a palace for her.'

'If she stays,' said Lydia.

'Why shouldn't she?' asked Edward. 'They get on a treat. She'll be OK now. I'm going over again tomorrow to start on the bedroom. I'll hitch a ride.'

'I'll drop you,' said Lydia. 'Thanks to you, all the jigsaws are done, so I'll take them back and see if there are more waiting for me. Maybe you could come back on the bus.'

'OK. Thanks,' said Edward. 'I might be late so don't wait your meal for me. I'll fix myself a sandwich if I'm hungry, if that's all right.' He might see what sort of night life Heronsmouth offered; not a lot, he thought. He took some money from his pocket and counted out twenty pounds. 'There. That's my next week's rent in advance,' he said. He was suddenly wildly happy. He had a place to live where he felt at home and work for the days ahead; what more did a fellow need?

'That's far too much,' said Lydia. 'You've already given me ten pounds.'

'That was for this week,' said Edward. 'And it's not enough. I should give you thirty pounds at least, as you give me so many meals.'

'I don't want to make a profit,' Lydia said.

'Why not? Everyone else does,' Edward said. 'And you give me the run of the house, and free baths and everything.'

'Well, of course,' Lydia said. Poor boy, where had he been living before he came here? 'I like having you around,' she said, the warmest remark she had made to a human soul for a very long time, although Edward was not to know that.

Lydia dropped him the next day at The Shieling. The house stood back from the road behind a small front garden; a short drive led up to the front door. It was a solid building with twin gables under a grey slate roof, the brickwork plastered over and painted white, the woodwork rather too blue. A prefabricated garage stood at one side.

'Ugly old place, isn't it, but it's nice inside,' said Edward. 'It's got big rooms and a garden running up behind. He grows lots of vegetables.'

Lydia read the name on the gateposts, which were freshly painted – Edward's work, she learned. Everything looked well kept. Lydia would have selected black for the paint-work, if the house were hers, but otherwise she could not fault it. Fuchsias leaned over the iron fencing, with among them tall, spiked dahlias, mainly yellow, not like Dorothy's multi-coloured display, and some old-fashioned blue Michaelmas daisies.

'See you later,' Edward said. 'Thanks.'

Lydia felt almost cheerful as she drove on. Edward's optimism was infectious. She carried out her errands at the charity shop, pointing out there was a piece missing from one of the puzzles; she always mentioned such details although it was written on the box. Then she went on to the car park, and had lunch in the department store again after giving Boris a short run. It was advisable to place oneself among other people occasionally, otherwise even speech became difficult and she had found that she sometimes felt quite unreal in crowds after days of isolation.

She had always been reserved but she had grown almost reclusive lately. It was like dreaming to look back at that summer so many years ago, when she had felt like bursting into song or laughter all the time. It had been so brief, just a few short weeks and then he was killed.

Lydia would not let herself think about it now. She selected a cheese salad and ate it quickly. No unattended children roamed the store today, and she went home with-out adventure.

Thelma's job wouldn't last; nothing did, with her; but it might take them past the performance of *The Seagull*.

Edward came in late. Lydia was in bed, but not asleep, when she heard him close the front door softly. Perhaps she should let him have a key; it wasn't a very good idea to leave the door on the latch, even in a peaceful place like this, if one took heed of what was in the papers. But things hadn't got to that pass in Milton St Gabriel: not yet.

When Betty came on Thursday, she was delighted to learn that Thelma had moved out and got a job.

'What's she doing, then?' she asked.

'She's housekeeper to some old man on Harbour Hill,' said Lydia. 'A widower. I don't know his name. He lives at The Shieling – the white house with the blue paint.'

'I know it,' Betty said. 'Used to belong to Phil Draper from the chemist, but the family moved after he died.' And the long established pharmacy had been bought by a multiple and lost its individuality. 'I heard a couple'd bought it and she died.'

'That would be right, then,' Lydia said.

'I don't know the new folk,' Betty said. 'Or rather him, as she's passed on.' That meant they were not members of Betty's chapel. 'The name's Anderson or Harrison – something like that. In the old days I'd have known all about him. When we had the shop. He'd have a paper delivered, that's for sure. Well, it sounds all right and she's old enough to know what she's about,' she added. 'I'll give her room a good going-over and then it'll be ready for Gerald next time he comes down.'

While she did so, Lydia listened to the morning story on the radio and began one of the new jigsaws. The house was almost back to normal; Edward was no trouble at all.

Gerald telephoned that evening, and when he learned that Thelma had taken his advice and had even moved out already, he was very relieved. He'd come down soon, he said, but he was taking a late holiday and going to France to visit Christopher. He'd suggested that Fiona might like to go with him, but she'd refused; she'd got some big date coming up in Scotland, it appeared, some lairdling's coming-of-age she'd been invited to attend.

'Mother, would you – ' Gerald began, then stopped. He had been on the point of asking her if she would like to go with him. How embarrassed she would be at having to find an excuse! Boris wouldn't do as one, with Edward there to see to him.

'Yes?'

'Oh – nothing. I've forgotten. It wasn't important,' Gerald said.

Two weeks passed tranquilly. Lydia saw little of Edward during the day as he was working either in the village or at

The Shieling, where he was tiling Thelma's new bathroom. He hadn't done such work before but he was learning. No more was said about him moving to his sister's place; Lydia supposed she had late guests. Some evenings he went out after the meal they had together, but often he sat helping with her jigsaw, one eye on television. Sometimes he spent the evening round at Karen's when she was alone, and he took her to the cinema in Lydia's car, a trip for which she gladly gave permission.

It was quite a shock when he told Lydia that he had been offered the post as boiler attendant and odd-job man at the hotel, taking over when the present man retired; he would eventually be given accommodation in staff quarters there. Meanwhile, he was spending time learning the ropes from his predecessor.

'Oh, that's splendid news,' said Lydia. He seemed happy working with his hands. 'I didn't know you'd applied for it.'

'I hadn't,' Edward answered. He hesitated. She still didn't know about Julie. 'I – er – I've got friends up there and I've done a few bits and pieces when they've been shorthanded. That's how it came up,' he said, which was more or less the truth.

He wasn't sure how long he'd stay. It might be too quiet in the winter, but now he'd be able to put down a deposit on a scooter and be independent. If a year went uneventfully by, with him keeping out of trouble, he'd trust himself enough to broaden out a bit. He'd been ready to tell Mrs Thomson about his past but it hadn't come up. She'd assumed he'd been made redundant by some normal process and had come to the village because of his sister. Julie was a good, reliable worker; no doubt her brother would be, too.

'I'll miss you,' Lydia said.

She smiled at him as she spoke. He'd noticed her smiling sometimes lately, a thing she hadn't done at all when he first arrived. It quite changed her face, wiping out the severe lines. She might have been pretty when she was a girl. Odd to think that she had once been young.

'I'd hoped I might get something a bit more up-market,' he admitted. 'Be a rep – something like that. I couldn't stand being stuck in an office all day.'

'You can regard it as experience,' Lydia said. 'You can always look for something else later. It's not like getting married, for better or for worse, until death.'

'No!' Edward was startled by this heavy comparison. 'Well, marriage isn't like that now, either, is it?' he said.

'I'm afraid not,' Lydia said. 'More's the pity.'

'Can I stay until my room's ready at the hotel?' Edward asked. 'It'll be a week or two yet.'

'Of course you may.' Lydia was delighted that his departure was to be delayed.

16

In some ways Edward was looking forward to having a place that was really his own, but he had never before lived anywhere with such a calm domestic atmosphere. Now that Thelma had moved out the place was as tranquil as a cloister.

'How do you like Thelma's flat?' he asked Lydia one day.

'I haven't seen it,' she replied.

'What? Haven't you been to visit her?' Edward was astonished.

'She hasn't asked me,' Lydia told him.

'But she's your daughter! Surely you don't need an invitation to drop in?' said Edward.

'I respect her privacy,' Lydia said.

'I bet she doesn't pay you the same compliment,' said Edward. 'If it suited her, she'd turn up at any time, even if you'd got the Queen coming to tea.'

That was perfectly true.

The next evening, Thelma rang up to invite her mother to dinner a week later. When Lydia accepted, Thelma said she would ask Dorothy as well. Lydia felt sure that the whole idea was Edward's and this took away some of her pleasure in receiving the invitation.

Soon afterwards, Dorothy telephoned to ask if she might stay at the lodge that night; it was quite a long way to go back to Wilcombe if the evening was a late one, and would mean, too, that a glass of sherry and perhaps a glass of wine would be all that she could safely drink in case a breathalysing constable was on the prowl. It only needed someone else to drive into her car, however blameless she was, for her to land in trouble, Dorothy declared.

When the evening came, she arrived in good time, ready changed, while Edward, who was going with them, was still in the bathroom. She had brought some cushions as a house-warming present for her god-daughter.

'Oh dear,' said Lydia. 'I never thought about a house-warming. She isn't going to be there long. It didn't cross my mind.

'Take her a bottle of sherry,' Dorothy advised. 'Have you got one that hasn't been opened?'

Thanks to Gerald, Lydia had. She found some gift-wrapping paper and put it round the bottle, feeling mortified. Why couldn't she think of these sort of gestures herself? And there was Dorothy looking so handsome in her lacy lilac knitted suit, with her abundant white hair smoothly set and rinsed a steely blue. Lydia, in the dress that she had worn to dine with Gerald at the Manor, felt inadequate and dowdy.

'Let's have a drink before we go,' she suggested, to Dorothy's surprise. She was always so abstemious.

She poured Dorothy a strong gin and tonic and a small glass of sherry for herself, and both were sitting comfortably in front of the electric fire when Edward made his entrance. He wore a pair of dark green slacks and a cream shirt with a dark green tie. He carried his bomber jacket.

'You do look smart,' said Lydia warmly.

'Yeah – well, I want to get a blazer but I'm still saving,' Edward said, obviously pleased by this reaction.

A blazer! How conventional! Lydia's reactionary influence was having its effect, thought Dorothy in amusement.

'Come along. We must go,' said Lydia, getting up.

He held their coats for them, faultlessly polite, and he drove the car. He must stand high in Lydia's favour, thought her friend.

They were able to park on the harbour front close to the block where Thelma lived.

She was ready for them, wearing a yellow dress which set off her gilded hair. Gold bracelets clattered on each wrist and gilt pendant earrings dangled from her ears.

Dorothy and Lydia handed over their presents which were received with apparent pleasure.

'This seems very comfortable,' said Lydia, glancing round the unremarkable sitting-room with its dull, serviceable furniture and its patterned carpet.

'It's convenient,' Thelma said. 'But my rooms at The Shieling will be really attractive. It's all being done up for me, you know,' she told Dorothy. 'Arthur's getting new curtains and things – I'm choosing everything myself.'

'Nothing's too good for her ladyship,' said Edward. 'Mr Morrison keeps finding me new jobs to do.' He laughed. 'I should worry.' Now that he was working regularly by day, he'd been up there in the evenings and at weekends carrying out the latest schemes. The old boy paid in cash, no questions asked.

'He was coming tonight,' said Thelma. 'But he's got a bit of a cold and he thought he'd keep it to himself, as he put it.'

'Oh dear! I hope it's nothing much,' said Dorothy, visualizing this ancient man succumbing to a fatal virus and thus relinquishing his role as Lydia's saviour.

'No – it's just a cold, but he has a weak chest,' Thelma said. 'Something to do with the war.'

'Was he wounded in it? His chest I mean?' asked Dorothy.

'I don't think so. No. In the legs – he walks quite stiffly, his left knee is fixed. He was lucky not to lose it,' Thelma said. 'He was shot down over Germany and taken prisoner. He said he was well looked after in hospital but he wasn't found for quite some time – he lay in a wood, unable to move, and got pneumonia. He nearly died.'

'Poor man,' said Dorothy.

'What did you say his name was?' Lydia asked. Betty had said it was Harrison, or Anderson, she wasn't sure. She hadn't heard his first name until now.

'Arthur Morrison,' said Thelma. Really, her mother was getting so forgetful; she must have heard his name a dozen times before. 'His wife was called Phyllis and he's got a son called Nicholas and several grandchildren. Anything more you want to know?'

'And he was in the Air Force?' Lydia said. Her head was spinning. She had once known an Arthur Morrison, common names enough, perhaps. The one she knew was dead. 'Was he a pilot?'

'I don't know,' said Thelma, who wasn't interested.

Lydia breathed deeply, trying to control the flutter in her

chest. It was so silly to get upset after all this time. Her Arthur was long dead, and this other man who bore his name was just a stranger.

Dorothy had begun to circle round the room inspecting the pictures the landlord had thought fit to put upon the walls – prints of the district – and the row of tattered paperbacks on a shelf. She pulled out a Dick Francis, one she had not read, and told Thelma that she wished to borrow it.

'Doesn't it go with the flat?' Lydia tried to speak normally though she felt that she was choking.

'I expect these have all been left by different tenants,' Dorothy said. 'But I'll give it back.'

'I'm sure no one will ever notice,' Thelma said, giving her mother a pitying look. 'The books aren't listed on the inventory. Dinner's ready. Shall we eat?'

She had made the table look very attractive, with yellow miniature chrysanthemums in a low bowl and some of her mother's linen table napkins. There were tall yellow candles in silver candlesticks which she had borrowed from The Shieling. She had taken trouble and the meal was delicious – beef fillets in a rich wine sauce after a frothy shrimp mousse. There was fresh fruit salad to follow. Lydia drank very little; someone must be in a proper condition to drive home. The other three enjoyed their wine, talking cheerfully. Edward wanted to hear about Dorothy's visit to Russia and was more interested in Peter the Great's boat, the forerunner of the Russian Navy, now in the Maritime Museum in Leningrad, than the glories of the Hermitage and the restored great palaces.

'They're such nice people, what I saw of them,' said Dorothy, and explained how she had tried to describe, by song and mime, which ballet she had seen to a delighted hotel maid who wore knee socks and bursting canvas shoes. 'I think I'll learn some Russian and go back.'

Lydia let the conversation ebb and flow around her, trying to do justice to the meal because she did not want to seem rude to Thelma, but her mind was haunted by the past.

'How does he occupy his time, your Mr Morrison?' she asked abruptly, interrupting Dorothy's description of delicious blinis.

'What – oh, he's in with the bridge-playing crowd,' said Thelma. 'More deeply than he wants to be, I think. His wife was rather keen and I gather they scooped him up after she died. The dear ladies keep trying to fix up games with him.'

'Bridge is such a waste of time,' said Lydia.

'People who play it don't think so,' Dorothy said. 'They might find your passion for jigsaws equally useless.'

'Yes. I'm sorry,' said Lydia, crumpling immediately.

'Oh Lydia, I'm only teasing.' Dorothy was instantly contrite.

'We all waste time in ways, don't we?' said Edward. 'Like watching telly when we could be painting a picture or learning Russian.'

'I'm too intolerant,' Lydia said. Her voice was harsh.

That was true, but Dorothy did not like to see her friend upset.

'One man's relaxation is another man's hard work,' she said lightly.

After the meal she insisted on helping Thelma wash up.

'We can't leave you like Cinderella at the sink after we've gone,' she said, putting on an apron that hung in the kitchen and setting to work while Thelma sorted things out and Edward put the coffee on. There were jokes about smears on plates and shiny stainless steel.

Dorothy was so good at making an evening go, thought Lydia, drying a wine glass. Thank goodness she had been included in the invitation. What if she hadn't been, and that Arthur Morrison had come? She would have been so thrown by hearing his name that no matter how different he was from the young man she had known, she would have found the evening a far worse strain even than it was. Dorothy never had any trouble finding things to talk about and drawing other people out. Now she had Edward telling some tale about a battle with the laundry-room door at the Manor. It had jammed with the ironing lady inside and she had felt claustrophobic. In the end he had extracted her through the window so that he could free the door in peace. Dorothy had always had a gift for putting people at their ease; it was one of the things that Henry had admired about her and when she came to stay they always entertained because then, he would say, he could be certain someone would see that things went properly.

'I hope we meet this old boy of yours before long,' Dorothy told Thelma as they left.

'He's not all that old,' Thelma said. 'No older than you are – not as old as Daddy would have been.'

Back at the lodge, when Edward had gone up to bed and she and Lydia were having a nightcap together – whisky for Dorothy and orange juice for Lydia – Dorothy uttered a thought that had come to her that evening.

'Do you think Thelma might want to marry this old man?' she asked. 'This Arthur, who isn't all that old? Be an old man's darling again?'

'What do you mean, again?'

'Well, she was the apple of her father's eye, wasn't she? She misses him,' said Dorothy. 'I expect this old chap makes a fuss of her too.'

'But she's working for him,' Lydia said.

'My dear, haven't you heard of housekeepers marrying their employers?' Dorothy inquired. 'What could be more likely? It would save him paying wages.'

'But she can't feel like that about him, at his age,' said Lydia. 'Or him either,' she added, ungrammatically.

'Lydia dear, age has nothing to do with it,' Dorothy said, and added, 'Would it be so very terrible, if he's nice? It might sort her out – steady her down – restore her confidence, if it lasted long enough. I think she misses being married – the status that it offers, I mean. She might learn to be content at last. Isn't that what you want for her?'

'Of course it is,' said Lydia slowly.

'I'll bet you,' Dorothy was saying. 'I'll give it a year but it's more likely to happen sooner. At his age, he won't want to waste precious time.'

17

To keep the ghosts at bay, Lydia took two sleeping pills. Some still remained from those the doctor had prescribed after Henry's death. Their effect wore off after only a few hours and she lay fretting restlessly until she could rise and take Dorothy a cup of tea. Her friend had slept soundly; she was anxious to return home promptly as she had some people coming to lunch, so she did not linger after breakfast.

In the morning light, Lydia suddenly looked every second of her age, which was, within three months, the same as Dorothy's. Old age did not begin until you let it encompass you, or physical deterioration restricted your life.

'You haven't had any more visits from the police, have you?' Dorothy asked.

'No. Why should I?' Lydia's answer came in her usual brusque tone.

'Why indeed.' Dorothy hesitated. 'Well, ring up if anything's bothering you,' she said. 'Take care.'

Lydia felt flat after she had gone. Edward had already left for work, and for once her precious solitude became oppressive. It was stupid to let herself be upset, she told herself. The coincidence of a name had brought back a rush of memories. That was understandable, and now she must forget it. But she had never been able to do that wholly; the past had marched along throughout her life beside the present, and she had harmed Henry just as much as he had hurt her. That was why she took the punishment. In the end, though, he had gone too far and she had let him die.

For Thelma was not Henry's child.

The pressure of her thoughts almost made Lydia forget that it was Thursday, Betty's day. She set off hastily to fetch her. All the scenery was grey and bleak today; odd to think that in spring the banks along the lanes would once again be starred with primroses. Winter, rarely severe down here, was even so a time of gales and penetrating damp.

Betty noticed that Lydia looked tired but put it down to the late night.

'Gave you a good dinner, did she? Thelma?' Betty asked.

'Yes, excellent. She is a first-class cook, you know,' said Lydia.

'Right enough. The gentleman she's working for – Morrison's the name,' said Betty. 'I meant to tell you. He's well thought of in the town. Credit good, all that. She's maybe fallen on her feet.'

'Nothing known against?' said Lydia, half smiling.

What a funny way to put it, but then Mrs Cunningham had always been unusual.

'That's right,' said Betty.

Lydia went into the garden while Betty was busy. She started digging up the vegetable bed, working hard, trying to think only of sending the spade in deep enough, leaving the soil level. Then, after she had taken Betty home, she drove into Heronsmouth, going up Harbour Hill to pass The Shieling in its quarter of an acre, a solid, safe house into which her daughter would be moving soon, a house owned by a man who had the same name as Thelma's natural father, and, like him, had been in the Royal Air Force.

Lydia drove on up the hill, past the Cliff Hotel, and turned at a fork in the road, then went back again. If she could just see the man, her fret would cease. Arthur, her Arthur, the lover of her youth, was dead, had died months before Thelma was born. This man was someone else. As she passed the house for the second time, no one came in or out; bald Mr Morrison was not to be seen. Thelma must be in there now; perhaps he was joking with her, planning her installation.

Why did she think he would be joking with her? Because Arthur – Lydia's Arthur – had always been so cheerful? He never admitted to the fear he must have felt as he went off on yet another bombing mission. He was shot down over Germany only a few hours after they had parted, leaving her pregnant. Such things happened to a lot of girls in those years.

On the way back, Lydia stopped to give Boris a walk, and once again trudged miles. Summer Time had ended the previous weekend, and dusk was falling when she reached home.

Lydia put the car away, closed the garage and went into the house, Boris shuffling ahead, her mind still full of Arthur Morrison, allowing herself to picture his fair wavy hair, his deep blue eyes, his smile. Thelma had his eyes and his fair, clear skin, but she had not inherited his happy temperament. Lydia put on the hall light, then went into the sitting-room and turned on a lamp.

Edward was sitting in a chair in the corner. He was crouched into a huddled ball, his arms hugging his knees.

'Why, Edward, what are you doing sitting here in the dark?' Lydia exclaimed. Then she realized that something was wrong, for he was making small keening sounds. Boris went up to him and began licking at him, trying to reach his hands with his pink rasping tongue. 'Whatever's happened?' she said, turning on another light.

He couldn't answer. At first she thought that he was ill, and then that he had lost his job, but he mumbled some negative response to both these theories.

'Edward, I can't help you unless you pull yourself together and tell me what's wrong,' she said. 'Now, let's have a cup of tea. Then you explain. Come along.'

He trailed after her into the kitchen in his socks. Whatever catastrophe had hit him had not prevented him from taking off his shoes before treading on the pale carpet.

Lydia brewed a pot of strong tea, let it stand, and then poured out two cups, ladling sugar into his.

'Drink it,' she instructed, and waited until he had swallowed quite a quantity before asking him again to explain.

'It's Karen,' he said at last.

'Karen? Why? Has something happened to her?'

'She's pregnant,' Edward said.

'Oh no! Oh, Edward, that is dreadful!' Lydia set her cup down. He'd seen a lot of Karen, come home from the Whites' quite late a good few times. He must have been responsible. Oh, the foolish pair! Then the full implication of what he had said struck her. 'Why, Edward, she's not sixteen yet, is she?'

'It wasn't me,' he said dully. 'I never went the whole way with her. Mind you, she would have.' He didn't know why he hadn't gone along with her and he certainly hadn't realized that she was only fifteen, though much good that would do him now. 'Her mum caught me on my way back from work. She's going to get the police and I'll be for it.'

'Not necessarily,' Lydia said. 'If it wasn't you, then it was someone else.'

'Karen told her mum it was me. She's annoyed because I've been seeing a bit of Cathy, up at the hotel,' said Edward.

'Edward, look at me,' Lydia commanded, sitting squarely facing him across the table.

He lifted his head and gazed back at her, his face blotched, eyes bloodshot.

'Do you promise that you didn't – that this child can't possibly be yours?' she asked.

'I do. It can't,' he answered, not evading her steady gaze. 'We necked, yes – but not the – the ultimate.'

'I believe you,' Lydia said. 'Now, let me think.' Life didn't change; the same old problems kept arising, only the solutions could be different. 'She'll have to have an abortion,' she said at last. 'There'll be no problem as she's under age.'

'She could marry the bloke. The real father,' Edward said.

'That's not the best way out, and anyway she can't till she's sixteen. Though she can't be far short of that.'

'Two weeks,' said Edward. 'That's enough to get me sent to prison.'

Lydia knew about the fever in the blood, though it took an effort to remember.

'It's the parents' fault,' she said. The mother out at night, the father away so much – what do they expect her to do but get into trouble? There's not enough to interest young people here – no youth club, no guides.' Once, many years ago, she'd run the guides. Eventually the scheme had died from want of recruits. She'd sometimes wondered if it was her fault.

'Guides!' The thought of Karen as a guide made Edward,

despite his predicament, give a feeble chuckle. Then he sat up straight and spoke firmly. 'I'm leaving,' he said. 'But I couldn't go without seeing you.'

'Don't be so silly, Edward,' Lydia said. 'That won't help. 'They'll soon find you if they mean to go ahead. Karen must be made to name the real father. He's the one to face the music. Have you seen her? Spoken to her about it?'

'No. Her mother's locked her in her room until her father comes back. He's due home sometime late tonight or else tomorrow,' Edward said. 'He'll certainly call the police, if he doesn't kill me first. Her mum's not going to work tonight. It's that bad.'

'Have another cup of tea,' said Lydia. She refilled both their cups. Some colour had returned to Edward's face.

'I was –' he began, then stopped. He had been going to confess about his prison sentence. And she still didn't know that Julie was a chambermaid.

'I suppose you haven't had time to tell your sister about this,' Lydia was saying, uncannily, in Edward's view, mirroring his own thoughts.

'No.'

'Hm.' Lydia finished her second cup of tea. 'When did you first meet Karen?'

'Just after I came here,' Edward said. He cast his mind back. 'I met her at a disco.'

'We can easily check the date,' said Lydia. 'You and Thelma arrived here on September the seventeenth. That's six weeks ago.' She rose and fetched a calendar depicting Scottish scenes on which she noted down her few engagements, then counted up. 'Yes – six weeks and two days.'

'What difference do the dates make?' Edward said. 'It's her word against mine. If she says it was me, they'll believe her.'

'Why shouldn't your word be as good as hers?' asked Lydia, busy calculating.

'Because I've been in prison,' he burst out. There! He'd told her! The deceit was over.

Lydia was silent for some time.

'What did you do?' she asked at last.

'Set fire to things,' said Edward. 'In the end I fired a car. No one was hurt,' he added quickly. 'It was in a parking lot, on a Sunday night. There was no one around and no other car nearby.' He stopped, remembering the blaze. He'd stood there gloating.

'Why did you do it?' Lydia asked.

'I like the brightness,' Edward said at once. 'The sparkle. But I wouldn't set another fire, Mrs Cunningham. Not if I can light a bonfire now and then.'

He might well be tempted to put a match to Karen, Lydia thought sourly.

'There's no reason for you to be blamed for something you haven't done,' she told him. 'I shall go and speak to Karen and her mother.' If they waited until the father came back, it might be too late; an angry man would not listen to what he would construe as the maunderings of an old woman. 'You must stay in Milton St Gabriel long enough for it to count when you want another job,' she added. 'You'd better come with me.' If she left him on his own while she did battle, his courage might not hold and he might flee – or go and start another fire. 'Go upstairs and change – have a good wash or bath and put on clean clothes and do your hair. I'll change too – I'm dusty after walking miles with Boris. But let's be quick.'

She didn't seem the least bit shocked by his confession. Like an obedient child, Edward went upstairs, and Lydia, left alone, felt the room start to sway around her. She gripped the back of a chair and breathed deeply, waiting till she steadied down. How did his crime weigh on the scales of justice, balanced against hers?

She must not faint. The only time she had ever done so was when a telephone call had come to the nurses' home where she was living while she did her training. It was one of Arthur's friends who had rung to tell her that he had not returned from a mission over Germany. Later, the same friend told her he had been presumed killed. She had never heard another word. If he had survived, as people who were reported lost sometimes did, he would have sent a message to her. So the man in Heronsmouth was not his resurrected ghost; just his namesake. There was no need to be upset.

She went upstairs and took her ten-year-old good suit from her wardrobe. Then she waited for Edward to finish in the bathroom. She washed her face, made sure her nails were clean, did her hair carefully, blotted a little powder on to her nose and dabbed her lips with pallid lipstick. This was an occasion for putting on a mask.

To his wounded surprise, Boris found himself shut into the house when she and Edward set off for the Whites' house those few short yards away. Edward had shaved; his face shone and he smelled of Imperial Leather soap.

Strangely, no sound of pop music came to greet them as they walked up to the door. Even with the windows shut, the place thrummed and throbbed when Karen or her mother was at home; now the silence itself was ominous.

'Leave the talking to me,' Lydia instructed quietly. 'Don't get angry. Don't start arguing.' She put a hand on his arm. 'Attack is the best method of defence,' she told him. She wasn't too sure if this was true but there was comfort in a cliché. Then she gave a little chuckle, an odd sound coming from her. 'And don't be tempted to strike a match,' she added.

Standing on the doorstep, Lydia pressed the Whites' bell which sent a two-tone jangle through the house. The door was opened by Karen's mother, a woman of about forty, her hair rinsed a gleaming chestnut with a metallic sheen.

'Good evening, Mrs White,' said Lydia. 'I have something to discuss with you.' Her voice was firm, assured; she was once more in the role of Mrs Cunningham, the lady of the manor.

Their visit had clearly taken Mrs White by surprise. She stood staring from the one to the other.

'I don't think we should have this conversation on your doorstep, Mrs White,' Lydia went on. 'We could be overheard if someone walks past.' That was unlikely to happen at this hour, but Mrs White would not want to risk it.

'I'm not letting him across my doorstep,' she said, glaring at Edward in the light that fell from the hallway.

'I'm afraid you must, Mrs White,' said Lydia. 'I'm sure you have no wish to be sued for slander, have you? But I think we can avoid that if we sit down and talk the matter over.'

Slander! The word struck home to both her hearers and for the first time since the accusation had been made,

Edward felt a flicker of hope. Mrs C. had something up her sleeve besides her arm.

Mrs White stood aside, and Edward followed Lydia into the house. Mrs White conducted them into her lounge, as she called the tiny sitting-room where a large electric fire filled the hearth and the carpet was heavily patterned with sprigs of flowers. More flowers danced over the curtains. The three-piece suite which took up most of the room was covered in gold Dralon and looked extremely comfortable. There was an enormous television set with a video recorder below it against one wall but no book or paper to be seen; indeed, there was no space for much else.

Lydia sat down in one of the armchairs.

'Will you fetch Karen, please?' she said, her tone turning the request into an order. 'Edward, sit down.' She nodded at the other chair.

Muttering, reluctant, but already at a disadvantage, Mrs White left the room and went upstairs. Edward opened his mouth to speak but Lydia put a finger to her lips. She sat up very straight in her chair and made signs to him to do the same. It seemed an age before the woman returned, but she did at last. Behind her came Karen, whose face was red and blotched from recent tears. Her hands were clasped before her over the spot where the ill-begotten infant must repose, and she twisted them together. Lydia, who had put on her bifocals, noticed two red marks across the back of one of them.

'Sit down, Mrs White and Karen,' she invited, as if she were in her own house. Because she and Edward were occupying the two chairs, Karen and her mother were forced into positions beside one another on the sofa so that they could not easily exchange glances if they were to face their interlocutor. Mrs White carefully smoothed her purple skirt beneath her buttocks and tucked her feet – she wore high-heeled sandals and sheer black patterned tights – close against the sofa. Karen sat as far away from her mother as she could.

'Now, Karen, will you tell me what you accuse Edward of having done?' Lydia asked in a cool, even voice.

'You know what it is,' interposed Mrs White. 'She's in trouble and he's the one responsible. She's under age, and that's a crime.'

'Her age is irrelevant to this discussion, since Edward is not the father of her child. Is he, Karen?' Lydia turned to address the girl.

'That's what I said,' muttered Karen, not looking at Lydia.

'Will you look at him and tell him to his face?' Lydia said.

'I've said he is,' reiterated Karen, still looking at her hands which she was twisting together in her lap.

Lydia turned to the girl's mother.

'Mrs White, did you suspect that Karen was pregnant or did she tell you?' she asked. She blanked down pity for the girl; this was no time for weakness.

'She's been being sick,' said Mrs White. 'And she's missed.'

'You always know when your daughter menstruates?' asked Lydia mildly.

The unfamiliar word threw Mrs White for a moment; then she caught on.

'Of course I do. Wants her Tampax, doesn't she?' she said, her careful accent wavering.

'She doesn't buy what she needs for herself?'

'I get it when I do the big monthly shop,' said Mrs White, who thought herself a caring mother.

'I see. When you get your own,' said Lydia, nodding.

'I've had a hysterectomy,' said Mrs White, speaking, as it seemed to Lydia, with some pride.

'Oh dear. Well, you buy your daughter's protection and she hasn't used it. Is that right? How did you know that?'

'She'd got two untouched packets in her drawer,' said Mrs White. 'There was one when I put the new one there. I thought it was a bit funny. Well, any mother would, wouldn't she?'

'Two untouched packets. I see. And she's been sick already. So you think she's missed two months? She's therefore seven weeks pregnant, maybe more,' said Lydia, and noticed Edward stir slightly in his chair. 'Is that right, Karen? Have you missed two months?'

A mumble came from Karen. Now she was pleating her cotton skirt through her fingers. Poor little girl, thought Lydia; she was too simple to see the trap ahead.

'I expect you've got a boyfriend at school, haven't you? Someone you're quite fond of?' Karen went on the school bus to Heronsmouth Comprehensive.

'I know lots of boys,' said Karen, with some defiance.

'I'm sure you do. You're a pretty girl, when you haven't spoiled yourself with silly make-up or with crying,' Lydia said. 'I expect plenty of boys like you. And you met Edward at a disco in the village, didn't you, the day after he arrived here, on September the eighteenth. I expect he danced with you because he liked the look of you. Is that so, Edward?' She nodded at him to show that she required an answer.

'That's right,' said Edward warily.

'But you were already late, weren't you?' asked Lydia smoothly.

The girl's miserable expression gave the answer, but Lydia would not let her get away with it.

'Well?' she asked.

'Right.' The word was barely audible.

Even the girl's mother had understood now.

'Why, you little liar,' she burst out and raised her hand. Karen had moved still further from her, edging close to the sofa arm.

'Mrs White, before you strike Karen again, hear what I have to say,' Lydia ordered. 'Karen, hold out your hands. No, palms down,' she corrected, as Karen slowly stretched them out towards her, palms uppermost.

The girl turned them over. In addition to the marks Lydia had already noticed, there were more on the other hand.

'Roll up your sleeves,' Lydia directed. Memories of Henry lashing out with his walking stick made her certain that she had correctly understood what had caused the weals.

As if mesmerized, Karen rolled up the sleeves of the white sweater she wore. Her already swollen breasts moved heavily beneath it. On the plump round arms were other lesions.

Lydia drew a deep breath. Her heart was thudding and a pulse had begun to pound in her head, but it was nearly over.

'Your mother beat you, didn't she, Karen? When she found out that you were in trouble?'

As Karen nodded, Edward gasped.

'And now you're afraid she'll beat you again because you've lied,' said Lydia. She turned to the woman who had been sitting rigidly throughout this dialogue, her lip caught between her teeth, her chin thrust forward. 'If you do, Mrs White, I shall find out and I shall report you to the police and the social services,' she warned. 'I mean that. Don't doubt it. Now, it's obvious that the father of this baby is some schoolboy, some friend of Karen's whom she's been seeing while you leave her here alone. What do you expect to happen, letting a girl of her age have so much licence? You're seldom home yourself until after midnight. Karen is lonely and she wants affection.' Into her head came the wistful hope that Karen, with her schoolboy lover, might have known some tender joy and that this was why she had tried to protect him by sacrificing Edward. 'You like this boy, don't you Karen?' she asked, speaking gently now. 'You're very fond of him?'

Karen scuffed the carpet with her foot and muttered, 'Yes.'

'I don't want to know his name,' said Lydia. 'And my advice to you, Mrs White, is to take your daughter to the doctor and arrange an abortion for her. She's too young to ruin her life, and so is this boy, whoever he is – too young to be trapped into marriage – oh, you could probably force him into that, after her birthday. He's probably over sixteen himself. He'd think it better than being prosecuted, I'm sure, and it would take her off your hands.' She looked at Karen. 'You're lucky in a way, Karen. When I was young, most girls had to have their illegitimate babies and it brought shame and disgrace on them and their families. Nowadays, you have a choice. You're just a child yourself. You'll get over this. Grow up, and see about some birth control next time.' She paused, then continued. 'If you have any difficulty, Mrs White, I will be able to tell you how to arrange things.' Dorothy would know what to do; she had seen pupils through worse crises than this one, and if necessary Lydia would find the money for a private clinic. 'And I advise you to keep this business from your husband, Mrs White,' she went on. 'He might be rather angry and blame you for what has happened. So lose no time. The sooner this is seen to, the better. Now, before we go, you'll just sign this piece of paper, Karen,' she went on, and took it and a ballpoint from her bag. 'It testifies that you never had full sexual intercourse with Edward Fletcher and that he is not the father of your baby.'

The girl signed it, her hand with the red marks across the back shaking a little. The document might have no legal value, Lydia thought, but it had moral force.

'And I meant what I said about your treatment of Karen, Mrs White. In fact I may report you anyway. Those scars will take some time to go away. I shall have to think about it. Now, Edward, come along.'

She rose to leave, and he sprang ahead of her to open the door, then stood aside to let her leave the room first. Turning, Lydia saw him exchange a glance with Karen. On the girl's face was pure anguish.

'I'm sorry, Eddie,' she whispered.

'That's OK. It wasn't your fault,' he answered.

'She called you Eddie,' Lydia remarked as they walked away. 'Do many people use that nickname? Ted or Teddy is more usual, isn't it?'

'Julie – my sister – always calls me Eddie,' Edward told her. 'Karen's heard her.'

'I see.'

He ought to tell her the rest now; it was minor after what she knew already, but first he had to thank her.

'You were a blooming miracle,' he said. 'How can I make it up to you?'

'By keeping out of trouble in the future,' Lydia told him, promptly.

'Oh, I will,' he answered, and the moment for a full confession passed as she went on speaking.

'And you can make the supper,' she said. She unlocked the front door and they went into the house, Boris coming forward to wrap himself about their legs, tail thumping. 'I need a drink. We both do. Pour us each some brandy. I'll have mine neat but you might prefer to add some ginger ale to yours.'

He cooked sausages while she sat in the sitting-room, hands folded, staring at the hearth where Betty had laid the fire ready for the autumn nights ahead. Was it right to kill that foetus? Would Karen, later, wish that she had carried it to fruition? If, as was unlikely, she went on with her schoolboy lover, yes, she might. Lydia herself had not let Arthur's baby go because it was all that remained to her of him. Even as long ago as that, there were ways to manage things and, if she could have brought herself to ask for help, someone in the hospital would have known how to set about it.

But Karen couldn't hope to escape all punishment; this one was, after all, not a lot to bear.

18

Lydia found it difficult to drag herself out of bed the next morning at her usual time. She went slowly downstairs in her dressing gown. A cup of tea might pull her round.

Edward already had the kettle boiling. He took one look at her and said, 'You go back to bed. I'll bring you up some breakfast.'

She stared at him.

'You don't look very well,' he said gently. 'Have a little lie-in. It will do you good.'

Her face, usually florid because the fine skin was etched with threadlike broken veins, was a curious grey colour and her eyes had sunk back into her skull.

'I've got a headache,' she admitted.

'Off you go,' he said. 'Please.'

No one, nowadays, except occasionally Dorothy, ever told her what to do. She felt too weak to argue, so she did as she was bidden.

'Have you got something you can take?' asked Edward, when he brought her tray.

Lying still, excused from making any effort, Lydia was feeling marginally better.

'I've got two aspirins here. Look,' she showed him. 'I'll have them with my coffee. What a lovely tray.' He had found her best Coalport china to make it look attractive. 'You're spoiling me,' she added.

'About time someone did,' he answered. 'Besides, I owe you, Mrs Cunningham.'

'We'll forget that now,' she said. A creaky smile softened her face. He'd learned a lesson: so had Karen, who would bear the brunt of her folly's consequences. Lydia had almost forgotten that Edward had come here as her daughter's latest acquisition. Remembering, her heart gave an anxious flutter.

'Edward, sit down a minute, if you can spare the time,' she said. He was due at work soon.

'Course I can,' said Edward. He perched on the edge of her bed, crooking one leg across the other thigh and exposing a pale hairy ankle.

Lydia looked at his ingenuous face and remembered what she had learned about him. It hadn't seemed important at the time because of his immediate predicament, but here, sitting on her bed, was a convicted arsonist.

A lot of people had secrets, though: look at her own.

'Ask your sister to lunch on Sunday,' she told him. 'It's time we met. If she can't come then, arrange another day – supper one evening soon.'

'Right,' said Edward.

'And now tell me about – er – Arthur Morrison.' She stumbled over the name. 'You said you like him.'

'Yes, I do. But I don't know all that much about him. You'd better ask Thelma anything you want to know. He's pretty fond of her.'

'I wondered about that,' said Lydia carefully.

'You mean he might fancy her? He's too old for her.'

'She might not think so,' Lydia said. 'After all, you're much younger than she is and that didn't prevent – prevent – ' she baulked at defining precisely what she meant.

'No.' Edward had the grace to blush.

'I don't blame you. I know my daughter.' Suddenly it struck her that Thelma's true father might have been a womanizer. All those years ago, she had believed that he really loved her and that they would have married if he had not been killed. That conviction had sustained her ever since, but perhaps she had been too credulous: perhaps he had said all those things she still remembered just to get her to give in: as if she could have stopped herself, in the end.

Such a thought was treachery.

'He was a navigator in a bomber,' Edward volunteered, eager to move the conversation away from himself.

'A navigator?' Lydia stared at him.

'Yes – steering by the stars,' said Edward. 'I've got to go now, Mrs C. You'll be all right, won't you? Take it easy.'

Lydia barely noticed him leaving the room. She felt as if

she were paralysed, unable to move a limb. She could scarcely breathe.

Her Arthur had been a navigator too.

It was coincidence, of course: he was dead, like countless other navigators who had been shot down and listed missing. There could have been ten or more with the same name. Lydia closed her eyes and lay beneath the bed-clothes, brooding.

What if he hadn't died? What if he had been merely a philanderer and grown bored with her? Too much love could be a burden: had she stifled him? Could he have thought so little of her that he had ignored her feelings altogether? Wouldn't he have got in touch with her eventually, even if only to say that everything between them was over? He could have written to her at the hospital; mail would have been sent on.

Perhaps his letter had got lost, she thought for a wistful moment.

But she didn't want him to be alive: not now, not living in Heronsmouth. He had died young and perfect, keeping their love immortal. He would never see her looking old and wrinkled.

She got out of bed and dressed, and when she had washed her breakfast things, she went into the garden. A few dead rose clippings and withered flowers discarded from the house lay on the ash pile at the bottom of the garden. Lydia glanced at them with sympathy for Edward's pyromania. If he had lived in the country, with space to let his anger out in some legitimate physical activity, he might never have started lighting fires. It would have relieved her to have lit a bonfire now, a really good one, the sort they used to have at the Manor where huge heaps of hedge trimmings and dead wood had been burnt up. But there wasn't enough today to make any sort of blaze.

She would have to meet this Arthur Morrison, or look at him, at least. It was the only way to regain her peace of mind. When she saw him for herself and realized how foolish she was being, the ghost would be laid.

She turned back towards the house, and as she entered it, the telephone began to ring.

Gerald had returned from France and wanted to come

down tomorrow for the weekend. He'd arrive in time for dinner.

Lydia had to do the weekend shopping anyway. Ordinarily, she would have made the best of what was available in the village but with Gerald coming, things were different. She set off for Heronsmouth where, in the delicatessen, she would be able to buy ripe Brie or Camembert. She'd get some fish, too; he liked that. He mustn't take them out again so soon; it cost too much.

Since Edward had been in the house, she had been cooking more than when she was alone, trying things she rarely prepared just for herself. He loved braised kidneys, liver and onions, shepherd's pie and kedgeree. No wonder he enjoyed home cooking if he'd only just come out of prison. She could see that he had put on weight in the past few weeks, and had more colour in his face. Did they ever get out, beyond walking in a courtyard? She must ask him; it might be good for him to talk about it.

On her way to the delicatessen, Lydia saw two people ahead of her going in the same direction. It was a second or two before she recognized the trousered figure of her daughter. She was talking animatedly to a man who walked beside her on the kerb edge of the pavement, slightly dragging one leg.

This was Arthur's namesake! Lydia's heart began to thump and her throat felt choked. She stopped abruptly, causing someone behind her to collide with her and drop the oranges she carried; the paper bag they were in burst and the fruit rolled into the gutter. Lydia, apologizing in a flustered manner, helped the woman pick them up, then walked on. Thelma and her companion had disappeared, but as she came up to the delicatessen, Lydia saw that they were inside, apparently discussing what to buy.

Lydia saw an old man wearing a tweed hat below which showed wisps of curly white hair. He had shaved in such a way as to leave pronounced sideboards on his pink cheeks, and his eyebrows were bushy. Young Arthur's hair had been cut so short that few curls were left, but they had been springy against her hand and lips. His brows had been strongly marked and in age might have thickened, but at this first glimpse, nothing about the man reminded Lydia of her lover. She was unaware of making a decision as her legs carried her into the shop and she heard herself speak.

'Thelma! What a lucky meeting! I was going to telephone to thank you for that delightful dinner the other evening.'

Thelma, startled, swung around.

'Hullo, Mother,' she said. 'What are you doing here today? I thought you only came to town on Thursdays.'

'Gerald's coming down tomorrow,' said Lydia. 'I need to buy some cheese.'

'You could get it in the village,' Thelma said.

'Not this selection,' Lydia explained. 'You know he loves ripe Brie, if they have some.' She peered at the counter lest she seem to be staring at the old man. He'd made a quick recovery from his chest infection, she thought inconsequentially.

'Oh yes, they have,' a male voice told her. 'We were just planning to buy some. And have you tried their home-made pâté?'

It was the voice. She knew the voice. That was the same warm tone, the slightly amused way of speaking. He had always been able to make her laugh. Lydia, who was wearing her bi-focal spectacles, slowly looked up. She saw the blue eyes, still merry though now a little faded, peering at her over half-glasses. She had only to look at Thelma to see them duplicated; surely the whole world could see the likeness? The face was fuller, lined and weatherbeaten like her own; he had put on several stone, and she would not have recognized him if she had not had what was to some extent a warning. But it was the voice that clinched it.

'Won't you introduce me, Thelma?' Again, that echo from the past.

'Mr Morrison – my mother, Mrs Cunningham,' said Thelma impatiently.

At least she'd done it formally, not in her normal casual manner using first names. Would hearing the name Lydia have sounded any knell with him?

'How do you do?' said Lydia faintly, gripping her bag and shopping basket tightly, not about to offer him her hand.

'We should have met on Wednesday,' he replied, and smiled.

'Yes. I hope you're better,' Lydia said conventionally, her own voice hoarse with shock.

'I've quite recovered,' he declared, and laughed. 'I'm sure I missed a splendid dinner. Thelma's such a tip-top cook. A great girl altogether.'

'Oh yes,' said Lydia, and inside her head was screaming, she's our daughter.

'Won't you come back with us now and have some lunch?' he was suggesting. 'We're just buying it – bread and cheese – you see the sort of thing.'

'No – no. I haven't time. I'm sorry. I must get home.' Lydia turned away to hide the fact that she was trembling. 'I'll go and get the fish now, and come back later when they're not so busy,' she said, and scuttled from the shop with Thelma staring after her in a pitying way. There was only one other customer waiting to be served.

'Mother's getting very stupid,' she said. 'I sometimes think she's going senile.'

'Oh, come now, Thelma,' Arthur said. 'Don't be naughty. You'll be old one day. She's just got too much to do, I expect.'

Thelma didn't mind the criticism.

'You don't know her,' was all she said, but in fact her mother had looked just as if she'd seen a ghost.

Lydia scurried to the fishmonger's and stood outside it gulping in deep breaths, trying to calm down enough to go in and buy some turbot. She had started on her way back to the car when she remembered the cheese for Gerald.

They'd be gone now. She walked cautiously towards the delicatessen but they were nowhere to be seen.

What if he asked Thelma about her parents? What if he wanted to know her mother's maiden name, found out that Thelma's grandfather had been a country parson? Or had he forgotten all about that young probationer nurse he'd met at a station dance to which she'd been persuaded to go by some bolder girls?

Lydia needed time to think about it. First, above all else, was her own sense of having been betrayed. A long time after that came the realization that another, dreadful danger threatened Thelma. For they had looked happy together;

that had been obvious as she followed them along the road.

What if Dorothy's prophecy should come true and Arthur Morrison should seek to marry his own daughter?

Years ago, Henry had hinted that his relationship with Thelma was not entirely fatherly, taunting Lydia that there was no blood barrier between them. She had not known whether to believe what he was saying, for he lost no opportunity of hurting her and she never knew when he was lying. So, when her chance had come, she had taken it without any hesitation. She had planned nothing, but as Henry suddenly clutched his chest and grunted with pain, gasping for breath, she had made no attempt to help him. She had felt a sudden surge of power as she watched his agony, ignoring the appeal in his protuberant eyes. He had tried to struggle from his chair and she had not prevented him. Then he had lurched across the room and fallen to the gound where she had let him lie.

He had not died at once; they were alone in the house and she had simply left the room. When she returned, he was dead.

Now, Thelma was under threat of being party to a most horrible offence.

She must be saved.

But how?

19

In Heronsmouth, Arthur Morrison was now a happy man.

A few short weeks ago he was inured to loneliness, doing his best to enjoy playing bridge, working in the garden, visits to the library. Life would be like this for ever, till gradually he ailed and failed and even these diversions were curtailed. There was not a lot to look forward to apart from visits to his family and occasional holidays. He and Phyllis had often been to France, touring with the car – he drove an automatic which spared his stiff leg – but that would be no fun alone. Last year, he'd taken the coastal steamer and sailed from Bergen all along the coast of Norway to Kirkenes on the Russian border. They'd planned to take the trip together, and he had gone by himself as a sort of seal on their compact. To his surprise, he had thoroughly enjoyed the voyage, finding pleasant company among the other passengers in the tiny boat and awed by the majestic scenery. He hadn't even minded a Force-Eight gale one night during a passage in the open sea.

Thelma might go with him on some trip or other; perhaps to China? He'd like to see those terra-cotta warriors. Would she enjoy that? The future seemed suddenly to be filled with possibilities instead of being just a slow decline towards death. He didn't know quite how he expected their relationship to develop, nor had he analysed his feelings towards her. She was attractive, full of spunk, and being with her made him feel half his actual age. People would talk, inevitably, but he didn't mind gossip of such a flattering variety; and Thelma, with her chequered matrimonial career, would probably treat it as a joke.

She wasn't very keen on sex. She'd told him so; she'd said she'd always found it very disappointing. She'd hardly have said that if she foresaw any intimate involvement between the two of them, and she didn't know he'd seen her naked by the swimming pool. Arthur was content to let things drift. An old man with a gammy leg was hardly an alluring prospect to a woman in her prime. He knew she needed some stability in her life; her mother seemed a nervy sort of woman, poor old soul, dashing from the shop like that, but he hadn't cared for Thelma's attitude towards her. He must invite Mrs Cunningham to the house another time. It seemed a bit hard, though, that Thelma should be caught between two elderly people, her mother and himself, when she was young enough to enjoy a full personal life – and should have one. Maybe she'd meet some fellow in the drama group, and he, Arthur, would be torn with jealousy.

The idea amused him. He'd be pleased if she were happy. Meanwhile, as he had done throughout his life, he would make the best of what was good about the present.

Years and years ago there'd been a girl. She'd had soft, silky brown hair, so fine it seemed like gossamer blowing across his face in a summer breeze. He'd met her at some dance or other organized to entertain servicemen like himself. She had large, frightened eyes and had looked lost and timid; he'd rescued her, then become entranced with the shy ardour she so surprisingly revealed. He'd hoped that they would marry – they'd talked about it, imprecisely, otherwise he was certain that she would not have contributed so willingly to her own seduction. They'd spent occasional nights at a pub near his station, signing in as Mr and Mrs Smith, giggling about it in the dipping double bed. Then he was shot down and badly wounded. By the time that he was well enough to write to her, he'd heard from someone in his squadron that she was married. So that was that. She hadn't even waited to find out his fate.

It had been a bitter blow to Arthur. In the prison camp his stiff leg excluded him from any chance of making a successful bid for freedom, so he decided to work towards some other goal. He had joined the Royal Air Force straight from school. As he had been good at figures, he embarked on an accountancy course. By the time he was released, he was nearly ready to take his final exams; his ultimate qualifications led him eventually to become company secretary in a light engineering firm. He had met Phyllis soon after he came home and they were married within a year. They had been very happy and he had almost forgotten Lydia. When he and Phyllis bought The Shieling, he remembered that she had come from somewhere in the West Country where her father was a parson. Lydia Newton was her name. She might be dead by now, for all he knew. He didn't know whom she had married, nor did he care; while he was in the camp, men were receiving Dear John letters all the time and his case was not at all unusual. He had made a monumental effort to put it all behind him and become, again, the cheerful person he had been before. He joined in amateur dramatics at the camp and found he had a talent for performing; in the end, through pretending that he was carefree, he became content. His good luck was to meet Phyllis so quickly and he made his mind up not to lose her.

Now, he missed her sadly but that was hidden from the world. People didn't want long faces round them; most had sorrows, aches and pains, and little tragedies.

On Saturday afternoon, Arthur was helping Thelma to go through her part as Arkadina in *The Seagull*. He was enjoying reading Trepliov's lines in Act Three when the doorbell rang, just as Arkadina said 'The doctor's late.' He laughed at the interruption and said 'I'm not expecting him, are you?' to Thelma, who shook her head and giggled.

'I'll go,' she said, pushing him gently back into his chair. Some days his leg was very painful.

She was astonished to find her brother Gerald standing on the doorstep.

'What do you want?' she asked sourly.

'What a welcome!' He spoke mildly. 'I called at your flat and you were out, so I thought you'd be up here.'

'Well?' She was quite put out at seeing him.

'I just came to see you,' Gerald said. He was determined not to let her irritate him.

Meanwhile, in the background, Arthur had heard unfriendly noises and came to find out what was happening.

'It's my brother,' Thelma said, turning a cross face towards him.

'Well, ask him in,' said Arthur.

Gerald stepped across the threshold, forcing Thelma to move aside, and held out his hand.

'Gerald Cunningham,' he said. 'I hope I'm not interrupting anything?'

'You are, in fact. A rehearsal of *The Seagull*,' Arthur said. 'Billed as comedy, I notice, but I wouldn't really call it one, would you? I'm sure you know it well, as Thelma tells me she's already played Nina.'

'I don't think any of those Russians are really funny,' Gerald said.

'They're all for ever setting off to Moscow,' Arthur said. 'They seem to have no other goal.'

He led the way into the square sitting-room where a bow window overlooked the estuary. A pair of field glasses lay on the windowsill; the old man probably spent hours watching what went on on the water, Gerald thought. The room was furnished in a pleasant, conventional way, rather like his mother's though it was much larger.

'I went to see Thelma at the flat and she was out.' Gerald repeated his explanation. 'I wondered if she'd already moved up here.' It occurred to him that he might have made a gaffe, and he added, 'She is moving, isn't she?'

'Yes,' said Thelma.

'It'll be better through the winter,' Arthur said. 'That haul up the hill can be quite a drag.'

She wouldn't be able to carry on with all and sundry under this nice old chap's roof; even Thelma would not do that, Gerald decided. Perhaps she'd settle for a spell of chastity.

'What a lovely view,' he said aloud.

'Isn't it?' Arthur moved to stand beside him at the window and they began discussing vessels in the estuary. Arthur knew who owned many of the boats which were still moored there, not yet hauled ashore for winter. Passing the field glasses to Gerald, he pointed out various interesting things to be observed and Thelma was forgotten by them both.

'I'll light the fire,' she said loudly.

Arthur had had a realistic gas fire installed after Phyllis died. It saved a lot of work and he derived enormous pleasure from its deceptive appearance.

'Do, do,' he said. 'Thank you, Thelma. And what about some tea? Shall we have some? You'd like a cup, I'm sure,' he said to Gerald.

'Yes, I would.' Gerald had not stopped, except for petrol, since he left London. 'But I mustn't stay too long. My mother's expecting me.'

'Telephone her,' Arthur said. 'Then she won't be watching for you at the window.'

As if she would, thought Gerald.

'The telephone's in the hall,' Arthur went on. 'Thelma will show you.'

'Mother was in Heronsmouth yesterday,' Thelma told Gerald as they went together to the hall, where a stream-lined in-phone rested on a table. 'She seemed quite dotty – came into the delicatessen and then dashed out again without buying anything. If you ask me, she's begun to lose her marbles.'

'She hasn't,' Gerald said. 'I expect she thought of something else she wanted.'

Thelma shrugged.

'Well, help yourself,' she said, and went into the kitchen.

Lydia answered the telephone promptly. Gerald told her where he was and said he would come on soon. Did she want anything from the town? He'd be on his way before the shops shut.

'No,' said Lydia; then she added, 'There is one thing you could do.'

'What's that?'

'Make sure he hasn't got a cat. That old man.' She would not speak his name. 'Because of Thelma's asthma,' she explained.

'I'll find out,' said Gerald.

He was smiling when he returned to the sitting-room where his host was admiring the leaping flames in the grate.

'Well, that's done,' he said. 'Thank you. My anxious mother asked me to find out if you have a cat. They give my sister asthma.'

'Do they? How strange,' said Arthur. 'I suffer from it too. It's got a little worse these last few years. Cats and boiler fumes and too much tobacco smoke are all hazardous for me. There are no cats here. You can reassure your mother.'

'I didn't think Thelma would take the job on if you had one,' Gerald said. 'It's beastly for her. And for you, of course.'

'It's a nuisance,' he admitted. 'I had injections once but they seem to have worn off now and I haven't bothered to be done again as I can usually avoid the cause of the trouble.'

At this point Thelma came in with a trolley bearing scones and home-made shortbread for tea.

'I'll put on too much weight with your sister's cooking,' Arthur said. He twinkled at them both. They were not at all alike, the one so fair, the other dark.

Gerald and his host found plenty to discuss since both had financial backgrounds, and Thelma soon began to fidget. When Arthur, quite aware that she was bored and jealous, changed the subject so that she could be included in the conversation, Gerald's own impatience with his sister's poor manners turned to admiring amusement. There were no flies on this old boy and he had a gift for cooling things; maybe a few weeks – or better, months – spent here would sort Thelma out.

'Thelma must bring you over to dinner some time when I'm down again,' he said, and added, 'At the hotel in the village where my mother lives, I mean. We go there now and then. The food is very good. It would be nice if she could meet you properly.'

'I'd like that,' Arthur said, and when he had gone, commented to Thelma, 'I like your brother.'

'You get on with everyone,' was Thelma's answer, given with a sulky frown. Then she softened the effect by smiling. This transformed her face and, as almost everyone had always done, he forgave her for her gracelessness.

'He gets asthma too,' Gerald told his mother. 'Would you believe it? So no cats. Why, Mother, are you ill?' For she had gasped suddenly and closed her eyes.

Lydia rallied quickly.

'It's all right – I caught my breath,' she said. How the body could betray, and in so many ways! Doctors had expressed surprise that there was no allergic history in the family to account for Thelma's complaint. Lydia had blue eyes, which explained Thelma's. Gerald's were brown, following his father. If Henry's had been blue and Thelma's brown, then any informed individual would have been suspicious.

'They were reading the play together – *The Seagull*,' Gerald went on. 'He seems to know it well. When's the performance?'

'In about two weeks' time,' said Lydia. 'I thought she'd know her part backwards by now.'

'I expect she does. I think she just enjoys any audience,' said Gerald. 'What'll she do afterwards? Be in a pantomime or something?'

'That would be a good idea,' said Lydia, taking him seriously. 'But there won't be much time to get one up, will there? When *The Seagull*'s over there'll be only a month or so till Christmas.'

'I was only joking, Mother,' Gerald said. 'I just thought she'd be lost without a part to play. Though she could be Wendy to this old boy's Peter Pan. I thought him a nice old chap and he seems to have her taped.' She'd gone off without a murmur to make the tea. 'I think they're somehow on the same wavelength. Let's hope it lasts.'

'Dorothy thinks that – er – that Mr Morrison – ' Lydia made herself enunciate the name '– that he might want to marry Thelma.

Good heavens, does she?' Gerald found the idea most surprising. He gave it his attention. 'Well, she could do a lot worse,' he said. 'She might be wise to jump at it, if she gets a chance. Still, he's getting on a bit; I shouldn't think he'd bother. It struck me that his manner towards her was paternalistic. What did you think of him? I hear you met him yesterday.'

It never occurred to Lydia to confide in Gerald. A lifetime's habit of concealment did not cease so easily.

'We barely spoke,' she said austerely. 'Thelma had to be reminded to introduce us.' And it was Arthur who had done the reminding, not her mother. The irony of this did not strike Lydia now any more than it had at the time.

But Gerald was registering the implicit criticism of Thelma and it amazed him.

'Well, you'll meet him properly soon enough,' he said.

'I'm going to invite them both to dinner at the Manor next time I'm down.' Then he had a thought. 'But why wait till then? We could all have lunch there tomorrow.'

'No, Gerald. It will have to wait,' said Lydia firmly. 'Edward's sister is visiting us tomorrow. One thing at a time.'

'Oh, very well. How is that young man?' asked Gerald.

'Working hard,' said Lydia. She would not tell even Gerald about Edward's narrow escape from litigation. 'He's a good boy, Gerald.'

'I'm sure he is.' Gerald was surprised at her insistence; he had already formed a favourable opinion of her guest.

Lydia had averted danger this time, but it would be impossible to avoid ultimately meeting Arthur, if Thelma went on working for him. Sooner or later she would find herself face to face with him, and she would not be able to endure it. Her tortured thoughts scurried round inside her aching head. His had been a gross betrayal for which she had sacrificed her whole life, and now, as she neared the end of the long pilgrimage, the daughter whose protection had been her main aim could be on the brink of committing an offence too terrible to contemplate.

Of course, she wouldn't be at risk unless they married. Or something.

The 'or something' was what mattered. It could have happened already, if the pair had had a mind to it, but now Lydia allowed Gerald's comments to offer her a little consolation. Thelma was not yet living in the house and she was busy with rehearsals for the play. Later, when these circumstances had changed, the opportunity would be there. And the temptation.

20

'I can't do it,' Julie had said. 'I haven't the nerve.'

'You must,' Edward had told her. 'Now I'm staying in the village, you've got to meet her some day. There's nothing to be afraid of. She's not one of your stuck-up kind. Look how she's treated me. She'll be really offended if you don't turn up. And you're not on duty. You can make it.'

She gave in eventually, persuaded because it would be just the three of them. Edward did not learn that Gerald was coming down until after he had got her to agree, and then he wouldn't warn her for fear she would cry off. Once, she'd been game for anything; odd how cautious she'd become, he thought.

'Think of yourself as an insurance clerk,' he told her. 'You were one once.'

When she arrived at the lodge at a quarter to one on Sunday, as instructed, Gerald recognized her immediately, though he did a quick double-take. Here was the bringer of his early tea, the waitress who had served them at dinner just a few weeks before. Now, she wore a cherry-coloured wool skirt, full and sweeping with unpressed pleats, and a tailored shirt in checks that toned with it. Her dark, shoulder-length hair, previously unremarkably secured in a ponytail, was drawn back from a centre parting and curled softly upwards at the ends. When she saw Gerald, she raised her chin as if to counter a challenge. She had arching brows like crescent moons above her hazel eyes and her effect on him was instantly erotic.

'Hullo,' he said, and put a glass of champagne in her hand. 'How nice to see you again.'

'Oh, have you met before?' asked Lydia.

'Yes – and so have you, Mother. Don't you remember? Up at the hotel,' said Gerald. His mother had got the wrong end of the stick somehow; she'd thought Edward's sister let rooms in the village. And he'd leaped to the wrong conclusion when he saw the pair at the window after that evening at the hotel. In case his mother still hadn't caught on, he asked Julie, 'How long have you worked there?'

'Only this season,' she answered. 'I came in March.'

'So that's how Edward got his new job, is it?' Gerald asked. 'You knew it was coming up?'

'Something like that,' said Julie. She took a gulp from her glass and it braced her. 'Is it someone's birthday?'

'No,' said Lydia. 'Gerald does this sometimes. Brings champagne, I mean. It's a thing his grandfather used to do.'

'It's a natural tonic,' said Gerald, smiling. He, however, was celebrating the fact that Thelma had left their mother's house for a new phase in her troubled life. 'Will Edward like working at the hotel? Won't he find it rather quiet?' he asked her.

'Well – I don't know.' He had expressed Julie's own fear.

'Hey – I'm here. Let me answer for myself,' said Edward. 'I've got a scooter now – I can get around.'

'Are you staying on?' asked Gerald.

'I'll have to, won't I?' Julie said. 'Now Eddie's here, I'll have to keep an eye on him.' She spoke lightly, suddenly at ease. Gerald's friendly manner, or the champagne, or both, had dispelled her nervousness. 'Is your sister coming?' she added. How would Gerald feel about her involvement with Eddie?

'No. She's living in Heronsmouth now,' said Gerald.

'She's an actress, isn't she?' said Julie. 'Eddie told me.'

'Well – sort of. She's appearing in an amateur production of *The Seagull.*'

'It's a Russian play,' Edward told her, sure that she would not have heard of it. 'Full of people all in love with the wrong ones and miserable.'

'Well, that's just like life, then,' Julie said practically. 'You've only got to read the paper.'

'True,' said Gerald. Even *The Times* offered such examples to its readers. 'Come and sit down, Julie – may I call you Julie? And tell me what you were doing before you came down here.'

He manoeuvred her towards the sofa and, before he sat

down beside her, refilled all their glasses.

'Gerald, this is really very nice,' said Lydia. 'You shouldn't, though. It's so extravagant. Sherry is quite adequate.'

Gerald decided not to take her remark as a reproof; he had seen his mother mellow after this medicine before. Just one glass was enough to do the trick.

'I think it's lovely,' Julie said. 'What else did your grand-father do?'

'Dabbled on the Stock Exchange, unfortunately,' said Gerald. 'But he was a nice old boy. I suppose he was a *bon viveur*. Would you say so, Mother? He knew how to get the utmost out of life.'

'You're like him in some ways,' said Lydia. Her father-in-law had given her bottles of Beaujolais from his cellar if he thought she looked a trifle pale during those war years when Henry was away. Now, Gerald brought her wine and spirits.

'I look like him,' said Gerald. 'He was short and dark and – ' he had been going to add 'ugly' but he bit back the word. 'He put on a lot of weight and got a drinker's nose. That hasn't happened to me so far.'

'You're very like him,' Lydia repeated. She stood up. 'Now, I'm going to dish up. Edward will help me. You two entertain each other.'

Julie turned amused eyes towards Gerald as the others left the room, as if to say, how shall we do that?

'Your brother's been good to my mother,' Gerald said. 'I don't mind admitting I was a bit doubtful about him staying on after Thelma left, but it's working well. She'll miss him when he moves into the hotel.'

'It's all over. Him and – and Thelma,' Julie said.

'I know,' said Gerald. 'I don't think it amounted to very much, do you?'

She shook her head. She'd made Eddie tell her the truth. He'd been lucky to get out of the entanglement so easily. The whole thing was an embarrassment to her. What had Eddie thought he was doing?

'One can drop into these things,' said Gerald. 'No harm done, anyway. Come and see the garden,' he suggested, and opened the french window. 'Will you be warm enough?' She had worn a showerproof jacket when she arrived.

'Yes, I'm fine,' said Julie. She walked ahead of him down the winding path between the rose bushes. 'It's a bit of a come-down for your mother, isn't it?' she asked. 'I mean, I think it's lovely, but after the Manor – ?'

'In a way, but I don't think she was very happy there,' said Gerald.

'Wasn't she?'

'She and my father didn't get along too well,' he said. 'I don't think they'd have married but for the war.'

'You couldn't get divorced then, could you?'

'Well, you could, but it wasn't easy like it is today, and a lot of people found it rather scandalous, unless you were a film star or a duchess,' Gerald said lightly. 'My sister was born very soon after they married. That would have stopped them from separating, even if they'd wanted to.'

'Still, they had space. They could get away from each other in a house that size,' she said, frowning.

What was her history? Had she been married? She was obviously several years older than her brother.

'I expect your mother's sorry you live so far away,' she was saying.

'Oh, I think she sees as much of me as she can take,' said Gerald. 'She's a lone bird. I don't descend on her too often.' He looked across to the Dennises' roof. 'She was upset when that huge expanse of ginger tiles rose up to block her view,' he added. 'Before that she could see across to the hills and know the sea was there beyond them.'

'I think it's lovely, even with the roof,' said Julie. 'I grew up in Birmingham.'

He'd picked up the hard G in her accent; she hadn't lost it altogether.

'What are you doing working as a chambermaid?' he asked her. 'You must have had other jobs before.'

'Better jobs, you mean? Status-wise?'

'I suppose I do.'

'I wanted to get away from – from everything,' she said. 'It was all found, and easy. A proper change.'

Some man, he thought, and he was right. Julie had had a long affair with a married man who, in the end, had elected to remain with his wife and she had cut and run away from him and from the perpetual problem of Eddie.

'Is there promotion? Could you change jobs?' he asked.

'Maybe, because it's small and we don't belong to unions,' she said. 'I hadn't really thought about it.'

He would, though. He'd talk to Paula Thomson about her, but not this weekend; it could wait.

Gerald had produced a bottle of claret to drink with the meal. Julie exhibited a hearty appetite which he found endearing.

'You are lucky, Eddie,' she declared. 'Living here, I mean, all this time. This is delicious.'

'The food's all right where you are too, isn't it?' asked Gerald with a smile. 'I expect the staff do quite well.' He hoped that was so.

'Oh yes, we do,' Julie hastened to assure him.

'Were you always such a good cook, Mother?' he inquired. 'Before you were married, I mean?'

'We ate plainly at the vicarage,' said Lydia. 'Milk puddings and mince.'

'Plain living and high thinking, eh?' said Gerald. 'It was different later. My father was a very particular man and if anything was not just as he thought it ought to be, he made a fearful fuss. If the meat was tough he always blamed mother, not the butcher.'

So he had noticed that, had he? Lydia was surprised.

'Tell us about life at the Manor,' Julie invited. 'Was it like *Upstairs, Downstairs*?'

'Gracious no,' said Lydia. 'Not in our time, anyway, though it may have been in the days of Gerald's great-grandfather. Most of the time we just had a woman from the village twice a week.' There'd been Betty sometimes, too. They'd shut up room after room; even so, Lydia had never seemed to cease cleaning and if she wasn't busy in the house, she was expected to labour in the garden where the help grew sketchier and sketchier as time went on.

'What was he like when he was little, Mrs Cunningham?' Julie asked. She looked at Gerald, not knowing what to call him. 'Your son, I mean,' she added, blushing slightly.

'Call me Gerald,' he instructed, and she blushed still more.

Lydia thought before she answered.

'Well, he was always very good,' she said. 'He worked hard at school and was hardly ever naughty.'

'I bet Thelma was naughty,' Edward said. 'She is still.'

'She doesn't change a lot,' Gerald agreed drily. 'Are you coming to the play, Edward? Julie, you must come with us.' He'd see her again if she joined them; he liked that prospect.

'It would be fun,' said Julie.

'Will you be free then?' Paula Thomson couldn't expect the girl to be always serving dinners as well as early-morning tea.

'That's no problem with some warning,' Julie said.

It was agreed that they would form a party for the Saturday performance, the last night of the run, and Gerald said that Arthur Morrison should be included in their group.

'He's bound to want to see it,' he said. 'We can't leave him out.'

'But – ' Lydia began, then stopped. How could she object? Gerald's was a reasonable suggestion.

Julie was still curious about life in Milton St Gabriel before the war, and Lydia turned to talk to her, concentrating on her questions so that she was distracted from the anxiety that was becoming an obsession. She grew loquacious, describing tennis parties given by the Cunninghams, with lemonade to refresh the players and sponge cake for tea. Her manner became almost hectic; Gerald looked at her, perplexed by this most untypical behaviour.

'They still went on early in the war,' she said. It was after one of them that she had found it easy to trap Henry. 'When Gerald's father was on leave. And before he was killed, his uncle, too.'

Gerald was discomfited by his mother's suddenly shrill voice and almost manic stare.

'My uncle was another short, dark swarthy Cunningham,' he said.

'Are your children like you?' Julie's attention was successfully deflected. She had learned some of Gerald's history from Ferdy at the hotel.

'No. Luckily they take after their mother,' Gerald

answered. 'I wouldn't wish my ugly mug on them.' He reached out with the wine bottle and refilled the glasses.

But Julie persisted.

'You aren't ugly,' she said. 'Whatever gave you that idea?'

'It's all right. I'm used to it after all this time,' he said cheerfully. 'Perhaps I'll look quite interesting when I'm old enough to be regarded as an ancient gargoyle.' He turned to his mother, whose expression during this exchange had become one of bewilderment. 'Mother, Christopher was in great shape when I saw him. His French is very good now.' He turned to the brother and sister. 'Christopher's my son. He's in France learning about wine.'

This diversion turned the talk into less personal channels. Gerald learned that Julie had once been on holiday to Spain, and on a day trip to Boulogne; that was the limit of her foreign travel. What fun it would be to take her to Paris – show her the Loire – the Dordogne. Images of a stone cottage in a grove of trees came to him; he pictured Julie barefoot, paddling in a stream, and laughing.

His mother had regained her normal control.

'Gerald, you're miles away,' she said. 'Come on, dear, and help me. We've got Queen of Puddings now.'

Gerald blinked himself back to the present. His mother, incredibly, had called him 'dear' and Julie had denied that he was ugly. Now he was being offered one of his favourite puddings: it was better than a birthday.

He left for London after Edward had gone with Julie back to the hotel.

'You shouldn't spend too much time alone,' his mother told him as he put his bag into the car.

'I don't,' said Gerald. She'd talked like this before, that day when they walked on the beach. What was on her mind?

'You get out of the way of it,' said Lydia.

'Out of the way of what?' Something was bugging her, that was certain, but it couldn't be him and his affairs; her concern had always been reserved for Thelma.

'Of – of – ' Lydia searched for words. 'Of sharing things, I suppose I mean. As I have done.'

She looked at him bleakly, a tall, thin woman, taller than

himself, so that he still looked up to her as the apprehensive little boy had done. And like that same anxious little boy who feared a snub, he could not find an answer and he did not dare to hug her.

'Goodbye, Mother,' he said, and got into his car.

She stood and watched him drive away, not waving, simply standing in the road until the car had vanished round the bend.

21

How could she avoid meeting Arthur at the play performance? Lydia could fake flu, or a cold: but she must witness Thelma's little triumph, if she had one.

Edward would know when she planned to move into The Shieling, and thus closer to real risk. Lydia asked him about it, and he said that it would not be for a while, at least until the play was over. He did not tell her that one of the actors, who had some leading role, was now a constant visitor at Thelma's flat in the evenings, ostensibly running through their scenes together. Knowing Thelma, more than rehearsing was involved, but at least she wasn't carrying on under the old man's nose.

Lydia clung to the fragile comfort of knowing that Thelma was, to some extent, protected for the present. There was time to prevent calamity, but she did not know how to do it, and meanwhile she kept having dreams. Sometimes it was the recurring house removal that she dreamed of, but at other times she was haunted by the past. She had nightmares about her life with Henry, imagining that it was he who had not died but who was about to thrust himself upon her as she lay in bed, or to beat her with his stick. She would wake tense and sweating, her heart pounding as if it would burst its way past her rib-cage. Sitting up in bed, clutching her nightgown to her thin chest, she would gasp with relief at finding it was just a nightmare.

Sometimes, Arthur came to her in dreams, as he had failed to do throughout the years. Now, he floated towards her through fluffy white clouds as though arriving from heaven, dressed in his blue uniform and smiling, his fair hair crisp against the sky. Then his image dissolved and there was an old, red face above the uniform and it was Henry who scowled down at her.

She would get up in the night and pace about, go quietly downstairs and sit at her jigsaw. Once, Edward heard her and came down. He made her go back to bed and took her up a cup of tea and, because he saw that she was shivering, brought her a hot-water bottle.

She couldn't read. Even the newspaper demanded too much concentration. She had been like that before, in the first dreadful days after Arthur was reported missing and she had to face both grief and her own predicament.

Her father had questioned the wisdom of marrying Henry in such haste, though the couple had, of course, known each other for years.

Her answer was to say that Henry might be killed. They had to take their chance.

Her parents had made no comment on Thelma's so-called premature arrival when she so obviously was a full-term baby, but a year later they moved to another living two hundred miles away and thereafter had seen little of their daughter and grandchildren.

Lydia had very soon discovered that her assumption that Henry would evoke a natural response in her had been false, the first illusion of so many that were soon to be dispelled as her punishing marriage began. She had been wicked, tricking him to protect her lover's child, but she had subsequently done her duty, played the role demanded of her in the village and never turned away from him until those final years together when she had, at last, moved her possessions from their shared bedroom to another far along the corridor. Even there, he had pursued her.

Round and round went her tormented thoughts. If only she had known that Arthur was alive! Even with no prospect of his imminent return, she would never have trapped Henry into imagining he was the father of their child. Setting out to fabricate that possibility had been the darkest action of her life. Even now, she could remember the scent of mown grass about them as they went into the summerhouse where Henry shut the door and wedged it with a chair. The plank floor was hard and rough; she'd got a splinter in her hand; but Henry, red-faced, sweating after playing tennis, had been oblivious. Oddly, treacherously, she had liked that strong male smell which later she had grown to hate. It had been over very quickly. Naively, she had expected that in the future, in more comfortable surroundings, it would be better. But there had once been a wood with Arthur which she could remember: trees above their heads with glimpses of the sky between the leafy branches; she'd noticed no discordance then. Perhaps that was when Thelma had been conceived.

As soon as Henry heard that she was pregnant – which she told him in a letter little more than two weeks later – he at once agreed to marry her. At that time his regiment was stationed on Salisbury Plain and it was speedily arranged.

Lydia had no idea that he had given Thelma a different version of these events.

Henry, captivated by the fair, pretty baby, had not at first realized the extent of Lydia's subterfuge when Thelma, weighing eight pounds and very sturdy, was born five months after the wedding. When the child was three weeks old, his father, half in admiration, had quizzed him about how skilfully he and Lydia had concealed their romance.

'Those quiet ones are often the best,' he'd said.

Then Henry had understood.

Pride made him connive at the deception, but he had allowed Lydia no more time to recover from the birth before, in fury, violently impregnating her again. After this virtual rape her hair fell out. She felt sick and ill through her second pregnancy and was bewildered by the strong attachment she felt to the dark, squalling baby that resulted. To protect them both, she hid it, for if Henry saw where she was vulnerable, she would be handing him a weapon to be used against her. Instead, she aimed at toughening her son.

Now, past and present had caught up with her and further payment was demanded. Thelma must be prevented from the risk of forming an incestuous relationship with her true father.

But how?

She could not telephone. That was out of the question. He would think she was a madwoman.

What if she wrote a letter?

Dear Arthur, she recited in her mind. *You will think it*

strange that I should write to you after so long an interval, but I believed you to be dead. We had a daughter, Thelma, and you know her. Yours, Lydia.

It would not do. She would have to go and see him.

She imagined herself going to The Shieling, parking in the narrow drive, ringing the doorbell.

Thelma might answer it. What then? What reason could she give for having called? Thelma would not take kindly to the notion that Lydia was paying a social call, and just suppose she did, how could she be dismissed while it was in progress, so that the true purpose of her visit could be revealed?

She could telephone while Thelma was rehearsing, ask him to meet her somewhere, say she had something important to discuss and beg him not to mention this request to Thelma. The idea terrified her. She could not do it.

She had made no decision by the time Edward moved down to the hotel. Lydia had grown so accustomed to his presence in the house that she had dreaded his departure, but now it released her from all need for concealment of her movements. She began going into Heronsmouth early in the morning. She would park in a side road above The Shieling and stand in the bus shelter which was almost opposite, dressed in her old gardening raincoat and a tweed hat bought at the charity shop. From this retreat she could watch the house unnoticed and she saw Thelma arrive on foot each day at half-past nine. Her hours were not demanding; Arthur clearly got his own breakfast.

Lydia could call on him before Thelma was due: she could go in and explain, and be gone again quite quickly. Once, she got as far as standing on the step, but she did not ring the bell. How could she face him, after what had been between them? How could she tell him what had happened? Most important of all, even if she managed that, how could she trust him to keep the secret she had guarded through the years?

She could not, even if he promised, and Thelma, who had idolized Henry, would be destroyed if she found out the truth.

She ran off quickly back to the car and drove away.

Most days Arthur and Thelma set out on expeditions of

one sort or another. Arthur would get the Renault out and lean across to open the passenger door for Thelma, who would clamber in beside him. At that distance, Lydia could not see their expressions, but she followed them several times, keeping well back so that Thelma would not recognize her car. They went for walks and had pub lunches, they visited museums and went shopping. At least, while occupied with these excursions, Thelma was not in moral danger.

Once, Lydia watched them through binoculars. Thelma took Arthur's arm and nestled up against him, looking happy. Lydia had not forgotten what joy there was in Arthur's touch; to think of sharing that with her daughter was horrifying. Lydia was not simply shocked, but jealous too.

After a number of journeys, Edward came to wash the Metro and check its oil and tyres, and he noticed her increased mileage.

'Well, you've been getting around,' he said. 'Been anywhere interesting?'

Lydia was missing him, but she snapped her answer back.

'Where I go is my business,' she retorted.

She had never spoken sharply to him before. Edward felt a chill wash over him.

'I'm sorry,' he said. 'Of course it is.'

Be like that, then, he thought bitterly, and did not linger. He did not come to see her again for several days and then they were very careful with each other, talking like two strangers.

Meanwhile, Arthur had suggested to Thelma that her mother should be invited to The Shieling, but Thelma made excuses.

'She's unsociable and odd,' she said.

'Perhaps she's lonely.'

'She's always been like it. That's how she prefers things,' Thelma insisted.

He let it pass. They would all meet at the performance of *The Seagull* and he would take it from there.

One day they went over to the Manor for a bar lunch.

'I've been there already,' he told her. 'But now I know

you once lived there, I'd like to go again.' He thought of telling her that he had seen her swimming, then decided not to; she was a tricky, prickly girl and it was easy to upset her. He suspected that she had become involved with the man who was playing Trigorin and that things weren't going too smoothly there. Perhaps she wasn't so different from her mother; even that old lady had been young once and may have had a few adventures before she settled down in what had evidently been an unsuccessful marriage. Thelma had revealed that her father had complained to her about her mother many times, and that he derided her in front of the children.

'She just used to crumple,' Thelma said. 'He'd have respected her if she'd stood up to him. He liked a bit of spunk. He told me so. I used to wonder if he'd made a play for Dorothy – that's my mother's friend, my godmother, quite a gutsy lady. But I never knew for sure.'

'People don't always play around, you know,' said Arthur. 'Some marriages last, and are happy. Mine was like that.'

'You were lucky,' Thelma said.

'Yes,' he agreed. 'I know it.'

'I'd like to be married again,' Thelma confessed, artlessly. 'It makes you feel respectable.'

'But you like your freedom, don't you?' he pointed out. 'Would you be faithful to another husband?'

'I don't know,' said Thelma honestly.

'You may be looking for something that doesn't exist,' he said. 'Some perfect fusion of two souls, like poets write about. It's very rare, and I question if it lasts.'

Long ago, when he was very young, he had felt lyrical about a girl, but she had soon forgotten him.

'I've never met anyone like you before,' Thelma said. 'You know I'm awful but you aren't shocked.' And you're not after me, she thought; I'm safe with you.

'I'm a father figure to you,' he declared, patting her hand. It was safer thus.

Ferdy served them in the Manor bar.

'How's Mrs Cunningham?' he asked. 'I haven't seen her lately.'

'She's all right,' said Thelma. 'How's Edward getting on?'

'Oh, very well. He's moved in here now. Very snug he is, in the stable block,' said Ferdy.

'So your mother's on her own again?' said Arthur as they ate their individual cottage pies.

'She was only helping out, letting him stay there,' Thelma answered.

'Let's call on her,' said Arthur. 'You can't be in the village and not look your mother up.'

But Lydia was out.

She had not gone to spy on them that day and had intended to go to the Manor, but when she walked up the drive she saw Arthur's Renault, whose number she now knew by heart, so she turned away and went over to inspect The Shieling itself; they would not return and catch her at it now.

Because she might be observed, she walked boldly up to the front door and rang the bell, as if on a genuine inquiry, and when no one came, went round to the back. The kitchen door was almost as solid as the front door; the windows were of the sash variety and there was double glazing. She didn't see how she could break in, and if she did, what then? She was no nearer a solution.

She couldn't trust him; not in any way. He'd never written to her; that was certain. A letter sent to the hospital would have found her, even months afterwards. He hadn't known her home address – luckily, as it now turned out, for surely, even after all this time, some small memory would have stirred.

She could not trust Gerald's assessment of the situation either. Paternalistic, he had said; well, Henry had been officially Thelma's father, and was, eventually, old. She had never known the full extent of what passed between them, but he had taunted her for years about it, knowing that she had no remedy. He could have been responsible for Thelma's adult problems. It need not have been a great deal, after all – not the completed act, 'the ultimate', as Edward called it, just some build-up towards it. Not that that was Henry's way of doing things.

What could she do?

Lydia drove home by a different route so that she ran no risk of meeting Thelma and Arthur as they returned to

Heronsmouth together.

She need take no action yet, but the deadline was the play, for then she would meet Arthur again. She knew he would not recognize her, but Dorothy had invited herself to join them, wanting to see her goddaughter's performance, and she would address Lydia by her first name. If he had not forgotten all about her, Arthur might say, 'I knew a Lydia once.'

Would that be the way to let it happen? Let the questions follow, his Lydia's surname be disclosed, amazement on all sides ensuing? Would he then realize the possibility that Thelma was his child?

At first, he wouldn't be able to realize that she, thin and scrawny, almost bald, was what had become of that happy, ardent girl. He would be shocked, incredulous: then hostile, surely, for his own emotions, long ago, were insincere.

She could not bear to see the horror in his eyes, and then the hatred that must follow.

Lydia telephoned Thelma and, awkwardly, because it was unusual for them to have such a conversation, asked how things were going. Thelma, who was expecting Trigorin to arrive at any minute, was anxious to get her mother off the line. She said that she had one becoming dress to wear and that the acting of the young woman playing Nina was pathetic.

'Have you many more rehearsals?' Lydia asked.

'Every night next week, then the dress rehearsal on Thursday,' Thelma answered. There were to be only two performances, on Friday and Saturday, and Arthur had wanted to take them all to dinner after the last one, but Thelma had said she would be at a party with the cast so that idea had perished.

Lydia went over to lunch with Dorothy on Sunday. She was very restless, walking round the garden looking for fallen apples in the grass – Dorothy's trees were prolific and she could not pick the highest branches – and refusing to settle with her coffee after the meal. They arranged that Dorothy, who was going to spend Saturday night at the lodge, after the play, should come over in plenty of time to set out with them for Heronsmouth. She was interested to learn that Edward's sister would be joining them.

'All her lodgers gone, then?' she asked.

'I don't know where we got that idea,' said Lydia. 'She works at the hotel.'

On Monday evening, when Thelma was rehearsing, Lydia drove again to Heronsmouth and once more parked in the side road near The Shieling. She walked to the bus shelter. Further up Harbour Hill, lights shone from the Cliff Hotel, and there was a faint glow showing behind the curtains at the bay window of The Shieling. One car went past but she saw no one out on foot. The people in the area were having their evening meal or watching television, and behind that bay window opposite was the man whose memory she had carried in her heart throughout her adult life, embellishing his image with careful touches, inventing what she did not know and rendering him more perfect than the truth could ever be. It was she, not Arthur, who had died all those years ago; her life since then had been one long charade. Oblivious of the cold and damp, Lydia stood there watching for an hour. He might come out, and she could follow him, though what she could do then, she didn't know.

The second night she took a torch, but once again her vigil brought no benefit. Behind his close-drawn curtains, Arthur Morrison occupied his evening unaware of the watcher in the road.

What was he doing in there? Reading? Watching television? Playing patience? She knew that he played bridge, but little else about his interests. He was a stranger.

Once again, she contemplated calling on him openly, ringing the bell and reintroducing herself as Thelma's mother, playing at small talk, then waiting for an opportunity. But for what? What did she mean to do? How could she silence him, the only person in the world who could reveal her secret – and might do so, less than three days hence.

On Wednesday, she approached the door, but as she raised her hand to press the bell, a car went past and she delayed, waiting till the sound of its engine faded in the distance. Then, shrill and distinct, she heard the telephone ring inside The Shieling. He'd be going to answer it, moving from whatever he was doing. Lydia scuttled off, back to the safety of her car.

Now time was running out if matters were to be resolved before the weekend. Lydia went to bed that night, but did not sleep. If she told Arthur the truth, the fear that he might react with joy and be pleased to acknowledge Thelma openly was almost as bad an alternative as the risk of incest, negating, as it would, the proud cover-up of over four decades. Lydia's own humiliation would be dreadful. There was no answer.

She got up and paced about the house. There was no Edward now to hear her, break the silence, send her back to bed and bring her up a cup of tea. Boris, in his basket, stared at her, unused to all these interruptions to his repose. She was still sitting in the kitchen when dawn rose, and that day, when she went for Betty, earned comments on her fatigued appearance.

'I'd have thought you'd be better now Thelma's moved out,' said Betty frankly. 'What you need's a holiday. Why not take yourself to Tenerife?'

She was missing that young lad: that was the trouble. It had done her good to have a bit of life about the place and someone who looked out for her, as he had done. Betty went home feeling quite concerned.

That evening, as Lydia walked slowly to the bus shelter along the grassy headland facing The Shieling, he emerged. She grasped her torch more firmly as, illuminated by a light over the porch, he went to the garage, opened it, and drove his Renault out. Laboriously, he got out of the car again and closed the garage doors, the cold engine running fast, exhaust fumes fogging the atmosphere. She walked on as he turned the car and came down the drive into the road thrusting one gloved hand into her pocket, the other grasping the torch, head down, not wanting him to pick her up in his headlights. His tyres swished on the damp road, twin red tail lights gradually diminishing as he went towards the town.

Perhaps it was a bridge night. He hadn't played that when she knew him, or if he had, she hadn't known about it. There was a lot she hadn't known about him, she had learned. Perhaps he took it up in the prison camp, or perhaps his wife had played. Her mind closed up at the thought of this unknown woman.

She walked straight up the drive to his front door and looked quickly round. No one was in sight. Harbour Hill, she had discovered, was a lonely place at night.

Lydia reached up with the torch and knocked out the porch light.

The noise seemed to her to be deafening, and glass splinters spattered round her as she ducked out of the way. She stood trembling on the gravel driveway waiting for windows to open and shouts to ask what was happening, but there was no reaction. There was just the sound of the sea below and the pale light from the widely spaced street lamps in the road.

Lydia went round to the back of the house and crouched there trying to decide what she meant to do when Arthur came home. The night was cold and raw, and she began to shiver. He might be gone for hours, certainly would be if he had gone out to dinner or was playing bridge. Holding her fingers over the torch so that only just enough light filtered through them to let her see her way, she went round to the front again. She could enter the garage, lie in wait for him there. But what then? Could she stun him with her torch, then start the car and leave the engine running, shut him in, let time do the rest?

She thought about it, standing there, then tried the garage doors, but they were locked.

Anyway, he'd see her when he put the car away.

She was reprieved.

She walked back to the car and sat there, shivering, for some minutes as she tried to achieve some calm. Then she started the engine and put the heater on full. She was about to move off down the road when she remembered that there was only one more night before she must meet Arthur properly – unless she found some excuse to miss the play – and that even if she managed that, Thelma would be moving to The Shieling very soon.

The truth was bound to come out. Eventually he'd ask about her mother, find out who she was, learn that she had been a nurse in training, and where.

Silence was the only safety. She, as well as Thelma,

needed that.

She let the engine run long enough to warm the car up. Then she sat and waited for Arthur to return.

She wouldn't see him, waiting here in a road above The Shieling. Lydia remained there for a while, then went back to the bus shelter. When a late bus came grinding up towards her, she walked off, letting it pass her near the Cliff Hotel, then turning back again. A few cars went by as she sat huddled there, but no one came that way on foot. Twice she returned to the car to warm up, hoping each time that Arthur would return during such an interval, and then she could postpone any decision once again. But she was in the shelter when, taking her by surprise, his Renault turned into the gateway of his house.

She was up the drive behind him and crouching round the side of the house as he closed the garage doors and walked towards the porch. He hesitated, and she heard him mutter something as he fumbled to fit his key into the lock. His feet scrunched on the broken glass on the tiled step as she came up behind him.

Lydia held the torch in her gloved right hand. She was nearly as tall as he was, and as she struck him down she was screaming in her head with hatred. Her thoughts, then, were not of Thelma but were for herself and her own pain. It was only as he fell that she remembered her daughter, and knew that she was safe.

Arthur Morrison fell inwards against the opening door and he gave a single grunt.

She could not leave him there. Lydia stepped over him into the narrow hall and put her torch down. Then she dragged him in by the shoulders until she could close the door. He was very heavy: dead weights were. But was he dead? She paused, panting, to look down at him. Light shone through the half-open door of a room on the right, and she could see his bald head gleaming above a little frill of silver curls. She picked up the torch to hit him again, but she could not do it. All her rage was spent. She set it down again and dragged him into the sitting-room. His shoes rasped against the carpet, setting her teeth on edge.

Was he dead?

She had bent to examine Henry without a qualm, but she could not touch this man again. Now he had become an object of horror.

Lydia looked round the room. A book lay on a table beside a big armchair; there were newspapers nearby. In the fireplace a fire was apparently laid, but without any kindling: fresh coals sat in the grate. Perhaps there was a gas poker. Living in the country without such refinements as mains gas, Lydia did not at first recognize the artificial device Arthur used with so much pleasure, but when she looked more closely and saw the gas tap, she understood. She tried to turn it and found you had to press it. Promptly she turned it off again; she had always been nervous of gas.

Now she felt a sudden calm. Perhaps this was what she had, without acknowledging it, planned all along. It was the only certain way, but she had to cover up her crime. Arthur's death must be made to seem an accident. Fire would destroy the evidence. She did not admit the conscious thought that if her victim were not already dead, it would complete what she had begun. She looked about for matches and saw some in a bowl on the mantelpiece; there was a long wax taper in a pretty pot.

Lydia picked up the newspapers that lay to hand and separated some pages, crumpling them up; she laid them in a trail from the fireplace across the room to the linen-covered sofa and on towards the long plum velvet curtains which hung at the window. Then she lit the taper, turned on the gas tap and plunged the flame among the coals. Because she did not know precisely where to place it there was a tiny delay before it caught and quite a loud plop as the gas ignited. Lydia left the taper alight beside the already burning *Cheverton Gazette*.

She was at the door, on the point of leaving, when she remembered her torch which she had put down in the hall. She snatched it up. Arthur's keys were still in the lock as she shut the front door behind her and scurried down the drive to the road, where she slowed to a walk and went rapidly back to the car, just a lean, shadowy figure in the night, if anyone had seen her.

But no one did.

*　　*　　*

Lydia had no memory at all of driving home, but when she arrived she stripped off all her clothes and made a bonfire of everything she had worn except her old gardening raincoat and her shoes which, naked otherwise, she wore while she burned the rest. She felt soiled, corrupted. Fire would wipe out contamination. She did not think of the other fire which she had left in Heronsmouth.

Then she had a bath.

Boris watched all these activities with indifference; he had ceased to be surprised at her departure from routine.

From their bungalow, the Dennises saw the bonfire sparks ascending to the heavens.

'What an hour to light it,' Roger said.

'The old girl's dotty,' answered Maureen. 'I hope it's under control.'

'Can't reach us,' said Roger comfortably. 'The wind's the other way.'

'You're safe now, Thelma,' Lydia told herself as she stoked up the flames. She went on muttering it as she soaped herself in the bath and washed her silky, skimpy hair. She wanted to think she'd done this for her daughter, not herself: that alone was justification.

There were no clothes to put away neatly that night and no underclothes to wash, for everything had been destroyed.

22

A woman taking her dog out for a final run noticed a beacon glow at a downstairs window in The Shieling. At first she did not understand the reason for it; when she realized that the place was on fire, she rushed back to her own house further up the road and dialled 999.

By this time, Lydia had been gone more than twenty minutes; when the fire brigade arrived, the sitting-room was full of dense toxic fumes from the smouldering upholstery. Anyone trapped inside the room would die very quickly. And there was somebody there: the first fireman almost fell over Arthur Morrison as he lay on the floor.

In some unreasoned action, Lydia had closed the sitting-room door when she left the house, and this had helped to contain the blaze. There had been no explosion; the gas fire went on burning in the grate but the curtains, flaring, had been what the passer-by had noticed. Though the rest of the house was saturated with water from the firemen's hoses, it was not severely damaged and the wreckage was restricted to the main room.

Men trampled to and fro, first the firemen, then the men who took away the body in a coffin shell. Gas board engineers and electricians disconnected the mains supply. It was not until the next morning, when experts inspected the building in daylight, that the broken porch light was noticed. By that time the shattered glass had been trampled everywhere and there was nothing to show that it had been deliberately smashed. It could easily have happened during the fire-fighting operation.

Chief Inspector Drummond, from Heronsmouth police station, stood among the debris with the district head fire officer. It was obvious that the dead man had just entered the house for he was wearing his overcoat and his keys were still in the front door.

'He must have gone out leaving the fire on and papers nearby. Perhaps a sudden draught blew one of them across the fire, and when he returned he smelled smoke and hurried into the room, and was overcome by the fumes immediately,' hazarded Drummond.

The fire officer indicated a fire extinguisher attached to the wall in the hall.

'Why didn't he use that?' he asked.

'Perhaps he opened the door to investigate and a wave of smoke engulfed him,' Drummond said.

It was possible. The smoke would have billowed towards him.

'But the door was closed,' the fire expert said. 'Our men found it closed.'

'It might have banged to behind him.'

'Possibly, if it was the sort of door that did that.' Such a thing would be hard to prove now, with the solid door warped and charred.

The dead man's car had been in the garage. There were no signs of any break-in, nothing to hint at something more than a domestic accident.

Thelma, arriving at her normal time of half-past nine, found the men still there, poking about among the devastation. She had heard the fire engines roar past the previous evening after she had returned from the dress rehearsal which, like most dress rehearsals, had been fraught with small disasters. Now, as she approached the house, she saw several cars parked in the road outside and a police car in the drive. An acrid smell of smoke hung in the damp wintry morning air, and she broke into a run when she realized that The Shieling was the source.

'What's happened? Where's Arthur?' she cried.

They broke it to her gently, first finding out her name and why she was involved. Drummond took her round to the rear of the house where the kitchen was undamaged apart from being drenched with water which was still running down the walls.

'Oh no!' she wailed. 'Oh no! I won't believe it! He was out last night playing bridge at the Frobishers'. There must be some mistake.'

Drummond put forward the theory about the fire: that Mr Morrison had left it burning and been careless with some papers.

'But he wouldn't leave it on,' Thelma insisted. 'He always turned it off when he went out, for economy. The heating system was good. He liked the fire just for cosiness.' Saying this, she began to weep.

A constable had been despatched next door to see if the neighbour would provide sanctuary and a cup of tea for Thelma until she had calmed down enough to be questioned. She might know where to find the next of kin, and could provide information about the deceased's movements the night before. The neighbour was delighted to comply; she had been intrigued by Thelma's constant presence in the house. While Thelma drank her tea, watched over by a youthful constable, the neighbour, in another room, declared that Arthur Morrison had kept himself to himself since his wife died, but he had given them raspberries from his garden in the summer and was a good neighbour in that he was quiet. There were no rowdy parties nor irritating barking dogs.

In her turn, Thelma knew that Arthur's son lived in Leeds, and she knew where Arthur kept an address book which might provide more details.

'What am I to do?' she sobbed, when Drummond, having established her address so that she could be interviewed again if necessary, sent her back to her flat in the police car. 'Oh, why do these things always happen to me?'

The young policeman, quite distressed, brewed more tea and asked her if there was someone who could come and keep her company until she had recovered from the shock.

'I'll ring my mother,' she said. 'She lives not far away.'

'You do that,' said the constable, relieved.

When the telephone rang, Lydia was doing her jigsaw, singing to herself. She felt entirely calm.

Thelma was hysterical, but Lydia had heard her in this mood before, first when Charles was killed and later when her second husband had deserted her. And when Henry died.

'What is the matter, Thelma? Try to control yourself,' she

directed. 'Take some deep breaths. I can't hear a word you're saying.'

'Arthur – dead – house on fire – ' jumbled phrases came across the wire among the sobs.

Lydia felt her whole body flood with sudden warmth as blood pumped around it.

'What are you saying?' she asked.

'I want to come home,' Thelma cried. 'You must come and fetch me.'

'Pull yourself together, Thelma,' Lydia instructed. 'Tell me what is wrong exactly. Are you ill?' For she must feign unawareness, that was crucial; she already knew that it was very easy to deceive.

Still sobbing, but somehow managing to utter, Thelma described what she had found when she went to The Shieling.

Lydia had given no thought to who would discover the body or when the fire would be detected. Her mind had blanked about the aftermath.

'The police think a paper blew across the fire while he was out.' Thelma spoke in a wail.

'I expect they're right,' said Lydia. 'How dreadful.' The words seemed meaningless.

'I'm most upset,' said Thelma. 'And I must come home, Mother. Please fetch me now.'

'Nonsense, Thelma,' Lydia said robustly. 'Of course it's sad and you're distressed. That's natural. But get things in proportion. This man was only your employer. You must make some effort. You're performing in a play tonight. Had you forgotten that?'

'I can't possibly go on stage after what's happened,' Thelma said.

'Yes, you can. You're acting now,' her mother told her firmly. 'I'll come in and see you this afternoon and not a moment earlier. Now, blow your nose and wash your face and have a cup of tea.'

She replaced the receiver and returned to her jigsaw. Soon she was humming again, a tuneless dirge. She had never before, in the whole of Thelma's life, spoken so sharply to her. But now all debts were paid.

*　　*　　*

Thelma was dressed in a grey velour tracksuit; her eyes were red and she wore no lipstick when she opened the door to Lydia later that day.

Once again, she related what had happened, the water streaming down the walls of the damaged house, the men investigating, the smoky smell.

Thelma still insisted that she could not perform that evening.

'You must,' said Lydia. 'You'll let the others down, if you don't. The show must go on, you know. Goodness me, Thelma, I know it's very dreadful but you'd only met the man a little while ago.'

'He was good to me.' Thelma dabbed her eyes with a tissue. 'We were friends. It was easy with him. I felt safe.'

'What was easy?' Lydia snapped.

'Just being with him. He was fond of me, and I was very fond of him,' said Thelma, with a curious dignity which moved her mother. This was genuine grief, not just Thelma acting up.

'You'll get over it,' she said, more gently.

'What do you know about such things?' Thelma rounded on her suddenly. 'You hated Daddy. I know you weren't a bit sad when he died.'

'He was old and ill. He no longer got much pleasure out of life,' Lydia said. 'Now, I'm going, Thelma. I've got things to do, with Gerald and Dorothy coming tomorrow for the play.'

'This isn't stomach ache, you know,' said Thelma bitterly.

'Time heals,' said Lydia tritely. 'You know that. This is not comparable with when Charles died. Now, that was a tragedy.'

Thelma was outraged at her mother's callous attitude; she stormed about the flat when Lydia had gone, and, because she needed an audience, she rang Gerald at the bank.

She got a much more sympathetic response from him. He was truly shocked, said how much he had liked Arthur, and added, 'You don't have much luck, do you, old girl? But hang on in there and make a success of the play.'

'Arthur would want me to do that, I know,' Thelma decided. She sniffed, partly mollified as she contemplated rescripting her role.

'Of course he would. Look, I'll leave as early as I can tomorrow morning,' Gerald said. 'I'll come in on my way to Mother's and we'll have lunch together, shall we? There's no point in my coming down tonight because you've got the performance. You'll feel better when you get among your friends.'

She might. She'd rung Trigorin in his dental surgery, managing to get past his receptionist, and he had expressed appropriate regret over what had happened, but, as he had not been encouraged to think of Arthur as more than just a kind employer, her grief had seemed to him excessive.

Oh dear, thought Gerald, hanging up. Poor Thelma was a sort of Jonah; everything she touched went wrong. He'd have to try to help her sort out the consequences of this disaster or it would all rebound again towards their mother. She must be persuaded to keep on the flat until she had another long-term plan to prevent her from running back to Milton St Gabriel again.

By the time Gerald reached Heronsmouth the next day, Thelma had cheered up a lot. She saw herself now as the pale heroine of a tragedy which was the main talking point in the town. Arthur, though relatively a newcomer, had been a familiar figure walking down the hill and going round the shops, and people stood on corners discussing what had happened, posing theories. The play had gone well the night before and Thelma's own performance had won special plaudits. Stress had put an edge on how she faced her part; her rather light voice had deepened and she had developed real presence.

Later, sleep had eluded her; she was, on several counts, over-stimulated. Trigorin had left her at her door, muttering that he could not linger, and for once she was not sorry. Eventually, she took a sleeping pill and did not wake until eleven.

At twelve, Gerald rang her bell, taking a deep breath and resolving to count ten before replying if she riled him. He had brought her a bottle of brandy; she might need it.

She repeated what she had already told him on the telephone about her arrival at The Shieling the previous morning.

'They'd taken him off somewhere by then, of course,' she said.

Charles, dead on arrival at the hospital after his car smash, had been taken to the mortuary, and to spare Thelma, Gerald had formally identified him.

He remembered that now.

'You didn't have to identify him, did you?' he asked her.

'No. They sent for his son. I suppose he did it,' Thelma said.

'There will have to be an inquest, I imagine.'

'Yes. It's on Monday,' Thelma said.

Would she have to go to it, and if so, must he stay and lend her his support? Gerald sighed inwardly at the prospect, determining to escape if possible, for surely Thelma might reasonably be expected to support herself? He reproved himself for base, unworthy thinking, and told his sister it was time for lunch.

He took her to the Swan, where several people in the bar had seen the play the night before and came up to congratulate her. Thelma at once began to glow, and, briefly, Arthur was forgotten. When Gerald left her at her flat again, she said she was going to get some rest before the evening's performance.

'Good idea,' he said.

She'd get over it once everything was tidied up and settled, but it was a wretched business. The old boy hadn't seemed the least bit casual; if the police really thought he'd let papers drift across the open fire, it sounded most untypical. Perhaps he'd felt ill, had a heart attack or something, or there'd been a gas fault of some kind. The police or the fire brigade would probably find out the truth in time; forensic science had developed many skills to aid them. He put his difficult sister and her problems out of his mind and thought instead of Julie Fletcher, whom he would see again this evening.

He played with the notion of taking her out somewhere, just the two of them, and seeing how they got along. Then he devised a scenario in which he stayed at the hotel once more and, when she brought his morning tea, persuaded her to join him in his bed. She might: the modern girl was seldom wholly chaste. She'd have other trays to take around, however; her time was not her own, he told himself, laughing at this fantasy. In theory, though, it might not be difficult to coax a hotel chambermaid into becoming his mistress, find a better job for her in London, set her up in a little flat. But he wanted none of that; Gerald was tired of meaningless encounters. He wanted love, and, in a rare moment of bitterness, he accepted that he had never known it in his life.

He found his mother looking rather better than the last time he was home and she seemed pleased to see him. He told her he had been to see Thelma who was bearing up quite well.

'I wonder what's the best way to help her now,' he said.

'She must stand on her own feet,' Lydia unexpectedly replied. 'She's independent. She has enough money to live on if she's not extravagant, and if she can't find a worthwhile job with a salary, she must look for some interest to occupy her time.'

Gerald could not believe what he was hearing. Always, in the past, excuses had been made for Thelma's failures and her failings.

'Had you anything in mind?' he asked.

'Aren't there training schemes she could go on? She could qualify for something,' Lydia said.

'Like what?'

'Oh, I don't know. Putting make-up on, something she's already good at,' Lydia said.

'Beauty counselling,' said Gerald, amazed that Lydia should suggest an occupation that in her view must seem worthless.

'Is that what it's called? How do you know?' Lydia asked.

'Some friend of Fiona's is doing it,' he answered. 'I wonder if she'd ever settle to it?' He could not see it happening. 'She likes being among people, of course. That's one of her difficulties. She can't bear being alone.'

'She picked Edward up on the train coming down here,' Lydia stated.

'Did she?' Gerald had not known that.

'She's so restless,' Lydia said. 'Always looking for something which she'll never find.'

'What sort of thing?'

'Some man. Some film star sort of man. A romantic falsity,' said Lydia.

'Or fantasy,' said Gerald.

'She's foolish about men, and she has no morals where they're concerned.'

'She's not a tart, Mother,' Gerald said gently.

'I don't suppose she asks for money,' Lydia said. 'That's not what she wants.'

'Maybe she's just a girl who can't say no.' Gerald spoke lightly, afraid of saying the wrong thing. 'She might have settled down with Arthur Morrison. What's happened is a tragedy and it was a dreadful way to die.'

'Thelma will get over it.' Lydia spoke abruptly.

The spell had broken. Gerald made some excuse and went upstairs with his small bag. Things didn't really change. When he had unpacked, he took a stroll down the garden. A few late roses bloomed but most of the withered herbaceous plants had been cut down and burned. Nothing waited on the bonfire site, only a pile of ash. He saw a wisp of blue and bent to look at it. It was a scrap of fabric, some old rag, perhaps.

He marvelled at his mother's new, tougher attitude towards Thelma. Would it last? How ironic that Thelma had had some sort of passage of arms with Edward while he now entertained thoughts of the same thing with Julie. But she probably had a boyfriend, one close to her in age; in a way he hoped she had because then he could back off without chancing his luck. Of course, he could always try to marry her himself. If she consented, they might have some years of happiness before he bored her and she moved on to someone more exciting.

But when Julie and Edward arrived, he forgot such thoughts and set out simply to enjoy the evening. Dorothy, magnificent in a gold and purple dress made from a sari she had bought in India, had arrived earlier, and they all piled into Gerald's car. Dorothy and the two young people were wedged into the back and Lydia sat in front with him although she was much thinner than her friend. It would be inappropriate to suggest to her that she should sit cramped up into a corner but Dorothy was used to a certain lack of style.

Julie was in a sparkling mood. She wore a pink, full-skirted dress, and her hair was different, cut much shorter. Before the performance, they had dinner at a restaurant in Heronsmouth which was noted for its lobster, and the subject of Arthur Morrison's death did not arise until they had begun their meal. Lydia had not mentioned it to Dorothy, and although hotel gossip had included news about a fatal fire in Heronsmouth, Edward and Julie were unaware of the connection.

Gerald raised the topic, saying that he had planned to invite Arthur Morrison to join them for the meal before the play.

'Why couldn't he come?' asked Edward.

As Gerald explained, Julie went quite white.

'When did it happen?' she asked.

'Some time on Thursday night,' said Gerald. 'He'd been out playing bridge, it seems. When he got home, he must have found the fire and been overcome by the smoke and fumes.'

'Oh!' Julie's colour slowly returned to her face. Last night, Eddie had been out late and she did not know where he'd gone. She'd wanted to find him to ask what time they were expected at the Cunninghams. On Thursday, though, they had been watching a film on Victor's video. But Eddie wouldn't set a fire like that; he liked the old man.

'Poor old geyser,' Edward said. 'How did it start?'

'Thelma says the police think a newspaper may have blown across the fire when he was out,' said Gerald.

'Would he have left it unguarded?' Dorothy asked.

'I expect he just forgot to turn it off,' said Lydia. 'People can be very careless.'

'Those coals don't fall out,' Gerald said. 'There's no need to use a spark guard.'

'Oh, it was a gas fire, was it?' Dorothy asked.

'Yes.'

They talked about the tragedy right through their first course – shrimps for Julie, who said she couldn't have too much shellfish, and the same for Edward, avocados for the others. When the lobster came, Gerald changed the subject; if they dwelt on the tragedy they would be in no mood to appreciate the evening's entertainment.

Edward had heard Thelma going through her part when he was working at The Shieling, but Julie did not know the story of the play. Dorothy outlined the plot, explaining how an older man had, for whim or simply vanity, destroyed a girl. Such things still happened, she declared.

'Or it could be the other way about,' said Julie. She looked across at Gerald as she spoke, and for a moment they held each other's gaze. She was the first to look away.

'It was so hot when I was in Moscow,' Dorothy was saying. 'There were specks of poplar dust dancing in the air like cotton buds. One could imagine the heat as they describe it in the play. You should get the feel of the humid, steamy atmosphere provoking tensions, ripe for festering jealousies. And of course none of them had enough to do and they were bored.'

When the play began, Julie sat forward on her upright chair in the school hall, peering round the head in front of her, entirely rapt. It was well done. Dorothy and Gerald, the two best qualified to judge, were both impressed by the quality of the acting and the production, and Thelma's performance was outstanding. Her face revealed unhappy passion, and when Trigorin started to encourage Nina, her anguish was made plain. Masha's drinking raised a laugh; the old man in his chair was appropriately irascible. The pace was slow enough to let the discontent seep through but with no longueurs.

There was great applause for Thelma at the end. They went round to see her before she left for a last-night party with the cast. She was elated, on another plane.

Edward and Julie walked up the Manor drive together after a final drink at the lodge. They parted at the side door of the hotel. There was an unfamiliar car in the yard outside the stable block, and when Edward reached his room, two plain-clothes police officers were waiting for him.

23

The post-mortem examination carried out earlier that day on Arthur Morrison had shown that death was due to suffocation from the fumes given out by the upholstery burning in the room. There was not a lot of actual fire damage to the body, and when it had been sluiced down and cleaned, a head wound was plainly visible. The skin across the scalp at the back of the bald head was lacerated and there was a depressed fracture of the skull. In the pathologist's opinion, the dead man had been struck from behind with some heavy object; because of the wound's position, and the fact that the body had been found centrally placed inside the room away from solid furniture, it was unlikely to have been sustained by accident, as in a fall.

Now the theory was that the deceased, returning from his evening's bridge, had surprised an intruder in the house. His assailant had then fired the house to avoid discovery. The police had looked for fingerprints and had found three distinct sets. Two were the dead man's and Thelma's; they had called to take hers after Gerald left on Saturday and because she was now mentally geared towards her dramatic performance in the evening, she had shown little interest in their reasons. 'For elimination,' they had said. The third set led them to Edward Fletcher, recently released from prison after serving a sentence for arson. Inquiries made during the day had enabled them to trace Fletcher's sister to the Manor Hotel in Milton St Gabriel, where they soon discovered that he had been taken on to the staff.

There was no charge of thieving recorded against him, but he would have fallen into bad company in custody and could have learned new skills and attitudes.

Detective Inspector Mobsby and his colleague, Detective

Sergeant Young, were very pleased to have their case wrapped up so soon. Such serious crimes were rare on their patch.

The two policemen had had a talk with Mrs Thomson, the hotel manageress; then they had played it quietly, waiting in the suspect's room for his return.

Edward went with them meekly.

Gerald had arranged to meet Julie on Sunday afternoon.

He said goodbye to his mother and Dorothy, who had stayed to lunch, leaving them to assume he was going straight back to London. Instead, he and Julie planned to go for a walk or a drive, depending on the weather. Then they'd have tea in some quiet spot. Julie was on duty at six o'clock and so brief a meeting committed neither of them to proceeding further.

They had arranged to meet beyond the hotel where the back drive emerged on the coast road. Gerald was there five minutes before the appointed time.

She didn't come.

When she was just five minutes late, he expected her to turn up very shortly. After another five, he began to think that she had stood him up. Ten minutes later he was certain.

His impulse was to drive away at once, writing the experience off as another bitter lesson in rejection. But surely he couldn't be so wrong about her? Surely, if she had wanted to cry off, she'd have telephoned with some excusing lie? He decided he would hunt her down and find out what had made her change her mind. She might, of course, be ill – upset, maybe, by the shellfish she had eaten.

He walked up the drive, went in through the swing doors and found Ferdy serving early teas in the lounge. Gerald asked him if he had seen Julie that day and where she was just now.

'They took the brother off,' he answered. 'She's quite upset.'

'Who took him off?'

'The police, Mr Cunningham. I don't know any more.'

'Oh God!' What had the wretched fellow done? Hit someone with his scooter? 'Where can I find her, Ferdy? We were going for a walk and she hasn't turned up. I thought she'd given me the brush-off.'

'I don't think she'd do that,' said Ferdy.

'Nor do I,' said Gerald. 'Now, where is she?'

Ferdy cast a glance round the lounge. Two elderly couples were tucking in to scones and cream; a middle-aged woman was waiting for her tray. He vanished beyond a service door and came out with a girl.

'This is Mavis. She'll show you,' he said, and went off to finish preparing the tea-tray Mavis had been getting ready.

Mavis led him up the back stairs, across a corridor, through several swing doors installed for fire safety, and up some more stairs to the attic floor.

'That's her door,' said Mavis, pointing. 'But I don't know if she's there. The police seem to think her brother had something to do with the fire in Heronsmouth on Thursday night. She's in an awful state about it.'

'But that's ridiculous,' said Gerald. Mavis must have got it wrong; the boy had probably simply landed himself in some silly scrape.

He tapped on Julie's door.

'Julie. Are you there? Can I come in? It's Gerald Cunningham,' he said.

Turning at the top of the stairs before returning to her duties, Mavis saw the door open and Julie stand there for a moment. Then Gerald went into the room.

She was distraught.

'I'll take you straight in to Heronsmouth,' he said. 'We'll soon sort it out.'

'He couldn't have started that fire,' Julie cried. 'He was here that evening. I know that, because he was with me. We were watching a video in one of the waiters' rooms. The police have been to see me and I told them so.'

'Of course he didn't do it,' Gerald said. 'Why ever should he? It's some stupid mistake.'

'It's because of his record, you see,' said Julie. 'That's why they'd pick him up.'

'His record?' Gerald tried to keep his voice level. In this context there could be only one sort of record and he knew he must tread warily, but in an odd way he was not surprised. It explained a lot.

'He's done time for arson,' Julie said. 'Your mother knows. Didn't you?'

Eddie had told her about Karen and how, in the aftermath, he had confessed to the old lady.

'No,' said Gerald.

'He wouldn't do it again. He'd no reason to,' said Julie.

Now Gerald remembered how white she had gone when she had heard about the fire and Arthur's death during dinner the previous evening and how she had asked particularly when the incident had happened.

'Fix your face, get your coat on, and we'll go,' he told her. 'You may not be back by six. You'd better let someone know – they'll have to let you go. This is serious.'

'Mavis will spell me,' Julie said.

He sat on her bed while she washed her face at the small basin in her room beneath the eaves. In his grandparents' day, this had been one of the servants' rooms and now, ironically, it had been returned to its original purpose. The walls were painted white and there were pretty print curtains at the window. The narrow divan had a pink padded headboard; there were shelves and a wicker armchair fitted up with several cushions. There were posters illustrating country scenes attached to the wall.

He must not seem inquisitive. He looked at Julie instead and watched her brush her short hair with quick strokes. He had always found the sight of a woman brushing her hair erotic. Luckily Julie's was soon done. She dabbed on lipstick, blotted it and turned to face him, then attempted a smile.

'That's better.' Gerald laid his hands gently on her shoulders. She was much the same height as himself. 'Good girl,' he said, and kissed her lightly, his own warm mouth just brushing her soft lips, not lingering.

A few minutes later they were speeding towards Heronsmouth in his car. Mavis had undertaken to see that Julie's evening duties were covered.

'Now, tell me all about your brother,' Gerald instructed, and she did, covering their mother's abandonment of the family, their father's second marriage, Edward's escapades at school and later the act which had ended in a prison sentence.

'But he'd no reason to want to harm Mr Morrison – why should he set a fire there?' she said.

'Not even if he thought the old boy had cut him out with Thelma?' asked Gerald.

'No. That was all over before he met Mr Morrison,' Julie said. 'He drifted into it. Anyway, what would your sister want with him?'

She could have dropped him abruptly, hurtfully, Gerald thought; if the boy had been made to feel slighted, he might have felt he had a score to settle. Still, there was no point in upsetting Julie with this theory, and anyway, it seemed that there was an alibi.

'It doesn't add up,' he agreed, aloud.

'They'll have found his dabs in the house,' Julie said. 'He did all that painting for the old man. That's how they picked him up, of course.'

Her pat use of the slang expression made Gerald smile.

'Mrs Thomson was very angry because she didn't know about Eddie when she took him on,' Julie said. 'I don't blame her, really. But if we'd told her, she wouldn't have given him the job.'

Probably not: as a shareholder, Gerald himself was not eager to have arsonists on the payroll.

'Don't let's worry about that now,' he said. 'Now that they know where he was on Thursday night, they'll release him.'

'You don't know the police,' said Julie. 'They can wear you down, once they've made up their minds about something.'

Gerald, however, still believed in police fairmindedness.

'We'll get him out,' he assured her.

It was not nearly as easy as he had expected, but in the end, because Edward had been held for some time already, they let him go, warning him that he would be required to appear again for further questioning. Gerald, who had been prepared to stand bail if necessary, found the whole business alarming and instructive. It seemed that a much more serious case than straightforward arson was under investigation, for Arthur had been attacked by whoever had started the fire.

'You're not arresting him, are you?' Gerald asked Detective Inspector Mobsby, when at last he managed to see the man himself.

'Not yet,' Mobsby said, for an officer had questioned Victor, who had corroborated the sister's tale of watching the video, the group separating at eleven o'clock. The Frobishers had stated that Arthur Morrison had left their house at about twenty minutes to eleven. They lived the far side of Heronsmouth, beyond the customs office, and it would have taken him ten minutes, at most, to reach The Shieling at that time of night.

Gerald saw that the police had grounds for their suspicions. He feared that, without another candidate in line, they'd pick Edward up again. The boy must have a solicitor to protect his interests.

Mobsby did not let him leave with Gerald and Julie, until a police officer had been sent to bring in Victor Hudson for further questioning, before the two could meet. The sister had to be a doubtful witness; if Hudson were persuaded that he might have made a mistake about the time, the case was on: or if it could be found that the old man had stopped somewhere on his way home, however briefly, for a late-night stroll or any other reason. Inquiries might produce a witness who had seen his car.

The officer escorting Hudson timed the journey, estimating that a determined young man pushing his scooter to its limits could make the distance in ten minutes when there was little other traffic to consider.

Thelma was desolate.

In the aftermath of her dramatic triumph, all was anticlimax and the world, as so frequently before, seemed a sad and empty place. Others in the cast were relieved at being free to prepare for Christmas, but for Thelma there was now no happy future.

Trigorin, too, had ended their fleeting affair.

'It's been fun,' he said. 'But it was naughty. Thanks for everything, Thelma.' He hadn't even kissed her when he dropped her at her door after the final party, driving off at speed back to his wife. He wanted no scandal, nor did he wish to see his home life threatened by what had been, to him, a minor and disappointing diversion.

Now there was no play, no job, no Arthur to make her feel that someone really cared about her, and she was genuinely grief-stricken, moved as she had not been since her own father's death. Why should such a dreadful thing have happened to so kind and harmless a person?

When the police came to see her on Sunday, she welcomed the interruption. She had not been up long, and was dressed in her grey tracksuit, no make-up on her face, just duty-free Je Reviens dabbed liberally on her pulse points. She seemed very attractive to Detective Sergeant Young, who was delighted with his assignment as he prepared to ask her some questions designed to support the case against Edward Fletcher.

First, he expressed regret over the sad circumstances which had provoked his call. Then he asked how well Edward Fletcher had known the deceased. Thelma confirmed that Edward had done a great deal of work in the house, painting and papering and simple carpentry. They'd got on well, he and Mr Morrison; indeed, no one could dislike Mr Morrison. There was a pause here for a small weep, large tears coursing down Thelma's cheeks without making her face blotchy; she switched them off before that happened as Young asked her how Fletcher and Mr Morrison had met.

'Through me,' Thelma said, blinking the last tear away and opening her eyes widely.

'And how was that?' Young hid his surprise. 'Had you known Fletcher long?'

'No. I met him on the train to Cheverton one night in September,' said Thelma. 'I'm not exactly sure of the date but I can probably check it. About the seventeenth, I think. A Tuesday. I'd just returned from America.'

Fletcher had been released from custody on the seventeenth.

'You got talking on the train?' prompted Young.

'Yes. It was a long journey and we ended up alone in the coach,' said Thelma. 'He was going to Milton St Gabriel to look up his sister. My mother lives there, so we gave him a lift – she came to meet me at the station.'

'I see.' Young made an entry in his notebook.

'Why do you want to know?' asked Thelma, genuinely puzzled.

'Did Fletcher tell you he'd just come out of prison?' asked Young.

There was no doubt about Thelma's genuine shock at this revelation.

'No,' she said. 'What had he done?'

'Served a sentence for arson,' said Young.

Slowly, the implications of this sank in.

'But he didn't – he couldn't – he wouldn't have –' Thelma looked at the stocky, red-haired sergeant in dismay. 'Oh no,' she said.

'His prints were everywhere in the house,' said Young.

'Well yes – he'd worked there,' said Thelma. 'They would be.'

'And he'd maybe have been able to take a key and get another cut. He maybe knew that Mr Morrison went out to bridge regularly. He could enter then, poke about, do a bit of thieving undisturbed.'

'I suppose he could, if he had a mind to,' said Thelma. 'But why should he? He'd got a job – he seemed happy enough.'

'Simple greed, perhaps,' said Young. 'Then the old man came back and caught him at it,' he went on. 'So he clobbered him from behind and set the place alight to hide what he'd done.'

'You mean he was attacked? Mr Morrison was attacked? Is that what you're saying?' Thelma exclaimed. 'That it wasn't an accident?'

'The post-mortem showed a head wound,' said Young.

'He didn't just fall and bang his head?' Thelma tried.

'No. He'd quite definitely been struck from behind with some heavy object,' said Young.

'I can't believe it.' Thelma hid her face in her hands. Her shoulders heaved. Then she sat up. 'Edward got on well with my mother,' she said. 'She invited him to stay and he was there for several weeks, till he moved into the hotel. My God, he might have attacked her! It might have been her who was killed.' The idea horrified her. All the same, she found it hard to accept that Edward could have so dark a side to his nature. He had been so gentle with her, unlike some men she had known, and had given up with good grace and no angry accusations. Even Trigorin had mentioned that they hadn't exactly set the estuary alight together.

Alight. Fire. Agony.

'He may have just snapped,' said Young. 'There are some people who go along steadily without any trouble for long periods. Then something happens to upset them and they hit out. It may be a very trivial thing that sets them off – a quarrel with a girl, a tiff at work. They take it out on someone else.'

Young left at last, having learned nothing that particularly advanced the case against Fletcher. At present it rested on the circumstantial evidence from his prints in the house and anything else the forensic scientists might turn up. Some of Fletcher's clothes had been sent to the lab, and a search of traces at the scene was going on, but after all the trampling to and fro since the incident, the chances of a vital clue appearing there were slender. The weapon might be found; meanwhile, the hope was that the suspect would crumple during questioning and confess.

After Young had gone, Nicholas Morrison, Arthur's son, who had come down from Leeds and was staying with some friends, rang up. He had tried to contact her the previous evening but in vain, because she was performing in the play.

He came round later, a shocked man, anxious to find the answers as to what had happened but eager, too, to return to his family as soon as possible.

Thelma told him what had passed between her and Detective Sergeant Young, and said she found it very hard to believe that Edward was responsible.

'They'll find out, I suppose,' said Nicholas. 'In a way it's a consolation to know Dad hadn't been simply careless. But it's dreadful. I can't take it in.'

'Nor can I,' said Thelma.

It was obvious to Nicholas that Thelma's grief was genuine. He was glad his father had found such an attractive woman to spend time with, whatever the true nature of their relationship. He asked her if she would keep an eye on things for him, a watching brief, during the police investigation.

'As a business arrangement, of course,' he added.

At the moment the house was under police guard while scientists sifted through the debris; it must be repaired as soon as that was permitted, and kept safe meanwhile against a further break-in.

Thelma was glad to agree.

'I don't want any money for it,' she said, and hesitated.

'Well?'

'Maybe, if the police agree, I could borrow the car. Just for a short time.'

'I'll see to it,' he told her. 'I'll have to make sure the insurance is in order first.'

Both were pleased with this arrangement. Thelma liked the freedom it would give her and Nicholas decided that if she had really been his father's mistress, as seemed possible, the least that could be done for her was, eventually, to make the car a gift. That should nicely solve the difficulty of what to do about her.

What a pity she couldn't use the car at once, thought Thelma. Then she could have driven straight over to Milton St Gabriel to find out what was going on. As it was, she could telephone her mother.

24

Lydia was sitting at the table with a large jigsaw that depicted the Tower of London spread before her. The edge had been completed but there was a big section in the middle waiting to be assembled. Outside, dusk was falling; the short winter afternoon had almost gone.

Over the weekend, Gerald had seemed in better spirits than for months; his holiday had done him good. He'd got on well with Julie who was a nice girl, but a serious attachment between the two would be most unsuitable; however, men had always been able to make discreet arrangements and she knew he could be trusted neither to take advantage of Julie nor to lose his head.

Thelma's telephone call was not a total surprise; some fresh appeal for sympathy was to be expected. But when Thelma told her that Edward was suspected of attacking Arthur and starting the fire to cover up his tracks, shock drove all vigour from her body. She felt icy cold and began to tremble.

'What are you saying?' she gasped.

Thelma described her interview with Detective Sergeant Young and the new police theory.

'Do you mean Edward's been arrested?' Lydia demanded.

'I suppose so,' Thelma said.

'But that's not possible,' said Lydia. 'Of course he didn't do it.'

'I know. I feel that, too,' said Thelma. For once they shared the same opinion. 'But the sergeant said that people can just snap. He'd been in prison, Mother. I didn't know that. If I had, I wouldn't have brought him home.'

Wouldn't you, her mother wondered: it was just the sort of challenge that would excite Thelma.

'I knew about it,' she said. 'He told me. But I'm certain he didn't do this. The police will find that out. He's only got to tell them where he was whenever it happened.'

'I hope you're right,' said Thelma. She went on to tell her mother that the inquest would be just a formality, to be completed later when the police had finished their investigation.

'That's how it was with Charles, if you remember,' Lydia reminded her. Though in his case no fresh evidence had emerged; no dose of drugs or alcohol explained that accident. 'I must go now, Thelma,' she said. She was shaking; surely Thelma must think her voice sounded strange? She needed time to pull herself together. She'd been so sure that the fire would obliterate all trace of the wound on Arthur's poor bald head. Now that he was dead, she could admit a little pity for him.

After Thelma had rung off, she poured herself a tot of brandy, then another, telling herself that the police would soon exonerate Edward. When Gerald returned, she was sitting before her jigsaw in the light of just one lamp, a trifle drunk.

'Gerald! But you've gone back to London!' she exclaimed, her words slurred.

'No, Mother. I've been at Heronsmouth police station,' Gerald said. 'You've heard about Edward?'

He had never seen her affected by drink before; indeed, he thought he had never seen her discomposed in any way.

'Thelma told me,' she said.

'The police have let him go,' said Gerald. 'For now, that is. I've found a solicitor for him – Roy Davis – you remember him.' Roy Davis was a junior partner in the firm that had helped Henry make his vengeful will. 'They won't give up, though – the police I mean – because of his record, although he was with Julie and one of the waiters on Thursday night at the time it must have happened.'

'Then he's all right,' Lydia said.

'No,' said Gerald. 'The police are trying to persuade them to admit that they broke up sooner. But don't distress yourself, Mother. I know you're fond of the boy and I'm sure he's innocent of this, but all the same I'm shocked to think you've been housing an ex-convict unawares.'

'I knew about it,' said Lydia.

'Yes, but not at first, did you?' Gerald said.

She had sobered up by the time he left. He had given Julie both his home and office telephone numbers, and had told her to get in touch immediately if there was further trouble. Edward was to do exactly as Roy Davis advised.

He'd ring her anyway, each evening. That was the silver lining in the present cloudy sky.

The police took Edward in once more after the inquest, which had gone along the lines foreseen. They questioned Victor again, as well, and Julie, but all three stood firm.

Julie said she had heard the church clock strike as she crossed the yard from the stable block, returning to her room.

Well, she would say that, Young reckoned, with her brother's liberty at stake.

At last Detective Inspector Mobsby let them all go; there was not enough to charge Fletcher on: not yet, but the suspect was by now thoroughly scared. When the lab had finished tests upon his clothes, the police would have their evidence; they'd get a confession, after that.

He had decided to run for it. With his record and the police determined to fasten this one on him, Edward knew he did not stand a chance.

As soon as they let him go, late on Monday night, he packed his few things into several carriers and his original holdall and got his scooter out, leaving a note for Julie in his room.

As he puttered out of the Manor gates, he saw a light on in the sitting-room at the lodge.

Mrs Cunningham was still up.

Edward slowed down, then stopped. He would say goodbye to her – explain, and ask her to thank Gerald. She wouldn't give him away; look at what she'd done for him over Karen. She'd believe him, too: he knew that.

He wheeled his scooter into the yard beside the garage, then went up the path to the french window and gently tapped on the glass.

Inside the room Boris had lifted his head when he heard a

movement outside in the night, so she had some warning.

'It's me, Mrs Cunningham. Eddie,' he called.

'Goodness!' Lydia had been startled by his tap at such an hour, but she did not fear muggers. As far as she knew, none had visited Milton St Gabriel yet. She got up and drew back the bolts to admit him. 'What are you doing, tiptoeing about at this time of night?' she asked. 'Come in, come in.'

She bustled him into the room and locked the door behind him. Boris welcomed him with wags of his tail and friendly snuffles.

'I'm leaving,' said Edward. 'I saw the light on and came to say goodbye.'

'Oh Edward, why? Have you been sacked because of the trouble?' she asked. 'Gerald told me about it. Surely all that's settled now?'

'It isn't,' Edward answered.

Mrs Thomson had already arranged for the retired man he had replaced to come back until someone else could be engaged. Edward could not really blame her; why should she believe him innocent?

'But why not?' Surely Roy Davis had attended to it all?

'The police think Victor and Julie are telling lies to save me,' Edward told her. 'We were all together, see, that night, until eleven. They've taken half my gear off for testing. They'll find plenty of proof that I've been in the house, because I have, more times than I can count. For sure I'll have picked up a hair or something, or some bit of thread. It needn't be a lot. There's nothing to say when it happened. It'll be my word against theirs.'

Listening to him, Lydia felt remote from the event: was it she who had found the strength to strike down an unsuspecting old man who had seemed like a stranger?

She pulled herself back to the present.

'You mustn't run away,' she said. 'That would be like admitting you were guilty.'

'It'll give me a chance,' he said. 'If I go now, I'll be a long way away by morning. Up in Birmingham.'

'They'll look for you there,' she said. 'You lived there once, didn't you?'

'Well, Wales then,' said Edward wildly. 'Anywhere but here.'

Shock was having its effect on him, and, as she had done on Sunday when she heard the news, he began to tremble. Lydia got out the brandy and two glasses. She poured plenty into both and gave him one.

'Here, drink this,' she instructed.

Edward obeyed. Lydia's authoritative manner, when she chose to employ it, had that effect on most people.

'Now you can't go,' she said, when he had swallowed it all. 'You might have an accident and be breathalysed. You'll stay here, Edward. I'll hide you. Then it won't be like running away at all. You'll simply move back into your old room and just lie low for a day or two, until things blow over.'

It took her more than half an hour, during which she got Edward to drink more brandy, to persuade him to agree and then he gave in because she had worn him down.

'I'm going tomorrow night,' he said.

'We'll see,' was her response.

When he had gone upstairs, she wheeled his scooter into the garden shed where it would be safe from observation.

Edward found it pleasant to be back in his old room. Exhausted after hours of interrogation, he fell asleep before she came up to bed.

Lydia was sure the police would be looking for him the next morning. She made him stay upstairs, bringing him up some jigsaws and a tray on which to do them, and the radio from the kitchen which she said he might use with the volume turned down very low.

'Turn if off if anyone comes to the house,' she warned.

At eleven o'clock, someone did: the doorbell rang, and she found a young man with red hair on the step. Detective Sergeant Young showed her his warrant card and asked if she knew where Edward Fletcher was.

What a simple question! There was no need to answer with a lie.

'Isn't he at the hotel?' she asked. 'He lives there now.'

'He's done a flit,' said Young. 'When did you last see him?'

'Let me think.' Lydia pondered her reply. 'We all went to Heronsmouth on Saturday – Edward and his sister, my son and I, and a friend – to see an amateur performance of *The Seagull*. My daughter had the leading role.'

'Your daughter?'

'Mrs Hallows. Thelma Hallows,' Lydia told him.

Young had not made the connection between Thelma and this weatherbeaten woman. It was difficult to believe that one so beautiful could have sprung from such a source.

'You've not seen him since?'

Lydia shook her head.

Would they search the house? Didn't they need a warrant for that? She'd make them get one before she would allow them to do it; that would give her time to move Edward, hide him on the cliffs or somewhere till the danger had passed.

'Why do you want him?' she asked. 'Has he had some mishap with his scooter? Parked it in the wrong place or something?'

'No, it's nothing like that,' said Young. 'We want to question him about the fire at The Shieling in Heronsmouth last week.'

'Surely he's not connected with that in any way?' said Lydia.

'We just want to talk to him,' said Young. 'I'm sorry to have troubled you, Mrs Cunningham. He's probably far away by now.'

After Young had gone Lydia allowed Edward to move more freely about the place as long as he kept away from the windows and did not go into the garden.

'It's like being in the Resistance,' she said, almost smiling. 'Hiding a prisoner on the run.'

What did she mean? Was she talking about the war? Edward stared at her, not understanding.

When Julie discovered that Edward had fled, she telephoned Gerald.

'Oh dear – yes, it is the worst thing he could have done,' he agreed. 'It will look like an admission of guilt. But try to keep calm, Julie.' He thought that the police would probably find their quarry fairly rapidly. 'It'll all work out in the end,' he tried to reassure her.

Later, he telephoned his mother, who might not have

heard the news.

'I know. The police came here to ask when I'd last seen him,' she reported. 'Silly boy.'

'There's no evidence against him,' Gerald said. 'They can't charge him without that. He should have sweated it out.'

It was easy to say that, Lydia thought, when you were not in Edward's shoes.

'They'll find traces of him in the house because he's worked there,' she said. 'How can he prove all that was legitimate?'

Gerald did not know.

'They'll soon find him,' he said. 'He can't hope to dodge them.'

That's where you're wrong, thought Lydia. Unless they looked in her shed and found the scooter, they'd be searching far away from the village.

That evening the regional television news showed film of Detective Superintendent Sawyer, from Cheverton, who told viewers that Edward Fletcher was wanted in connection with the death of Arthur Morrison in Heronsmouth on Thursday night. He appealed for help. A photograph of Edward – a prison mug shot – was displayed, and the registration number of his scooter was supplied.

The matter was extremely serious. That was evident.

25

Edward and Lydia had watched the programme. The curtains were drawn against the night and the fear of prying eyes; all the doors were locked and bolted and the windows tightly fastened.

'I'll have to move on,' he said. 'If they find me here, you'll be for it too. You'll be an accessory.'

'They aren't going to find you here,' said Lydia.

Thus it must have been in France and Belgium: young men concealed in barns and attics, smuggled on to safety. Had Arthur been concealed like that before his final capture?

She allowed Edward into the garden later, making him do exercises on the lawn in the darkness, running on the spot and press-ups.

'Otherwise you'll get flabby and unfit,' she declared.

He felt very silly carrying out her instructions, but he obeyed. When he returned to the house, she turned off the lights, so that no one could see him slip through the french window, not that anyone could look into her garden unless they were perched on the Dennises' angry orange tiles.

'You'd make a good conspirator,' he told her, almost laughing despite his predicament. Things had come right between them now; the faint, flaring hostility had vanished in his adversity.

That night, Lydia did not sleep at all. She spent hours sitting by her bedroom window, the curtains drawn back, looking out over the quiet garden. A thin moon slid into view between the clouds and cast a hasp of light across the steep, monstrous roof which blocked out so much of the sky. Would the moss ever grow there?

She was downstairs very early, leaving Boris behind after giving him a quick run in the garden while she went to the shed and let the air out of the scooter's tyres. Then she took Edward's huge helmet and put it in the boot of her car. For him to ride off without it would be to invite instant arrest. She shut Boris back into the house and went quietly out again.

Less than half an hour later she was in Heronsmouth police station, asking to see the officer in charge of the investigation at The Shieling.

Neither Detective Inspector Mobsby nor Detective Sergeant Young had yet arrived. The desk sergeant invited Lydia to tell him whatever it was she wished to say.

'I want to see the officer in charge,' Lydia repeated.

'I'm afraid you'll have to wait, then, madam,' was the answer.

'Very well.' Lydia sat down on a bench across the small front office, folding her hands across her worn but once expensive leather handbag. After several minutes she looked up at him and said, 'I did it.'

'Excuse me, madam. What did you say?' asked the sergeant.

'I did it,' Lydia declared again.

The sergeant looked at the faded elderly woman with her neatly arranged grey hair firmly secured beneath its velvet band, her padded Husky jacket and her grey flannel skirt, and sighed. He put her in the interview room, ordered a cup of tea for her from a duty constable, and rang Young at his home.

'We've got a nutter here,' he said. 'Says she did The Shieling job. A nice old lady. Mrs Cunningham from Milton St Gabriel.'

'Mrs Cunningham, eh? You must have got it wrong,' said Young.

'That's what she says,' the sergeant told him.

'Probably remembered something about the suspect,' Young hazarded. 'I'll be over right away.'

When he arrived, Lydia recognized the red-headed man who had called at the lodge. This wasn't the officer who had been on television the night before, but he would have to do, otherwise she would be waiting all day and Edward might commit some further folly.

'Well, Mrs Cunningham,' Young said briskly. 'I hear you

want to tell me something.'

'I did it, Mr Young.' Lydia's voice was firm. 'I waited for Mr Morrison to come home and then I hit him on the head. He fell dead. I lit the fire to hide what I had done.'

Poor old trout, thought Young.

'Why did you do this, Mrs Cunningham?' he sked.

She remembered what Edward had told her, and so her reply was, to the sergeant, inconsequential.

'I wanted to see the sparkle,' she said.

'What sparkle?'

'The fire, of course,' said Lydia.

'Why should you want to harm Mr Morrison?' asked Young.

'He got in the way,' said Lydia.

'The way of what?'

'My daughter's way,' said Lydia. 'Her pathway to the future.'

'Suppose you tell me about it.' He'd get rid of her faster if he listened to her maunderings, Young thought. 'Why should Mr Morrison be a threat to Mrs Hallows?'

'He would have tied her down. Curtailed her liberty,' said Lydia. 'He was an old man. If he grew frail she might feel she could not leave him. She was his housekeeper, you know.'

'Yes,' said Young.

The motive she had supplied was a weak one, and Lydia hurried on to tell him what had happened.She told the truth, not mentioning how she had watched the house for several evenings first.

'The house was a little distance from its neighbours. I didn't think there would be a risk to them,' she said.

'I see,' said Young, when she had finished. 'Well, thank you for coming in. I'll bear in mind what you have said. Now, I'll get a car to run you home.'

'But aren't you going to arrest me?' Lydia asked.

'No,' he said gently. 'What you've said will have to be investigated.'

'I see,' said Lydia. 'I used my torch to hit him with,' she added.

'I'll note it down,' said Young.

Lydia rose to her feet.

'My car is in your yard,' she said. 'There's no need for you to take me home. You'll know where to find me when you want me.'

Was she all right to drive? He supposed so. Perhaps he'd better telephone her doctor. He asked her who that was and Lydia said that she was on Dr Garfield's list but had not consulted him for years.

'I'm quite well, I assure you,' she insisted.

As she left the station, a uniformed policewoman was walking through the front office. It was WPC Cotton, who had come to talk to her about little Melanie Smith's disappearance from the motorway service station.

She told Young about that incident when Lydia had gone.

Edward had come downstairs to find a note.

Have gone out. Stay inside until you hear. Don't answer phone. Look after Boris. L.C.

What a strange message. Until he heard what? Her return, presumably. She must have gone out shopping but she'd left extremely early. He made himself some breakfast and switched on the radio. The news had nothing about the fire. He turned to the local radio station and learned that a ship had been marooned on the rocks further west; that was the most important local item.

He could slip away now. By this time the police would expect him to have left the district. He quickly packed his few possessions and went to get his scooter from the shed, where he discovered what Lydia had done to stop him leaving. He had no means of pumping up his tyres. Lydia had a footpump, but that was in the Metro.

He couldn't hope to get away on foot. He'd have to wait for her.

She was a long time. Once, the telephone rang and Edward went to answer it, then remembered that he mustn't. The caller did not hang up until after fourteen rings; he counted them.

At last he heard the car.

She came in looking pale but seemed extremely calm. She brought no parcels with her.

'I've told them that I did it, Eddie,' she said, for the first time using his sister's name for him. 'I don't think they believed me but they'll check.'

'You did what?' He did not understand.

'I told the police that I hit Arthur Morrison on the head and lit the fire,' said Lydia.

Edward stared at her in horror.

'Oh Jesus! What a thing to do!' he cried.

'There were reasons,' Lydia said primly.

'But to go and tell the police such a story!' Edward said. 'I know you thought you'd be helping me, but you shouldn't do a thing like that.'

'But it's the truth, Eddie,' Lydia said. 'I couldn't have them arresting you for something you hadn't done. I never thought they'd accuse you. I imagined they'd think it was an accident.'

'I don't blame them for picking on me,' said Edward. 'It was bound to happen, given the evidence and my record.'

'But I did do it, Eddie,' Lydia said again.

'Of course you didn't. Why should you want to hurt him? You hadn't even met him,' Edward said.

'I met him and Thelma in a shop,' said Lydia. 'I thought he was too fond of her and she would be at risk. That was my reason. Thelma makes mistakes and I wanted to protect her from another.'

'You thought what?'

Lydia put the kettle on.

'I'd like a cup of coffee,' she declared.

'About Thelma,' he prompted. 'You wanted to protect her. Why?'

'He was much too old for her,' said Lydia. 'It wasn't suitable.'

'But he wasn't going to marry her, for Christ's sake! And even if he wanted to, what's wrong with that? He was a nice old guy – he'd be good to her. And she can't make it with younger men. She might have been all right with someone older.'

'What do you mean, she can't make it?' Lydia asked.

Edward stared down at the table top, tracing a pattern on it with his finger. Lydia resisted the urge to tell him to stop fidgeting and answer her.

'Sex,' he said. 'She doesn't like it. Never has, I think.

There are girls like that.' He swept on. 'But an old man like Arthur mightn't want a lot.'

He was wrong, of course: Lydia knew that Thelma's trouble was her appetite.

'It wasn't suitable,' she reaffirmed.

Mrs Cunningham had gone and flipped her lid. The police had realized that and sent her home. People did make false confessions.

'How did you do it?' he asked. He'd soon shoot her story down.

'I waited till he went out. I'd been watching him – you said what a mileage I'd been doing with the car,' she told him. 'I wanted to surprise him, otherwise he'd be too strong for me.'

At her mention of the car, bile rose in Edward's throat. This was what had caused the little rift between them. Could she be telling the truth?

'When he came back on Thursday night, I hit him as he opened the front door. I'd already smashed the porch light and I came up the drive behind him. He fell down and I was able to drag him into the sitting-room. I thought a fire would hide what I had done.' She paused. 'He was very heavy. Bodies are,' she stated. Then she continued. 'I thought the fire was real at first, but it wasn't laid with sticks or paper. Then I realized it was gas. It made a popping noise when I lit it. I scattered papers round the room so that they would catch and make it look as if it was an accident. Then I left.'

'And he was lying there, perhaps not dead. You left him there to burn to death?' asked Edward, still only half believing her.

'He was unconscious,' Lydia said.

Edward had heard men in prison speaking callously about their victims, but Lydia's three words made him shudder. Why was she talking like this? Then he remembered their discussion in the restaurant on Saturday: they had wondered how Arthur had been careless enough to cause an accidental fire.

'I expect he forgot to turn it off,' Lydia had said.

She had known that there was a gas fire in The Shieling before they had mentioned it in the conversation.

She might have heard someone talk about it: he or Thelma might have done so, even Gerald. But Mrs Cunningham had shown no interest in the house or in its owner, and she'd just told him, now, how she had found out about the fire.

Oh God! It was the truth.

Edward felt quite sick. Without another word he left the room and ran upstairs.

Left alone, Lydia hummed to herself as she made some coffee and cut herself some sandwiches. There was plenty of cheddar cheese and she felt hungry.

It was natural that Edward should be upset by what she had told him. He would soon come to terms with his new knowledge when he realized that now he was safe. She made some sandwiches for him and put them on a plate which she covered with foil. He'd eat them later.Then, because there was nothing else to do but wait, she went to fit more pieces into her jigsaw.

She was still sitting there when Detective Sergeant Young arrived, this time with an older man who had a small moustache and said he was Detective Inspector Mobsby. Mobsby had talked by telephone to the pathologist who had carried out the post-mortem on Arthur Morrison; the wound could have been caused by a heavy torch, the doctor said, and if the article could be produced, tests could be made. Because of the lack of firm evidence with which to make a case against Edward Fletcher, Mobsby had decided that Lydia Cunningham's weird confession must be thoroughly investigated. Most cranks were not connected with the crime for which they claimed responsibility, but she was linked with this one through her daughter. That business about the child was odd, too, and should be borne in mind.

'We'd like to see the torch you mentioned,' Mobsby told her. 'And we'd like to take a proper statement.'

'I'll fetch the torch,' Lydia said.

'No, let me,' said Young, and he followed her to the cloakroom where the torch rested, head downwards, on the shelf beside the washbasin, kept there in case of some emergency. Young picked it up gingerly. If she'd really used it as she said, wouldn't she have wiped it clean? He dropped it into a plastic bag and sealed it, while Lydia watched with interest. Betty hadn't been to clean since that evening, or she would have dusted it. What would they find on it?

'What about the clothes you wore that night?' asked Mobsby.

'I burnt them,' Lydia said. 'All except my shoes and raincoat.'

'We'll take those, then,' said the detective inspector.

'They're in the cloakroom,' Lydia said. 'The old beige raincoat and the walking shoes.'

This time, since he knew the way, she allowed Young to fetch them unaccompanied.

Then, sitting in her own armchair, she described what she had done, including how she had watched the house for several nights while waiting for her opportunity. Young wrote it down while she was speaking; she marshalled her narrative so methodically that he took it down verbatim; she waited while he caught up with her. Mobsby sat there with her while she read it though before she signed it, and Young went down the garden.

Lydia worried, while he was absent, lest he peer into the shed. He came back with some more little plastic bags containing fabric fragments he had found on the bonfire pile.

Lydia signed her statement in a small, neat hand. Then she looked up at them.

'Edward Fletcher is exonerated now,' she said. It was a statement, not a question.

'We still want to talk to him,' said Mobsby.

'But you'll be arresting me,' she said.

'We'll be pursuing more inquiries first,' said Mobsby. There was no point in taking the old woman into custody; she would hardly do a flit and there would be a dreadful rumpus if they took her in without sufficient grounds. From what WPC Cotton had said, she was a little odd, maybe paranoiac, but that did not mean she was a murderer. And this was murder; whoever injured Arthur Morrison had not dealt him a lethal blow though the injury was serious; but by setting a fire and leaving the man unconscious in the room, the arsonist had definitely planned a killing.

They left the house without searching it or looking at her car, and they did not go into the kitchen where they might have seen the plate of sandwiches.

Edward had remained silently in his room while they were in the house. He would wait upon the consequences. When they had gone, he came downstairs.

'Do they believe you now?' he said. If they did, wouldn't they have arrested her? Had they cautioned her?

'They took away some things – my raincoat and the torch I used to hit him with,' she said. 'And my shoes.'

'Oh,' he said. They might find something on the shoes: soil from the old man's garden, maybe. Surely she'd cleaned the torch? He didn't ask her because he didn't want to know the answer, either way.

'You'd never stand it,' he said.

'What?'

'Prison.'

'I've been in prison nearly all my adult life,' said Lydia.

He did not understand her.

'You're ill,' he said.

'I'm not. I knew exactly what I was doing,' Lydia said. 'The thing I hadn't thought of was that you would get the blame. That was the unexpected factor.'

'You'll go to Holloway,' he said.

She hadn't thought that far ahead.

'I suppose I will,' she said.

'But it's dreadful there, if you're ill.' It was dreadful anyway, but psychiatric patients needed treatment, not incarceration. She'd end up a gibbering idiot. 'Oh, why did you do it?' he wailed, like a child, and he knuckled his eyes to hold back the tears.

'I told you. It was for Thelma. All her life, everything I've done has been for her,' said Lydia. 'Now, don't grieve, Edward. It won't be for long. I'm quite old, you know.'

'You're not.' People lived to ninety these days. She could face years of horror and he could not bear the thought of it. Miserably, he cast himself against her, and Lydia found herself gently embracing a young male creature in distress. A pleasant, warm sensation filled her thin body as she held him to her, smelled his clean, crisp, curly hair. He was just a little taller than herself – much Arthur's height.

'Dear Eddie,' she said. 'Don't take on so.' She gave him a little hug, then she released him. 'Let's forget it now,' she said. 'They'll come for me when they are ready.'

What should he do? Should he ring Gerald? Edward did not know at all. He wouldn't leave her here alone, however; he must stay with her until the police made their move.

In the end they spent a peaceful time, talking very little. Without discussion, they left the television off for neither wished to see the local news. This would be their last evening together; somehow both knew that. Earlier, Lydia had gone upstairs to make sure her hair was orderly, and while in her room had taken the telephone off the hook. She wanted no incoming calls or further complications now.

That night, while Edward tossed and turned in bed, she slept well. She had tidied up as carefully as always, washing her tights and underwear, putting her skirt away and covering her sweater.

Edward was tormented by visions of her shambling round a prison yard, set upon by other, madder women. When on remand, he'd known the worst himself. Things had been better for him later at a prison set aside for young offenders.

She'd only owned up to save him.

He could still take the rap for her. He could confess. The police would rather believe him guilty than accept her story. She'd told him that they'd taken the torch away; he'd say he'd used it. But she'd stick to her confession; she was stubborn. Now that they had something to look for, they might discover other evidence against her. Those scientists could find a needle in a haystack.

He could still save her from a sentence. There was a way. Which was the worst offence, to let her go to prison or to release her from the possibility? Edward did not know the answer, but he couldn't let her suffer, either way.

At two o'clock in the morning, after racking his brains for a different solution, Edward got out of bed and, carrying his pillow which now was damp with tears and sweat, he tiptoed across the landing and opened Lydia's door. Soft, regular breathing could be heard. He stepped over the carpet to the bed, the pillow raised. Faint light coming from his room across the landing revealed to him that she lay sleeping on her side, knees drawn up, a hand beneath her cheek. Edward pressed the pillow down over her face, but as he did so he could not hold back his sobs. In the same moment, she woke up and, without much difficulty, pushed his attempt at suffocation aside.

She sat up, gasping slightly, and turned on her bedside lamp, not at all frightened but anxious to show no physical signs that might alarm him.

'Eddie, dear, what are you thinking of?' she asked him.

Edward had collapsed backwards, the pillow clasped against his body, near hysteria.

'I couldn't let you go to prison,' he sobbed. 'It would kill you.'

Lydia put a hand to her head. The fine hairnet that she wore in bed was slightly disarranged by Edward's action. She adjusted it, pulling down a fold of hair.

'And have I done it all for nothing?' she demanded. 'You'd be charged with murder. I'll probably get off with manslaughter if Gerald finds a clever counsel. Nonsense, Eddie. It's bad enough as things are. We can't have murder in the village. What would Gerald think? And Julie? They're quite fond of one another. That would all be spoiled.'

It would be anyway. There would be no hope for either of them now, thought Edward. He felt as if a ton of lead was weighing on his heart.

'Go down and put the kettle on,' Lydia instructed. 'We'll have some tea and settle down again. Oh, and don't forget your pillow.'

26

Lydia had foreseen no dreadful consequences of her violent action because she had not expected it to be detected. Would the examination of the torch and of her clothing yield enough evidence to make the police believe her story? What more could she do to convince them? Someone might have seen her car in the side road where she had left it while she reconnoitred. Detective Inspector Mobsby had said he would make inquiries, but one blue Metro looked much like another. In a way, it would be a relief to have the struggle ended. She had a vision of herself in an overall among a lot of other women, queueing for food which would be served in a tin dish. It would be like going back to boarding-school but without the opportunity to lift herself above the rest as her success at games had done in youth. There would be smells and noise.There would be rough treatment, even bullying. She might have to share a cell and lose her solitude. If only she could be sent to some retreat: a cool convent with a bare, lonely room where she could leave behind the pain of life.

In saving Thelma, she had unwittingly endangered Edward, and now his rescue would bring shame and disgrace upon Gerald and his children.

When Edward had gone back to bed, Lydia again sat by her bedroom window waiting for the dawn, and again, when it arrived, she left the house, but this time she took Boris with her.

She drove to Worton Bay and parked the car on the headland where she had come with Gerald before the start of all this horror.They had walked together on the beach and talked more frankly than ever in their lives.

One way out, assuming the police were going to accept what she had told them without further testament, would be to drive straight over the edge of the cliff. That might not be interpreted as an accident, however, and if it were not, it would be another cruel legacy. She would have to devise some other means, such as driving round a bend apparently too fast and running into a tree, as Charles had done.

For the first time since his death, it came to Lydia that it might have been suicide. She pushed it from her mind: not that, to add to Thelma's other failures.

Lydia got out of the car and set off with Boris to walk along the headland. Gulls called below, and two cormorants dived for fish, but she took no heed of them, head down, staring at the tussocky grass while Boris rooted on ahead hoping to find a rabbit. They'd go round by the golf course and return along the shore, thus pleasing both of them for Lydia preferred walking on the sand.

The day was damp. Lydia took a scarf from the pocket of her jacket and tied it round her head. Hands in pockets, on she trudged, and after a while a course of action she could follow came into her mind. She would write a careful statement of everything she had already told the police and address it to the Chief Constable. She would describe the things she had noticed at The Shieling – the details of where the matches were, and the taper, the colour of the carpet – things she could not have known if she had not been inside the house. She would mention Henry's position in the county and request the Chief Constable's discretion in settling the case; influence might still count for something and at last, after death, she would make use of Henry. She must trust the man to manage that.

Gerald would never understand, of course: even Edward had found her explanation unacceptable, but the only motive she could offer was the one she had already given the police. They would just have to believe she had been temporarily deranged.She saw now that one could not escape retribution; all those years ago she had sinned against the truth, and the devil, laughing, had caught up with her. Well, she'd beat him in the end.

Gerald would pick the pieces up, put his life together, settle with some woman. Men usually did: it was women who forged on alone, whether from chance or choice.

From ahead came a single sudden bark.

Boris had been snuffling on in front of her, seeking intriguing scents in the hollows and crannies of the headland. Now he had vanished.

Probably he'd found a rabbit hole.

'Boris,' she called, then called again, 'Boris? Boris?'

He did not reappear, but she heard another bark and then a frightened whining. Lydia went to the edge of the cliff and looked over. There, on a ledge below, stood Boris, trembling. Scrabbling at an interesting hollow in the ground, he had disturbed the soft topsoil and caused a tiny avalanche of earth, enough to carry him over.

'Oh, Boris, you silly boy! Look where you've got to,' Lydia cried aloud.She peered down.The ledge was no great distance below her and if she could reach it, she would be able to lift him back to the top. 'Stay there. Stay,' she instructed.

Trustingly, Boris looked up at his mistress, his large strong tail waving gently. Lydia looked about for a way to climb down to his level. To his side, there were footholds in the cliff face. Ignoring the menace of the rocks below, she took off her jacket so that it would not impede her movements and lay down on her stomach, her head facing inland, easing her long thin legs in their ribbed navy tights over the edge. Some small hard object in her skirt pocket pressed against her skinny hipbone as she moved backwards, feeling about with her feet for a place to rest them. She found a hold for one foot, inched down and reached out for another, her hands on the top. There was no scrubby bush to grab to keep herself secure.

In Worton Bay, an old retired seaman who lived with his daughter and son-in-law in a bungalow where he spent much of his time watching the local life through his binoculars, saw the whole thing. He had noticed the small blue car earlier; at this time of year there were few headland walkers and he had seen this one before. He saw the dog running on ahead and he witnessed the whole rescue, the woman edging her way along the cliff to where her pet was marooned. She successfully lifted him back and the dog was safe when the ledge on which he had been stranded gave way and she fell to the rocks below.

She died before help could arrive.

PENSIONER DIES SAVING PET ran the headline in the *Cheverton Gazette*, with below it the eye-witness account, as told to their reporter, of Lydia's heroism.

A small paragraph on the same page announced that the police investigation into the tragedy at The Shieling in Heronsmouth had been concluded and no charges would be preferred.

Lucky for her, I reckon,' said Detective Superintendent Sawyer. The police had been forced to accept that her death was an accident, since a witness attested to the whole thing and she had left no suicide note. She was taken to Cheverton Hospital, and her identity was only discovered by means of the tag on Boris's collar: he had stayed at the cliff top, barking continuously, looking down at the recumbent form of his mistress while the ambulance men summoned by the watcher in the bungalow loaded her on to a stretcher. The Cheverton police dealt with the details and it was a little time before their colleagues in Heronsmouth heard what had happened.

A single fragment of a jigsaw puzzle was found in the pocket of her skirt. Later, Edward could fit it into none of those waiting to be completed at the lodge; then he remembered the jungle scene with one piece missing; here it was.

Meanwhile, the forensic pathologist who had carried out the post-mortem examination on Arthur Morrison had concluded that the wound on his skull matched Lydia's torch, on which had been found traces of tissue which, on analysis, had come from the dead man. There were scorch marks on Lydia's old raincoat more likely to have come from tending a bonfire than from the fire at The Shieling, but earth particles found on her shoes were being checked to see if they matched soil from the garden of the house where she claimed to have set the fire. It was too late to seek a footprint, and too much traffic had passed the house for one to be found inside.

'She must have gone right round the twist,' said Mobsby. It tied in with her action when she had abducted a small girl apparently to teach the parents a lesson. 'Didn't like what the daughter might be up to and tried to play God.'

'Something like that,' agreed Detective Superintendent Sawyer, who seldom made moral judgements. He was a just man and had told Edward Fletcher – who had been found at the lodge when Gerald Cunningham arrived there after his mother's accident – that the case against him had been dropped.

Mud stuck, though; Edward knew that well. His always precarious world, which had briefly seemed secure, had fallen apart again; and he grieved for Lydia.

He found enough courage to ask Sawyer about her confession. The fact that he had been in the house the whole time Mobsby and Young were taking her statement was now known to the police.

'I suppose you didn't believe her,' Edward said.

'We needed proof,' said Sawyer.

'And you've got it now?'

'Enough.' The boy could have used the torch, of course, but he would have had the sense to wipe it clean, or dump it.

'Must you tell her family?' asked Edward.

Sawyer looked at him, weighing him up: a thin-faced ex-con who gazed back at him unswervingly.

'I shan't let on,' Edward said. 'It would shock them something rotten, a lady like her doing such a thing.'

'It won't be my decision,' Sawyer replied. 'But I'll see what I can do.'

It might all die down. No journalist had got hold of the story and unless any member of the force blabbed, the truth might remain locked in the files, though the coroner would have to be told and Morrison's son might need reassuring that there had been no miscarriage of justice.

He could be told that the attack came from an intruder known to the police but who subsequently had died. Time would tell if that would satisfy him.

On a grey day Lydia's ashes were interred in her husband's grave at Milton St Gabriel. She had left no instructions about a funeral and this seemed the best compromise between the various choices.

Gerald still felt stunned by the finality of it, the suddeness of her death. Now he would never win her love or her approval, and he felt as though the core had gone from his life. Julie found him still in the graveyard after the small

ceremony which only he had attended. At the crema-
torium, some days earlier, a respectable number of
mourners had put in an appearance out of respect for Henry
if for no other reason.

'Come on,' said Julie. 'It's over now,' and she took
Gerald's hand to lead him away. They went back to the
lodge together and walked down the garden to look at the
angry orange roof which had so annoyed his mother.

'Look, there's some moss growing on it,' Julie said. 'See –
up there in the gully.'

Gerald followed her gaze and descried a small thread of
dark green adhering to a tile.

'That'll improve it,' he said.

'What will you do with the lodge?' Julie asked.

'It's only leased from the developers,' he said. 'That was
arranged for her lifetime. They'll pull it down and put up
two or three bungalows, I expect.'

'I see.' Julie had thought he might use it for weekends.

'I never want to come down here again, once everything's settled,' he declared.

'Never's a long time,' said Julie.

'I know.' He turned to face her. 'Will you come to London
with me?'

She nodded, trying to control the huge smile of joy which
she felt stretching across her face.

'What about Eddie?' she asked.

Gerald laughed at that.

'And her brother came too?' he said.

'He needs a job and he's very sad,' said Julie. 'He loved
Mrs Cunningham.'

'I'm going into business on my own,' said Gerald. He had
decided to take his money out of the hotel group. 'I don't
know what, or where,' he added. 'Maybe the wine trade. I
was quite taken with all I saw when I went to visit my son.'

'So you might have a post for a strong young man?' Julie
said.

'I daresay,' Gerald answered, smiling. He took her hand
and held it against his cheek, then kissed it. No one had
ever kissed Julie's hand before and her inside lurched.

'What about Thelma?' She tried to speak in level tones.
There was no need to fall on his neck; there was plenty of

time.

'Oh – I suppose you haven't heard the latest. She's taken a shine to that old man's son – Nicholas Morrison. A nice bloke, too, as you'd expect. She's off to Leeds, where he lives. Says she doesn't know that part of the world and it's time she had a look around.'

'What'll she do?'

'Find a job if she can, I suppose,' said Gerald. 'She's going to rent a flat for the rest of the winter. Maybe she'll join another dramatic society. But she's chasing him, of course.'

'Isn't he married?'

'Yes, but that won't stop Thelma,' Gerald said.

'Perhaps she won't catch him,' said Julie.

'Perhaps not,' Gerald agreed. 'Who can tell?'